Sanctuary

RACHEL JAMES

Published by
Crimson Romance
an imprint of F+W Media, Inc.
10151 Carver Road, Suite 200
Blue Ash, OH 45242. U.S.A.
www.crimsonromance.com

ISBN 10: 1-4405-9451-1
ISBN 13: 978-1-4405-9451-9
eISBN 10: 1-4405-9449-X
eISBN 13: 978-1-4405-9449-6

Cover art © 123RF/ostill, 123R/Fandreykuzmin.

CHAPTER ONE

Jenny Flores lay on the table, staring at the ceiling with lifeless eyes. What the man was doing to her was obscene. Yet, for some unknown reason, she couldn't find the courage to make him stop.

"Kiss me," a pleasant, deep voice said.

A hand slipped beneath Jenny's back and lifted her torso up. She raised her face, and warm lips smothered hers. "And where are you now?" a different voice asked; it was louder, less distant.

Her breathing became erratic.

"I'm having sex with Phil. He's a wonderful lover. We make love two or three times a week … "

"And where are you now?" asked the voice.

"I'm in the park with Phil and the kids. It's Sunday. We always picnic in the park on Sundays. The weather is picture-perfect, and the kids are playing with our dog, Scruggs."

"Kiss me," the pleasant voice interrupted again.

Jenny fell back, staring up at the ceiling with lifeless eyes. What the man was doing to her was obscene. Yet, for some unknown reason, she couldn't find the courage to make him stop.

• • •

Hurled out of a white vortex and back to reality, empath Sonny Blake hugged the bedpost. Something was wrong with her skills. The same vision was replaying over and over—one she couldn't make sense of, or stop.

An icy fear snaked around her heart muscle and squeezed. Was she finally going mad after all these years? Had her mind been flung in and out of time and space so many times that it could no longer tell one vision from another?

The young girl's face swam through her mind again. Who was the girl, and why couldn't she identify where she was?

And who owns that distant sexy voice requesting a kiss? Sonny's inner voice asked.

And why are two visions overlapping one another? she shot back. *We never mix and match our visions.*

You're the interpreter, Miss Empath. You tell me.

Her inner voice fell silent, and Sonny sighed. She was talking to herself—a clear sign that she needed to start using her brain for something more rational than stolen kisses and frightened girls. There were bills to pay, schedules to keep, and a host of employees to manage.

She attempted to haul her body away from the post, only to cling to it again as a bout of nausea swept over her. The vision had not only drained her psychic energy, but her physical energy as well. *Not a good sign*, her inner voice chided. No, if she kept on, she would be hauled off to the funny farm and dropped down a rabbit hole so deep not even her family would be able to find her. *And who belongs to that sexy voice that keeps requesting the kiss?* her inner voice prodded. *He sounds delish—not like the other one.*

Annoyed by her ego's fixation on erotic kisses, Sonny crawled back under the covers. There'd be plenty of time to look for answers after she got her nausea under control. She closed her eyes, snuggling into her pillow. She needed to realign her body and mind with her personal mantra. *Down the rabbit hole, one, two, three; out the rabbit hole, fiddle-dee-dee ...*

Sonny smiled at her self-mockery. The similarity between her and *Alice in Wonderland* wasn't far off the mark. They both went down rabbit holes in pursuit of a White Rabbit—or, in her case, a white vortex. And while in Wonderland, they both endured trials that tested their souls, yet managed to re-energize their spirits.

Swallowing a growing lump in her throat, Sonny concentrated on her breathing. *In, out, breathe.* Twenty exhalations later, the image of the High Priestess Tarot card swam into view. She attuned her energy to the card, her mind sweeping past the dual pillars, through the door of knowledge, and down into a different kind of rabbit hole. This hole was filled with the shimmering, golden light of the Sun. She turned her face to the orb and basked in its glory.

When a feeling of peaceful euphoria settled over her frame, she snuggled deeper under the covers.

Goodnight, Alice, her inner voice called, as she drifted down, down, down ...

• • •

Ned Chalmers closed the office door and locked it. His sessions had gone incredibly well today. Two of the clients had actually shown a flair for the therapy. Tomorrow, he'd look for others he could manipulate.

Turning, he hit the light switch and stood in the darkness. There was nothing better than moving through the scrim of darkness—except for when the darkness moved through *him*. Then, he was godlike, the power showering his entire aura and energizing it with a magic that couldn't be halted, or described in human words.

Recalling the elation, he smiled. He had spent years training his senses to align with the dark's spatial energy, and now that he had succeeded, he knew he had earned the skill of seeing, hearing, and moving without detection. The nightly alignment was downright addictive, and, unlike those around him, he considered the darkness his trusted friend.

He moved now, reaching the short staircase without bumping any piece of furniture. A few moments later, his foot hit the bottom step of the staircase, and he paused. Abducting and killing Sonny Blake was his current objective. The bitch was poking her nose into his business. She was questioning his trip schedules, asking for airline and hotel receipts, and demanding to view his therapy session tapes. He'd make her pay for that aggravation when he had her under his thumb and begging for her life. But before he killed her, he'd merge her talent with his power of darkness and, once united, be unstoppable.

He'd have to be careful, though. The bitch could sense any dark thought that came against her. Thankfully, she treated him like a favorite uncle, and that helped him stay in close proximity to her. It also fueled his desire to wound her to the core. Her ability to project her mind into spatial energy and interpret it gave her an edge over him. And that rankled. There was too much on the line. If she learned about his pet project, Pandora, he'd have to go underground again and stay there. No, killing Sonny Blake was his only option. But how to do it? And when?

When no answer surfaced, he bounded up the steps and entered a makeshift bedroom. He made a beeline for the large bed, where he shed his clothes and slipped beneath the sheets. He rolled over and checked the shackles tied to the bedposts.

A frightened scream floated through the darkness at the dip in the mattress. He smiled smugly, moving his fingers down the chains to a pair of magnificent breasts. In seconds, he was mounting the young girl and introducing her to the ways of the dark.

CHAPTER TWO

Logan Reed nudged the petite body on the floor with his toe. Shit. Another dead empath—and another goddamned Tarot card. You'd think the bastard would add some variety to his killing ritual. Logan stared down at the purple hair, nose ring, and colorfully tattooed arms. Amy Carlyle was certainly not your average-looking empath. Her talent had obviously hitched itself to the wrong crowd. His gaze swept the needle in the fold of the young girl's left elbow. The mouse might still be alive if Logan had ignored his grumbling stomach and skipped lunch.

He scanned the tank top and cut-off jeans, and then the Death card peeping from beneath her bare torso. Reaching into his back pocket, he pulled out a pair of gloves and donned them. Seconds later, he was studying the skeletal image on horseback with a frown. Meta Corps would be pissed about another sudden death of one of its empathic clients. If and when he reported the teen's death, he would be screwed. The teen had been his to keep safe.

He smacked the face of the card with his fingers. Could he walk away and let somebody else find the body? He could, but ... His gaze landed on the delicately carved, heart-shaped face. No, the teen had parents who loved her—no matter her addictions. Backing out of the doorway of the four-story brownstone, Logan reached for his cell phone and dialed 9-1-1.

...

Idly slapping the encased Tarot card in his hand, Logan listened to the police chatter emanating from the two-way radio atop the interrogation table. The investigation at the brownstone was winding down at last, and in less than twenty minutes, his boss, Dresden Charles, would be seeking a written statement from him.

The two-way radio continued its crackle and then fell silent. Logan sighed loudly. His Meta Corps instincts had taken an unexpected holiday today.

Every day, his inner voice chided.

No need to remind me, he told the voice.

The radio took up its crackle again, dispatching the med techs to a new crime scene. Hearing the line go dead, Logan dropped the baggie onto the table and fished in his pocket for a cigarette. He wished he could kick his nicotine habit permanently. He had managed to cut down his intake after the shooting last summer, but to his disgust, he hadn't quite managed to kick the habit flat out.

Raised voices filtered through the plate-glass window, and Logan saw that the first of the evidence teams had arrived back at the station. Hearing the radio in front of him squawk loudly, Logan reminded himself to watch his mouth during the interview. Dresden abhorred his sarcasm.

The figure in question appeared outside the door, sending a brief glance Logan's way and then concentrating on the file a young med tech was offering him. Watching Dresden sign off on it, Logan's frown deepened. Dresden was pissed; he could see it through the glass.

A folder suddenly slapped down in front of him.

"Two dead empaths in six months—and both of them female."

Logan gave a twisted smile. "The bastard is bold; I'll give him that."

"I want him stopped."

"So do I. He's fixated on my clients."

Dresden flipped the folder on the desk open. "Any thoughts? Leads?"

"No leads, but plenty of thoughts," Logan replied. He leaned over and placed the cards encased in plastic in a straight line. He tapped each of the different Tarot cards. "I did a little digging after the first murder and found there have been sixteen similar deaths of female empaths in the last three years. Eight here in the East, four in the Midwest, and four in New Mexico."

"Sixteen!" Dresden crowed. "That's a hell of a coincidence. Any common thread?"

"One. The Sanctuary."

Dresden's head popped up. "The spiritual retreat?"

"Afraid so," Logan said. "From what I've managed to discover, it appears each of the empaths visited the retreat before their deaths."

Dresden dropped into a chair across from Logan. "You realize that Sonny Blake, our prize empath, lives there."

Logan nodded. "Puts Meta Corps in the crosshairs, I should think."

Dresden shuffled the baggies back into the folder and then spun the folder towards Logan.

"Only one way to tell if we're right. You need to go there and scout it out. I'll e-mail a copy of the Tarot cards to Sonny and ask her to use her skills to verify your findings. By the time you get there, she should have some answers for you—what dates the women stayed there, their agenda while there, etc. She's a whiz when it comes to solving Meta Corps cases."

Annoyed, Logan studied the folder. "Why the hell would we ask her to look into the deaths when she might be involved?"

"She might be the next empath to die."

Logan pushed the folder away. "Assign someone else to verify my findings with her. I'm knee-deep in cases and can't go."

"Don't bullshit a bullshitter," Dresden advised. "I'm your boss. I know your caseload. You have time to put this one to bed. This case is hinky, to say the least, and it needs our best agent to handle it. And at the moment, our best is *you*."

"I'm tired, burned out," Logan argued. "Send someone else. Besides, when the press gets wind of this latest victim, they'll fry my ass in negative headlines like before. It's best I keep a low profile."

"And the best way to do that is to not be in the city. You'll take this case and get the hell out of Dodge pronto. That's an order."

Surprised by the command, Logan squirmed in his chair. Dresden was copping an attitude with him, and it wasn't like him. Had the man finally decided to write him off as a screw-up?

"What's your problem, Dresden?" Logan asked. "I'm doing the agency a favor by wanting to keep a low profile. One bloodbath of negative headlines is certainly enough, don't you think?"

Dresden shot from the table. "Do you think anyone's going to believe you suddenly don't give a shit about solving a serial killing? You're a goddammed legend in this place, Logan." He began pacing the floor. "You may have become a royal screw-up the last six months, but I am *not* going to let you shy away from another case with a female empath because it's uncomfortable for you. What you're going to do is get on a plane and solve these cases with Sonny Blake's help." He rejoined Logan at the table, and Logan felt the first stirring of anger at his tone. "Now, I'll overnight the original Tarot cards on the company jet and give Sonny a heads-up you're coming, but not the precise date or time. Sometimes, surprise is a great ally."

Annoyed, Logan sprang to his feet. "Why are you railroading me into taking this case? Can't you see empaths are nothing more than damn charlatans getting rich off of other people's dreams?"

"Don't condemn all empaths because one skidded off the rails and shot you."

"She put me in the hospital for months, Dresden."

"Be grateful. She made you take the best vacation of your life, which is something I could never make you do."

"That isn't funny. I damn near died."

"Well, that's not Sonny Blake's fault. Besides, we need her. Her ability to touch an object and obtain facts that no ordinary agent can deduce on their own is something that Meta Corps has no intention of discarding any time soon. Her reputation, not to mention the reputation of The Sanctuary, is beyond reproach."

Logan sniffed his disgust. "I've a good mind to go to the director and ask him to reassign me to a different Meta Corps division."

A similar growl mocked his. "Fine. But if you do, I'll see to it that your Meta Corps career comes to a screeching halt. I'll yank your license and make sure you never work in this city—or any other city—ever again. And if you think I'm bluffing, just try me."

Logan crushed out his cigarette, wishing the stub was Dresden's jaw; he would have loved to sucker-punch the bastard. But what would it get him? He'd still be sent to New Mexico. He returned his attention to the folder and swirled it absently. Perhaps he *should* meet with Sonny Blake. Even though he no longer believed in all the touchy-feely crap of empaths, the woman had a success rate that defied belief. While there, he might even gain some brilliant insight into how to resurrect his sagging career. His gaze lifted to Dresden, who was studying his expression with an eagle eye.

"I suppose you'll want a full accounting once I meet this paragon of virtue and take stock of things?" he asked.

A smirk came his way. "A quick e-mail will do," Dresden replied. "As a courtesy to the agency, though, you might ask Sonny Blake to share some insight into your sudden career meltdown."

"And if she senses nothing?"

Dresden rapped his knuckles on the desk. "She'll sense *something*, you can bet on it."

"No, *you* can bet on it," Logan chided. "I prefer my bets to be tangible—something I can see and touch—not supernatural."

"One more thing," Dresden cautioned, handing Logan the file folder. "When you get there, use the shuttle to the retreat. It runs every hour."

"I can rent my own vehicle," Logan stated. "You know I work better on my own."

"No car—and no working alone this time. I need you to be inside the family structure. Go where they go, eat what they eat, begin to think like they think. And remember to keep Sonny in your sight at all times … You're scowling. What now?"

"If Sonny Blake's accuracy is so damned high, why hasn't she sensed her life is in danger and contacted Meta Corps?"

"Now that's a great question," Dresden said. "Go and find the answer, but tread lightly. Blake Industries owns half of the New Mexico desert, not to mention it runs numerous spiritual retreats around the world. The family is constantly on the go, which makes each one of them a prime target for abduction."

"Have there been any hints of a kidnapping attempt?" Logan asked, reseating himself. "I like to know what I'm walking into before I get there."

"Another great question. It shows your brain is still functioning at some level. And no, there haven't been any attempts yet, but if your info is correct, our killer has already picked out his next victim."

"Who may be at the retreat already," Logan said.

"Well, let's hope that scenario doesn't play out when you get there. Instead, let's hope you spend a month in paradise getting in touch with your spiritual side."

Logan drummed his fingers on the table. Did he have a spiritual side? Not any longer. All he had was a bruised and battered ego. Besides, he never liked going into a case blind. It smacked of suicide. His gaze lifted. Perhaps The Sanctuary would turn out to be his fast track to the grave.

"Your integrity has never been in question, Logan," Dresden added. "All the young agents look up to you and aspire to be like you. And as for your peers, they're devoted fans. You've simply hit a bad patch. It happens sometimes. I'd like to think you understand why I'm giving you this assignment."

"I understand perfectly. You want the case solved, and you're sending the best to work with the best."

"Humility is certainly not your middle name, is it?" Logan grinned suddenly, but Dresden went on. "Do the right thing when you get there. Listen to Sonny and then use your logic to solve these murders, because it would be a real shame if your gravestone read: 'Here lies a pompous has-been.'" He left the table without glancing back; however, when he reached the door, he paused. "I'm sure you'll be clever enough to avoid any media hounds lurking outside. But just in case, I'll play the decoy. Take the earliest flight out you can, preferably tonight's red-eye."

He left the room as quickly as he had come in, and Logan eyed the file folder with a twisted smirk. He had been reduced to a fucking babysitter. Worse, an empath's babysitter. Was he ready to be around another empath? It had been, what, thirty minutes since he'd found his last one?" *Pompous has-been* ... The words had him launching himself from the table with a growl. Pompous? Maybe. Has-been? Not bloody likely.

Cradling the file folder, Logan left the room and crossed the squad room to the rear exit stairwell. Passing through, he let his mind shift gears. He'd show the Meta Corps bastards he still had what it took to close a case with his client still alive. He'd work with Sonny Blake. He'd even pretend to believe in her supernatural powers. But that's all he'd do—pretend to believe.

He tripped out the basement door into the parking garage, and his spirits suddenly lifted. The desert landscape would be awash in colorful cactus blooms this time of the year. And the night sky, filled with exotic perfumes, would be a starry expanse that let a man breathe—a far cry from the neon lights of big-city streets. He slipped from the building into the rear alleyway and headed west towards Broadway. When he hit the sidewalk and turned south towards home, he began to whistle softly. By this time tomorrow, he'd be basking in the New Mexico sun and enjoying the best vacation he'd had in years. And best of all, he could charge all his expenses to the Meta Corps bastards.

CHAPTER THREE

A heavy downpour swept the arid landscape, angling towards the cottages dotting The Sanctuary Spiritual Retreat. The yoga group meditating on an open-air platform ignored the first of the raindrops—until a huge crack of thunder shook the stage and sent them scurrying for cover. Two miles away, sunbathers heard the crack, followed by an ominous series of lightning arcs, and wisely fled the pool area for the clubhouse.

Once inside, they watched the approaching light show, snacking on fruit and cheese and joking about Mother Nature's ability to go berserk at a moment's notice. In minutes, the usually dry streambeds surrounding the buildings brimmed with excess runoff, and surly winds whipped sand into abrasive blankets.

In the heart of the Serenity offices, Sonny Blake took no notice of the light show going on outside the windows. Instead, she was immersed in bringing Lydia Summers out of her past life-regression session in the gentlest way possible.

"Three, two, one. Open your eyes, Lydia."

The young girl's eyes fluttered open, and her gaze found the ring of chairs encircling her. "Did it work?" she asked, her eyes scanning her companions.

Giggles showered the air at her question. Babe Armstrong was the first to speak.

"Of course it worked, you dolt! Miss Blake took you back at least two lifetimes."

Lydia's eyes widened even more. "Really. I went back *two* lifetimes?"

The girls giggled again. Becky Sanders spoke this time.

"You should've heard your voice. It was sexy as hell. You were some kind of prostitute, we think."

Hearing the statement, Sonny stepped in. The girls' imaginations were taking flight. "I think that's enough excitement for today, ladies," she declared. "This session is now officially over."

The girls sprang from their chairs, gathering up their belongings and giving Sonny exuberant bear hugs as they left.

"You're the best, Miss Blake," Becky complimented her, squeezing her arm. "You make the sessions so much fun, we forget to be afraid."

"Becky's right. You're scary good, Miss Blake."

Sonny laughed outright. "I like the good part, but the scary part—not so much."

The girls drifted away, chatting amongst themselves as they made a beeline out the front door and off towards the hiking trails. When they were out of sight, Sonny closed the door with a relieved sigh. The session had drained her energy more than she cared to admit. For a brief moment during the last regression, she had caught a glimpse of the frightened girl from her dreams, only this time the girl had been begging for mercy from her captor. Why the hell wouldn't the image go away and stay away?

A sudden thought of the girl's body being buried beneath one of the trees in the meditation garden assailed Sonny's senses, and she fled back to her desk quickly. Once there, she picked up a bagged Tarot card and held it in her gloved hand. She needed to concentrate on something challenging right now. She scanned the card's image, looking for a hidden meaning. When none came, she flung the card back onto her desk.

The Tarot cards had arrived by overnight mail from Meta Corps, and she was damn sorry she had agreed to look at them. Each time she looked at the images, she felt violated—a sure sign that she was identifying with the slain women.

The card left at the first murder scene had been The Fool—dressed in jester attire and walking off a monstrous cliff. The second card, Judgment, had depicted the opposite feeling, with its angel blowing Saint Gabriel's horn. The third card, The High Priestess, had resonated strongly within her, and she knew without even touching the card that she had met the murdered girl here at the retreat sometime in the last two years. The fourth card she hadn't even bothered to look at. She could sense its evil right through the plastic, and her soul had shied away from imprinting it on her memory. It would lie on her desk till hell froze over, she decided. The fifth card, The Tower, she had slipped into her desk drawer after scanning. Why, she didn't know. It had just felt like the right thing to do. However, pieces of it still peeped from the corner of the drawer, as if to say, "You're not quite through with me yet."

Realizing she needed an energy boost badly, Sonny shoved her chair back and sprang to her feet. The sound of fabric ripping made her emit a heated curse. Now the damn cards had cost her a perfectly beautiful blouse. She fingered the tattered fabric, wishing some arrogant agent from Meta Corps' office was standing in front of her. She would have loved to knock him to the floor and damn him to hell.

Delighted by such a perverse thought, she tore off her owl-framed glasses and tossed them onto the desk. What agent was Meta Corps sending? And when would he show his arrogant face? It wasn't like Meta Corps to be so vague about an agent's name. *Perhaps you're under the microscope*, her inner voice suggested. *After all, you've been declining their requests for help the last several months.*

Dismissing the dig, she fled to the windows that overlooked the carefully manicured lawns beyond the terrace. Her gaze sought the signpost marked "Serenity," but all she saw was sheets of pelting rain. She drew in her breath. When had the storm started? Usually she sensed an impending storm coming and took pains to close the blinds. She hated storms. They played havoc with her empathic skills.

Mesmerized by the light show over the distant mountaintops, Sonny was surprised when a beam of light illuminated her reflection in the glass. She had a nice pear-shaped face, but it looked like someone else's face today—crow's feet, tension lines along the forehead ... She gave a sigh, returning her attention to the hammering rain and her scattered thoughts. A face with a haunted look was appropriate for a woman suffering from a psychotic break.

A sound mind isn't everything, her inner voice chided. *It can't hold a candle to hot, sweaty sex with a devastatingly handsome man.*

Sonny made a face at her reflection. *As if we'd ever meet a man like that,* she shot back. *You have to be out in the world to accomplish that deed. And when was the last time we were out in the world?* No answer came from her ego, and Sonny's smile switched to laughter. *That's right, Miss Empath. Cross "one sexy hunk" off our Christmas list this year.*

Sonny's mouth twisted into a cynical smile at her rambling mind; however, her thoughts soon switched back to the mysterious Meta Corps agent. What was his name? Was he one of their best? And why didn't he call?

"Here, drink this," a pleasant voice said from behind her. "You look like you could use a refreshing pick-me-up."

Sonny turned, smiling at the tall woman offering her a mug of steaming liquid. "You're an angel, Cassy," she said, grabbing the mug and taking a quick sip. "Mm. Chamomile tea. Just the thing to calm my rattled nerves."

"As usual, you've been conducting too many sessions in one day."

"Those sessions pay the bills, Cassy."

A haughty sniff came from her friend.

"You have enough money for two lifetimes. Why put yourself through such mental distress when you don't need to?"

"I have to help people, Cassy. It's my job."

Her sniff came again, followed by the soft sound of something dropping to the floor.

"You really must be rattled today. You've dropped one of your fancy cards on the floor."

Picking it up, Cassy offered it to Sonny, who took one look at it and turned away. *Ugh!* The Death card. Whose Death did it indicate? The frightened girl's? Or her own? *Who cares,* she answered her own question. *We are through thinking about hypnotic voices that bury bodies under the trees.*

Sighing, she returned to her desk and kicked off her shoes. "It's time to stop focusing on Death cards and focus on work; otherwise, we'll be days behind in arranging my aura portrait classes." She leaned forward, riffling through the pile of letters Cassy had brought with the tea and laid on her desk "Anything pressing in the mail?"

"Just more requests for your services."

"Turn them all down," Sonny said suddenly. She handed the stack back to Cassy. "You're right. It's time I take a break from absorbing people's energy for a while."

"Well, hallelujah," Cassy crowed. She sketched a wave and sashayed from the room, not bothering to the close the door behind her. Sonny grinned and then let her gaze drift to the High Priestess painting on her far wall.

The Seeress. The Empath. The Guardian of the Doorway.

But what doorway? her inner voice asked. *And why are our talents showing signs of deterioration after all these years?*

Stop asking questions we can't answer, she advised her ego. *Focus on ones we can.*

Her gaze scanned the top of her desk, spotting the peekaboo card still taunting her. She opened the drawer, pulled it out, and tossed the card back onto the top of the desk. It skittered across the smooth glass, stalling at the edge. It was time to focus on the Tarot cards and discern an answer. She collected the baggies and laid the cards out in a straight line. Did she want to know the answer?

Touch them, her inner voice nudged. *Just take off your gloves and touch one of them. You'll know the killer's identity immediately.*

Sonny squirmed in her chair. *No thank you, Miss Empath. You know we've given up touching objects that send us down rabbit holes filled with visions we can't interpret. The price is too high. We're just going to get a "feel" for the evidence.* She shifted her torso and settled back in her chair. Thank God she hadn't told anyone about Meta Corps' request. She'd appear more of a fool than the Fool card.

She let her gloved fingers slide over the cloaked skeleton with a giant scythe. A sudden tremor of an image started to emerge, and she pulled her fingers back rapidly. What the hell was that? She had almost initiated a vision *through* her gloves. Her current stress level must be higher than she thought. In the past, her talent had no way of setting off as long as she was wearing gloves. She took a last look at the skeleton.

"You are nothing but a big, fat jokester," she told the card. "You have no power over me." A flash of words assailed her mind.

I KNOW YOUR NAME AND
WHERE YOU LIVE.

Absorbing the words, Sonny felt tears ring her eyelashes. The victim had been taunted through a phone call by an annoying, arrogant bastard. No wonder she'd stopped going out and cried all the time. Sonny dropped the baggie back onto the desk and wiped her wet cheeks. She wasn't quite ready to "feel" what this victim had felt.

She turned her attention to the Judgment card. Lifting the baggie, she studied the figures rising out of the coffin. Had the second victim been buried alive? *Make a note to ask the sexy Meta Corps hunk that they send,* her inner voice advised. *And when he confirms your suspicion, give him a big, fat, juicy kiss as a reward.*

Exasperated, Sonny dropped the card. *What is your problem, Miss Empath? You've become fixated on all things sexual. Get your mind out of the bedroom and concentrate.* No further jabs came, but drops of blood did—all over the plastic baggie.

Seeing the mess, Sonny sprang to her feet, snatching a tissue from a box on her desk and wiping down the plastic. Holding her nose, she fled to the bathroom and attempted to staunch the flow of blood. She dropped her head back and wondered whether it wasn't time to see a doctor. She was showing signs of a complete unraveling. First, her mind; now, her body.

The sound of voices floated through the bathroom door, and Sonny recognized them immediately. Great. Now, on top of bleeding all over police evidence, she had to deal with her aunt and Ned. What the hell did they want?

She checked her face in the mirror, pleased to see no red marks stained it, and then, taking a deep breath, she straightened her shoulders and exited the bathroom. Her lips snaked upward as she joined the pair.

"Both of you at once?" she quipped, dropping into her desk chair. "To what do I owe the pleasure?"

Ned spoke first. "I've brought your damn receipts," he said, dropping a fat file-folder in front of her. He motioned to a metal box on the edge of her desk. "And here are the damn discs you demanded to see."

Sonny's eyebrows rose. "I didn't demand to see anything, Ned. Daddy did."

"What? You could've told me that sooner." He dropped his massive frame into a chair and glared at her. "You take perverse enjoyment in telling people only half truths, don't you?"

"Oh, leave her alone, Ned," her aunt interrupted. "If David told her to acquire the discs, she had no choice but to do it."

"He could've asked me himself," Ned scoffed. "His telephone works."

Sonny saw her aunt begin fidgeting. A clash between them was imminent; she could feel it. She took back the conversation quickly.

"I've a lucid dreaming class in a few minutes, so if anyone has anything important to say, say it now." Her gaze impaled her aunt. "Aunt Charlotte?"

"You've been oddly preoccupied all week, Sonny. I want to be sure nothing serious is going on with your health."

"Define serious." *Time to break the news*, her inner voice advised. Sonny waved her hands at the baggies in front of her. "Meta Corps has requested I look at some evidence involving a serial killer."

"Dear God! You didn't accept?" Her aunt looked repulsed by such a request.

"Of course I did."

Ned settled back in his chair, fussing with a pleat in his trousers. "I should think by now, Charlotte, you would've learned that Sonny does what she damn well pleases—regardless of what anyone else thinks or says."

Hearing the annoyance in Ned's tone, Sonny matched it. "I do it to irk you, Ned—as payback for all the ragging you do on me."

"If we rag on you, it's because we love you and want to protect you," her aunt threw in. She leaned forward, placing her jeweled fingers over Sonny's gloved ones. "I know how terrible it was for you to lose your mother at twelve and then be homeschooled by me. You missed out on a lot of friendships."

"It can't have been pleasant for Daddy to lose his wife and gain an empath at the same time," Sonny retorted. "But I always appreciated your trying to keep the press from learning my secret and plastering it all over the news."

Her aunt released her hand and then lifted one of the evidence baggies. Sonny tamped down an urge to snatch it from her fingers. Instead, she switched the subject.

"If there's nothing more you need from me, I need you both to leave. I've got to prepare my mind for the upcoming session. And I can't do that with your negative vibes stuck to me." The pair continued to stare at her, rather than rising. "What? Spit it out, Aunt Charlotte," she demanded.

"You've grown into quite a stunning woman over the years, Sonny," her aunt remarked.

Sonny schooled her features. *Here we go. Bash the ego.* "Do you think so?" she finally asked. "Stunning enough for a rugged, good-looking man to offer me hot, sweaty sex?"

"Don't be vulgar. You know I abhor vulgarity—especially in you."

"Lighten up, Aunt Charlotte. You know I'm only joking. Where is your sense of humor today?"

An odd silence descended on the room, and then, out of nowhere, Ned spoke up.

"As your aunt has just pointed out, you've been off your game lately. Both of us wonder whether you shouldn't back off your schedule and take a vacation. Why don't you and I go to Europe? It's been years since we've enjoyed a holiday together."

Sonny's mouth turned down. "If I remember right, we took a holiday together not because you wanted to go, but because Daddy ordered you to take me to Europe as a graduation present. Now that I'm a grown woman, I can't imagine a worse trip. We'd be arguing the whole time. I'd rather go with a man I adore, and we're on our honeymoon."

"I can give you the names of at least three suitable men who'd like nothing better than to marry you, Sonny," her aunt interjected crisply. "Just say the word and I'll set up a date night."

Sonny fired up at the offer. "Get out of my office, Aunt Charlotte, and take Ned with you, before I forget that you are family and I love you. And for your information, I am capable of finding a man on my own, preferably a virile one who can take me past naked desire to ecstatic fulfillment."

Her aunt's scowl reappeared. "You're being vulgar again."

"No, being vulgar is pointing out that sex doesn't take place in the hands, but between the thighs."

Her aunt shot to her feet. "If you insist on talking like a common whore, this conversation is over." She whirled around and strode out the door without a backward glance. Watching her disappear, Sonny sighed. One down; one to go. Her gaze drifted to Ned, who hoisted his large frame out of the chair.

"You can be an awful bitch sometimes, Sonny."

Sonny's mouth snapped open, as if to vent an objection; however, seeing the fire behind Ned's eyes, she wisely backed down.

"I'll apologize to Aunt Charlotte as soon as my class is through."

"See that you do." He approached the desk and studied the plastic bags spread out on the desk. "Is it wise to help Meta Corps with such a big case?" he asked. "Your talent is fine in small doses, but to burden yourself with a serial killing seems like psychic suicide." He fingered the plastic coverings, and it took all of Sonny's willpower not to snatch the bags away. She admonished him verbally instead.

"You know better than to touch pieces I'm working on, Ned. You'll smudge the vibrations with your own energy."

His fingers drew back. "You really *are* a bitch, Sonny." He whirled from the desk and exited the room, leaving Sonny to curse softly.

"In my world, it takes a cunning bastard to recognize a cunning bitch. Welcome to my world, Ned."

CHAPTER FOUR

Glancing at the three women assembled beyond the two-way mirror, Ned Chalmers smiled. It was going to be a very productive morning fulfilling these women's desires. Their pleasure always got his juices flowing. He studied the woman closest to the window. Sarah Winters was a mid-fifties empty nester who longed to relieve her boredom by reliving her youth. She paid him big bucks for the adventure, and he always paid special attention to her desires when he put her under.

His gaze tripped to the teen seated beside her. Troubled Maddie Sharp. She sought a different way out of her problems, besides heroin and coke. He always paid special attention to her, too. Once under, he gave her the ultimate high—a new and improved sex life. He snickered at the thought. He hoped her boyfriend back home was grateful for his new-found sex slave.

Next, his gaze landed on a blonde in a yellow tank top and matching shorts. Margie Hunt was a frequent visitor to the retreat, and while here, she always spent her time and money delving into past-life regressions. To her credit, she wasn't one of the messed-up ones. Her sparkling personality was always in force, and that joy never wavered, not even under hypnosis. It was as if her spirit was so good that no amount of negativity could touch it.

She was his first appointment today, and by the looks on the other women's faces, she was regaling them with some past remembrance of a therapy session. They were all laughing, and the sound filtered through the mirror, reminding him of his last session with Margie. She had gone under fast and stayed under longer than he expected. And for that he had been paid handsomely when she woke.

A familiar figure appeared in the waiting room, greeting the women and then heading for the chamber door. As it opened, Ned turned.

"You're up early, Charlotte," he greeted her.

She shut the door quietly. "We're heavy on appointments today. I noticed an odd thrumming in the headpieces yesterday, so I'm recalibrating all of them before the sessions start. We can't risk being sued because we've electrocuted one of our guests."

Ned frowned at her words. "I check my headpieces daily. They don't need any further monitoring."

"That doesn't seem to stop you from checking my equipment daily, though, does it?"

"You're hallucinating," Ned said. "I've never interfered with your dream lab equipment."

She ignored his statement, moving to the mirror instead. She gazed out at the seated women. "I see Margie Hunt's here again. Perhaps we should restrict how many sessions she's allowed to indulge in while she's here."

"It's her money," Ned retorted. "Let her spend it how she wants. Besides, it's clients like her that bring in other clients. When she leaves here, she recommends The Sanctuary to all her friends. I have no intention of telling her she's unwelcome."

The woman beside him sighed. "Very well. Do as you like. You always do." She moved from the window to a raised chair on a platform. Once there, she lifted a green headpiece from its holster and studied the dials situated on either side of the crown. Obviously not liking what she saw, she withdrew a small screwdriver from her pocket and adjusted the screws.

Giving her space, Ned returned to the main console and waited for her nod. When it came, he powered up the circuit board. Green lights rolled on one by one, and in seconds, the entire system was set to go. He moved to the door and then stepped back as Charlotte swept past him, back into the waiting room.

"You're first, Margie," she called. "Have a great session."

The woman sprang from her chair, her face glowing with an eagerness Ned couldn't help but savor. The woman couldn't wait to go under, and he couldn't wait to give her what she wanted. She took her seat in the chamber chair quickly, settled the green headpiece on her head, and then waited patiently for Ned to acknowledge her readiness. He hit the "on" button, and a prerecorded voice came through the room's speakers.

"It's only moments before dawn. It's a beautiful summer morning, and you're outside, enjoying the beginning of a new day. You notice a gentle, warm breeze and the scent of the morning air. You can hear birds chirping in the distance, and the sound is muted and pleasant as they welcome the dawn of a new day ... In front of you, you see a very beautiful, gated gazebo. There are four steps up to a gate. It's a green gate ... Can you see it?"

"I see it."

"You walk towards it, thinking it's the perfect place to relax and watch the sunrise from ... And now you're going beyond the sunrise ... beyond the colors of dawn, into the center of the sunrise ... Where are you now?"

"I'm riding in a gondola in Venice. Monte and I are on vacation. The sky is blue, and music is playing from an apartment building nearby. We're happier than we've ever been ... "

"And where are you now?"

"Monte and I are having incredible sex in the moonlight. The stars are shimmering like silver. Monte's a wonderful lover, knows just where to touch me ... "

"And where are you now?"

CHAPTER FIVE

Panting heavily, Logan rubbed his right side. He wasn't used to hiking up steep hillsides, and his body was rejecting the climb with every step he took. So far, he had stalled by two rocks, clung to a tree, and pleaded for a refreshing drink of water. When he didn't oblige his body, his brain complained of all the dirt and rubble on the path. He grimaced. Dirt *had* been his only companion as he ascended the hill, and he was damn tired of breathing in the particles.

Glancing up, Logan was grateful to see he was finally closing in on the jutting overhang above him. He had been following the marked path of arrows since starting his climb, and he wondered if he was ever going to reach the scenic overlook.

Bent on reaching the overlook in less than two minutes, he doubled his pace. Three minutes later, he reached the scenic plateau, wheezing lightly. Studying the vista now spread out before him, Logan immediately took in its beauty. The Sanctuary was a magnificent piece of real estate; Dresden hadn't lied about that. Down the hillside, the canyon floor was awash with colorful blooms of purple, yellow, and blue. To his right, adobe cottages dotted the hillside, and off to his left, tall buildings surrounded a large lake. Serenity, the shuttle driver had called it, as the van had circled the lake—the side of the retreat that catered to the guests' desire to take classes, have personal readings, or indulge in a variety of metaphysical pursuits.

Seeing the sparkling sheen on the water, Logan realized the retreat had a true Southwestern charm. Pools, gardens, waterfalls—it had "rich and classy" stapled all over it. He grinned. Dresden hadn't lied about The Sanctuary's elegant reputation either. All the buildings were beautifully tailored and sculpted. He could also see why Sonny conducted her Sunday-morning classes two miles up from the hotel. Up here, the guests got a two-for-one bargain. Spiritual solace, plus a spectacular view of the countryside.

His gaze scoured the landscape below again, pleased when a cool breeze swept up from the desert floor and licked his face. Suddenly in no hurry, he leaned against a post marked "Mystic Overlook." Crossing his legs, he chuckled at the name etched into the wood. Since he had exited the shuttle, he hadn't seen a name that didn't have a spiritual tie. Spirit Lake, Mystical Gardens, Sacred Path, Holistic Gardens.

He glanced north, realizing that the turquoise sky, winding trails, and hiking paths also added charm to the desert locale. To its credit, the Loop, formally known as The Spiritual Path, paid homage to the natural beauty of the hillside.

Logan glanced at his watch. The receptionist had told him Sonny's class would end at eleven, and by the sound of the New Age music blaring above his head, the class was running late. He let another five minutes slide by, enjoying a smoke while he waited. When another five minutes passed and the music still blared, he sighed loudly. How long did it take for people to get in tune with their auras? Surely not the two hours listed on the retreat brochure.

The music suddenly stopped, and Logan hoisted himself from the column. At last. He squashed his cigarette in a nearby garbage bin and continued his climb. As he trudged upward, his mind circled back to the question he had been asking himself since he had boarded the plane at JFK. Did Sonny Blake have any clue she might be harboring a serial killer at the retreat? If she was so damn good at reading people, she must've at least had an inkling of something sinister.

His foot hit the end of the path, where he found an empty clearing, but no people. Where the hell had everyone gone? He scanned the rows of chairs, looking for signs of life. When he heard the sound of fading voices, he realized the group was leaving the plateau by a separate route.

Swinging left, he studied a decimated buffet table. Only a scant tray of food was left. It was clear doing aura portraits made one ravenous. Entering the canopy, he plucked two last croissants from the tray and leisurely popped the first one in his mouth. His eyes watered at once, and he dove for the pitcher sitting in the middle of the table. Holy crap! Talk about a spicy kick! He poured water into a glass and then chugged the refreshing liquid down. The burning fire coating his larynx quickly eased.

He poured a second glass, pleased when his tongue and throat stopped burning. Chucking the second croissant in a trash container at the end of the table, Logan ducked back out from under the canopy and studied the rest of the mesa. Looking northeast, he spotted a sign marked "Chapel" and headed for the structure. What else did he have to do? Sonny Blake had obviously escorted her group to a descent path, and he didn't intend to stand around, twiddling his thumbs, while the woman took her time coming back.

Following a paved-stone sidewalk, Logan reached the chapel and ascended two wide steps into the small, yet cool, dwelling. He headed for the large open-air window at the front of the church. When he reached it, he drew in his breath. Another magnificent vista with God's name scribbled on it. Up this high, it was easy to believe God existed, and that all was right in the world.

Embarrassed by such spiritual whimsy, Logan whirled rapidly and slipped into the first pew. He studied the cross hanging over the small altar and wondered when he had become such a jaded ass.

• • •

Returning to the rows of chairs, Sonny rubbed her face. Thank God the class was over. She had barely made it through the last portrait without throwing up. She plopped into a seat and dropped her head into her hands. There was no denying it now. Something major was wrong with her skills. Ever since she had pulled herself from her bed this morning, she had been besieged with a fear so paralyzing she could hardly breathe.

Lifting her head, she glanced down at her gloved fingers, willing them to stop shaking. She'd make an awful criminal, she knew. She made an awful empath, too. How could she help a client when her hands were shaking like fruit whirring in a blender? Shaking hands screamed fear, and fear screamed mental breakdown. Last night's nightmare hadn't helped. She had dreamed of thousands of Death cards being hurled at her by a shadowy figure who kept shouting: "I know who you are and where you live!"

A stark thought hit her. Perhaps she had been wrong to agree to Meta Corps' request. She was clearly in some kind of personal meltdown, and getting into the head of a serial killer might be the final push that sent her into a rabbit hole filled with dead bodies and no way out.

Relax, Sonny. Rely on your spiritual prowess to get you through, her inner voice advised. The thought was so ludicrous that Sonny laughed. Hadn't she been doing that? The question gave her a chance to take a closer look at the table. The setting had been sweet at the start, the stemware elegant and the wine glasses celebratory. That was before the hordes had descended and devoured all the canapés. Now, it looked like a team of pigs had stampeded through.

Hit by a sudden desire to clean up, Sonny jumped up and entered the canopy, shivering when a cool gust of air fanned her uncovered arms. She tilted her face to study the wind chimes dangling from the canopy edges. The chimes were also sweet, as if announcing to the world: "Here lies God's goodness." She shifted her gaze to the majestic landscape and beyond. No crouching tigers or hidden dragons, she mused.

The arbor is a perfect backdrop for an ambush, though, her inner voice warned.

Stow that kind of thinking, Miss Empath, she responded. *We're already stressed to the max.*

Hearing a soft scurry on the ground behind her, Sonny glanced over her shoulder quickly. She spotted a large iguana darting under the edge of the buffet table and stomped her foot, hoping to scare it away. Cleaning tables with a determined lizard was not how she wanted to end her morning. When she saw no sign of its body, she sighed in relief.

Now what? her inner voice asked. We shift our thoughts to physical activity and hope to God we don't get hit with any more surprises today. *Amen,* her ego replied. Agreeing, Sonny popped one last, stray cheese ball into her mouth and munched on it with relish. Leaning over, she began collecting the paper plates into a pile and scooping them into the garbage.

• • •

The dining hall was filled, but Ned found the trio he was looking for right away. He zigzagged his way between tables, and, reaching the group, he plopped down in an empty chair.

"You need to talk to Sonny," he told the mustached figure on his right.

"Why? What has she done now?" David Blake asked, glancing at Ned over the rim of his coffee cup.

"She's brought Meta Corps down on us."

Charlotte Fletcher stopped smearing jam on her toast. "Meta Corps is here?"

The lanky figure to her right dropped the piece of toast he was buttering. "Bloody hell! That's all we need. A government agent poking into our business." Brad Fletcher glared at Ned. "You're sure your info is right? You've seen the man? Talked to him?"

Ned shook his head. "I heard him checking in, but before I could touch base with him, Jessie sent him up to the mesa to meet with Sonny."

"It's that damn case she's looking into," Charlotte exclaimed, shivering. "Touching the evidence of a serial killer is just plain crazy. You know how sensitive she is to negative vibes. She could have a meltdown or something." She glanced at her brother. "You need to talk to her, David. Convince her to send this agent packing."

David frowned, setting his cup down. "You know I never poke my nose into Sonny's business. She's a grown woman with a mind, and a schedule, of her own."

"She's a bitch, you mean," Ned said heatedly.

Brad stirred. "That's my niece you're talking about, Ned. She's no bitch; she's just remarkably smart when it comes to reading people—and their vices."

"What's that supposed to mean?" Ned asked.

"It means, like the rest of us, she's noticed how much time you're spending in late night sessions with the same female clients," David cut in. He poured himself another cup of coffee. "We cater to all of our guests here, not just a select few. It sends the wrong message to our guests when the appointment ledgers are filled with the same client names all the time."

Ned's stomach curdled at the criticism. He obviously had been too overt in his session scheduling. He'd have to back off some.

"I wasn't aware I was hogging the limelight," he finally chided. "From here on out, I'll turn down some clients. Shall I send them your way, Brad?"

Brad shoved his plate away. "Don't be an ass. Just put a little more variety in your scheduling from now on."

Suppressing the urge to throttle the man beside him, Ned rose instead. It was time to beat a hasty retreat up to the mesa. He needed to put a little scare into Sonny and her companion. He shoved his chair back.

"I need to see you privately," David said, seeing him prepare to leave. "Company business. When can we meet?"

"In a couple of hours. I'm having brunch with a friend today."

A snicker echoed from Brad.

"How old is she? Sixteen? Seventeen?"

"Fuck you, Brad!" Ned whirled from the table and struck out for the entrance. Fucking prick! He'd see to it that Brad paid for that cutting remark. But first, he had to learn how safe his secret was from Sonny and her companion.

• • •

Coming out of the chapel, Logan heard a husky laugh and halted. What the hell? He stopped on the bottom step, studying the figure beneath the canopy. Thin, but not too thin. Nice legs. Nice ass. His gaze swept higher. Full, rounded breasts, tiny waist. He felt a nudge in his groin and winced.

Store those insane desires to touch and feel, Reed, his inner voice warned. *Desires like that landed you in a hospital bed last time.*

Yeah, but a well-stacked mouse had an amazing beauty. He left the steps and started across the stone pavers. As he strode, his thoughts turned to his ongoing bad luck with women. *Fool me once, shame on you; fool me twice, shame on me.* He let his gaze rest on the figure again. Damn, but she had a gorgeous body, even from the back. Would the face match the figure?

Whoa, forget that kind of question, his inner voice urged. *It doesn't matter how gorgeous the mouse is. We're here to solve a case, nothing more. Besides, we've given up trifling with mice. They're trouble, with a capital T. And the one thing we don't need at the moment is more trouble in our life.*

Right, he agreed. *Just keep on walking.*

CHAPTER SIX

Sonny popped the last chocolate pastry into her mouth and chewed on it thoughtfully. If she didn't figure out what was causing her overwhelming shutdown soon, plus her sudden uncontrollable urge to eat everything in sight, she'd end up eating herself to death. This chocolate pastry was heavenly.

Thirsty, Sonny turned to the standing coffee urn, bent on taking a shot of caffeine; however, her hand paused over an empty cup when she spied a white envelope propped in the center of the mugs. She scooped up the note, spotting her name on the front. *A secret admirer?* her inner voice asked. She ripped open the flap. Probably a thank you note from a guest.

Feel the texture of the envelope with your fingers, her inner voice prodded. *It's probably the owner of that distant, sexy voice wanting to make mad, passionate love to us.*

Shut up, she told the nagging voice.

She peered inside the envelope, spotting a splay of colors. Her heart tripped suddenly. A Tarot card?

Curiouser and curiouser, Miss Alice in Wonderland, her inner voice mocked her.

Sonny peeped about her.

No White Rabbit today, Miss Empath; we are alone.

She pulled the Tarot card from the envelope, studying the image depicted. The Lovers. Naked bodies entwined in a highly erotic pose. She shivered at the thought. Just whose naked bodies did the card represent? She examined the card more closely. It was from the Morgan Greer deck, and that, in itself, was odd. She had stopped using that deck for readings a long time ago, and her spirit guides knew it. So, who had left the mysterious card for her?

She turned the card over and saw a typed note Scotch-taped to the center. She read the words.

Sonny:

   We need to talk. You are in grave danger. Meet me in the bungalow after your class on the mesa is finished. And don't tell anyone you're coming. Your life depends on it. Trust no one. DAD.

The cryptic words made Sonny's mouth turn dry as dust. *Trust no one.* Not even her aunt? Her gaze strayed to the bottom of the hill. Meet him in the bungalow. *Done,* she decided. She slid the Tarot card in her dress pocket and whirled around. She hit a rock-solid wall of chest. Long arms came up and around her, encircling her like strands of a spider web. Stunned, she glanced up and then inhaled sharply. God, what a magnificently sculpted face! Her thoughts soured immediately. *Trust no one.* Not even a gorgeous face with electric blue eyes and a disarming lopsided grin.

Trust no one, Sonny, her inner voice stressed. *Don't even think about how well your curves mold against the contours of his lean body. Forget the divine, masculine smell of his aftershave. Get out of his arms!* Sonny lifted her hands and pushed at the chest. To her surprise, the man didn't budge. The word "nice" echoed in the air, and she wondered what was "nice." The sky? The trees? Her breasts tucked tightly against his warm chest?

Embarrassed by such a starkly erotic thought in the face of such uncertainty, Sonny squirmed. The movement caused her breasts to sway across his chest, and a rush of pink stained her cheeks. They were welded so close that she couldn't tell which of their heartbeats was racing faster—his or hers. Should she scream for help?

Yeah, her inner voice chided. *Scream for help. See who comes.*

Sonny bit her lip at the rebuke. *Right, we're alone, in the arms of a man who smells divine and whose embrace feels safe.*

Get a life, Sonny, her inner voice scoffed. *And get out of his arms.*

Luckily, she didn't have to push him again. The arms holding her released her from his embrace. She retreated a step, unnerved by his piercing stare.

"May I see what you've just tucked in your pocket, Miss Blake?" The voice was deep and pleasant, and sounded familiar. Sonny felt her heartbeat quicken but ignored it. She was acting like a starstruck tween focused on Justin Bieber when she should've been telling the stranger to go to hell. Trust no one, her father had warned.

Before she could utter the word "no," the stranger's hand slipped inside her dress pocket and foraged for the card. Outraged, she slapped at the fingers.

"What the hell do you think you're doing? How dare you? Give that back to me!"

She attempted to snatch the card back but found her gloved fingers slapped. Fast, she concluded—he had soft, gentle, and fast hands. She watched as he scanned the card leisurely.

"I suppose you know what the picture on this card represents?"

The question hung in the air, and her response was filled with dripping sarcasm. "Of course."

"I thought as much." Looking her over, he handed the card back. "I don't suppose you'd care to translate it for me?"

"I think it's pretty self-explanatory," she retorted. Who the hell was this man? And why was he quizzing her on the Tarot card?

"Somehow, I *knew* you'd be a stubborn wench." Reaching into his left shirt pocket, he hauled out a cigarette and lighter, and Sonny saw him grimace as the cigarette flared, leaving smoke trails skimming his nose. His bold stare continued, and this time, she tried to ignore it by stuffing the card back into her dress pocket.

An uncomfortable silence descended between them, and Sonny cleared her throat. What was the man thinking about so intently? His keen, thoughtful gaze was lingering on her shape, his interest curious and obvious, but his mind elsewhere. Clearing her throat again, Sonny centered her thoughts on the stranger's identity.

"What can I do for you, Mr. ... ?"

"Reed. Logan Reed. And to answer your next question, no, I'm not a guest."

Smoke coiled, hiding his expression, and Sonny frowned. Why was he here then? And blast it, why did she have to be more interested in learning what his taste in women was, rather than finding out what he wanted from her? And he did want something from her. She could sense it.

"Surely you must want something from me," Sonny stated. "You tracked me all the way up here."

Crusty laughter startled her. "Hopefully you've already done what I need, and I can get the hell out of here."

Sonny's brow furrowed. "You seem familiar. Did I do an aura reading for you recently?"

"Not bloody likely. I don't do spiritual shit."

"What do you do then?" Sonny asked, surprised by how offended she was by his "spiritual shit" insult.

His hand reached into his back pocket, and she saw his amused grin emerge again. "I'm from Meta Corps. You're expecting me." He flashed his ID badge in front of her face and she scanned the name quickly. Logan Reed, out of New York City. The wallet snapped shut and was pocketed again.

Caught off guard by his sudden arrival, Sonny bristled. "How could I be expecting you, when Meta Corps refused to tell me when you were coming?"

"Surprise has its advantages, Miss Blake." His wry grin came again. "Surely, with your amazing talent, you knew I was on the way."

Sonny frowned. He was disparaging her talent again. What an odious toad he was turning out to be. It was time to put him in his place.

"I did have a vision of an agent coming; however, his demeanor was extremely kind and pleasant. It appears Meta Corps changed agents at the last minute and sent an arrogant toad instead."

"It's more likely you misinterpreted the vision."

At his jibe, Sonny felt her blood begin to boil. This meeting was so over. With a flounce of her skirt, she whirled about. She was whipped back around before she could even take a step. Blue eyes pinned her face.

"Simmer down. I meant no insult."

Sonny's anger evaporated instantly, but her curiosity didn't. "Pardon me for asking, but if you don't do 'spiritual shit,' why did Meta Corps assign you this case?"

"Because I'm the best," he replied. "And you always send the best to work with the best. And according to Meta Corps files, you're the best."

Sonny's pulse lurched at the compliment, but she managed to keep her surprise from showing. "Do you know anything at all about what empaths do?" she asked.

"I'm not a newbie to empaths. I know what you do. You excel at psychic bullshit."

Sonny was astonished by his words. The man obviously hated metaphysics in any form. "I see. You're a nonbeliever?"

"No, I'm a believer," he corrected. "I just believe in tangible things you can see and touch."

"So do I," she mocked him. "But I also *see* intangible things as well."

"So your file says. It reeks of adoring fans."

"Really? They don't find me too flashy?" Sonny asked sarcastically.

His expression pulled into a sour grin. "Now who's being unpleasant?"

"Touché." She took a step. "Shall we go?"

Sonny took another step, only to find her wrist snatched roughly. His sudden grip dislodged the edge of her glove, and his warm fingers connected with the bottom of her palm. In seconds, her empathic skills set off, tossing the pair into a white, blinding light, where they skittered down a rabbit hole filled with jarring bumps and skids.

•••

Shock waves shook Logan's frame, and in one brief instant, he sank into a pool of throbbing pain and a mysterious ripple of moving images. His mind was suddenly pitched through a white vortex and then thrown out the other side. A vision of an alleyway washed through his mind, and he recognized the place at once.

And then he saw himself standing next to the mouse, both of them witnessing a replay of his deadly shooting last summer as if standing behind a plate-glass window. He saw his "other" self. Arm raised, gun poised out front, moving towards an approaching figure. In the span of an instant, he saw another gun firing and a speeding bullet heading his way. He winced as he saw the bullet hit its mark and watched as his "other" self collapsed to the pavement.

His rib cage suddenly ignited with tremendous pain, and as quickly as he had been whipped into the vortex, he was whipped back out. He gasped under the barrage of floating pain and then willed his head to stop swimming. He came back to reality with a mental thud, firmly clutching the mouse's hand, and then, out of the blue, he heard tortured gasps. He followed the sound, spotting Sonny's short, red hair glistening in the sun. Mesmerized by the sight, Logan drew in his breath. And then his gaze slid to her face. Once again, he felt an insane urge to sweep her into his arms and taste her lips. He chucked that thought, and her hand.

Free of his grasp, the mouse grabbed her torso and doubled over. At the same time, Logan's rib cage started throbbing again. The pain lasted all of ten seconds and then waned; however, Logan realized the mouse was absorbing his injury into her own body. He didn't know how she was doing it or how she was standing the pain. All he knew was she was experiencing the exact moment his world had come crashing down, a bullet ripping through his flesh.

The scar on his rib cage suddenly stopped aching, but the mouse's look of pain morphed into distress before she collapsed to her knees and threw her arms around her chest, rocking back and forth. Alarmed, Logan dropped beside her.

"Miss Blake!"

"Don't touch me," she warned through gritted teeth. "The exchange isn't c-c-complete." Her last word was stuttered, and Logan fell silent. Not complete? What else was left? His rib cage was without pain for the first time since the shooting. She had quite literally taken the pain away, and that was impossible. He glanced at the mouse's face again, noting the blood now dripping from her nose. He reached in his back pocket and hauled out a handkerchief.

"You're bleeding."

Her fingers shot to her nose. "Perks of the trade," she quipped. She pulled a handkerchief from her pocket and threw her head back in an attempt to staunch the flow of blood.

Logan frowned at her sarcasm and shoved her fingers away, mopping the streaming blood with her hankie.

"You're an insane wench, you know that?"

"And a danger to everyone I meet," she mumbled. "Why do you think they keep me hidden away?"

"Don't joke. You could've been killed absorbing that wound."

She pushed the hankie away from her face. "Don't be so melodramatic. You caused the connection, not me. The bleeding will stop momentarily. It always does."

True to her words, the flow soon stopped, and she scrambled to her feet, settling her gloves back into place quickly. He handed her the hankie again, and finding a dry spot on it, she wiped the base of her nose. In seconds, her face was dry, and she was pocketing the hankie.

"How come the Meta Corps files are incomplete?" Logan asked. "Why don't they say you've the ability to link minds?"

"If you were Meta Corps, would you want the public to know?" Sonny asked. "People are frightened enough of talking with the Other Side; would you place more fear in them by telling them it's possible for two minds to link up and experience the same moment together?"

She bit down on her lower lip, and Logan sensed she'd been about to add something else. She obviously didn't trust him enough to reveal it.

"Very well," she continued. "You've managed to convince me it makes perfect sense for Meta Corps to monitor me from time to time. After all, they own a piece of me."

He growled impatiently. "I'm no babysitter, Miss Blake. I'm here to find a serial killer. You happen to have an incredible talent for touching objects and getting supernatural answers. And as you know, that's a talent Meta Corps uses to its advantage. Besides, your personal file reveals you've saved countless lives over the years."

Sonny made a face at him. "Admitting that must've hurt your ego."

"More than you think."

She laughed at the confession. "But just think. If you hadn't come, you would've missed seeing my incredible talent in person, and of course, if you hadn't come, you would've had no one to insult every five minutes."

"I haven't insulted you every five minutes. Perhaps only every ten."

A small hiss pummeled his ears. "How on earth have you managed to stay alive without some woman bludgeoning you to death?" She whirled around. "It really is time we parted company permanently."

"Have I insulted you again too soon?" he mocked her.

"You've managed to insult me quite thoroughly, and you know it," Sonny answered, whirling back. "So rather than inflict my 'spiritual shit' on you any further, I'll return you to the front desk of the hotel and bid you good-bye."

"Without telling me whether you've had a chance to look at the evidence I sent?" he queried, as she stepped away. She swung back, her eyes widening in surprise.

"Good heavens! No one said this was a rush job."

"Well, it is."

"Well, if you paid more attention to what you call 'spiritual shit,' you'd know that Spirit can't be rushed. It reveals its truth in its own time and in its own way, and not before."

"I'm not a patient man, Miss Blake."

"Well, then, Spirit is about to teach you a very *big* lesson."

A glimmer of a smile surfaced on his lips. "At least Spirit sent me a gorgeous teacher to look at. It should make the lesson very entertaining."

His gaze met hers, as if expecting her to mount a comeback; however, a loud boom rocked the crisp air, startling the pair. A split second later, a bullet shattered the water pitcher beside them, sending shards of glass splintering in all directions. Sonny whirled away with a screech, clutching the front of her dress in fright.

Logan's fight-or-flight instincts kicked in at once. He upended the table, grabbed the mouse's elbow, and jerked her down. Another bullet ricocheted over their heads, and he forced her to the ground, covering her body with his.

"Bloody hell!" he cursed. "I knew the moment I saw you you'd be trouble. Why the hell do I always have to be right?"

• • •

"Call the bastard off, Miss Blake, or I'll strangle you, here and now." He made a move to throttle her, but Sonny deflected the chokehold by grabbing his hands. Good Lord, he thought she had set him up to be killed. Locked in his stare, Sonny felt nothing, heard nothing, except the loud beating of both their hearts. A second later, a cluster of pinpricks settled in front of her eyes, and she knew she was going to faint. Closing her eyes, she let her mind float away.

Out of nowhere, pain jarred her cheekbone, followed by a sudden rush of air coursing back into her windpipe. Immediately, strong fingers hauled her to a sitting position against the back of the overturned table. Sonny's eyes flew open at the contact. The rotten swine had hit her. She could feel the imprint of his palm on her cheek. Her hand flew upward, along with a scathing comment about men who hit women; however, a spasm of coughs erupted from her vocal cords, slicing off the taunt. Swallowing air, she managed a hoarse croak.

"Who wants you dead?"

An icy silence greeted her question, and Sonny realized she had asked the wrong question. Someone wanted *her* dead.

You are in grave danger. Hadn't that been her father's words?

Once again, she found her face and hair under intense scrutiny, and then, lightning-quick, Logan hunched in front of her, shading her from another round of shrapnel whizzing over their heads.

"I can tell by your face you know you asked the wrong question," he finally stated, craning his head as the air around them went quiet. "The question really is, how the hell are we going to stay out of the bastard's line of fire? This table is going to come apart if it gets hit a few more times."

Before she could offer a suggestion, another barrage of gunfire chewed the canopy above their heads. Once again, the pair clung to each other. The arbor on their left sheared, sending wood shavings and mangled flowers raining down on their heads. Sonny clutched Logan's chest. Once again, her breath was cut off midstream, but this time she knew it was from the smell of a cowhide jacket.

Almost as soon as it began, the gunfire stopped, leaving an unearthly smell of gunpowder hanging in the air. Sonny covered her nose to suppress a sneeze. Lightning-quick, a gun appeared in front of her face, and she gasped. Her fingers clenched the barrel, sliding it away from her nose. For the first time, she felt a real tremor of fear. Someone did want her dead.

An image of the Lovers card floated through her brain, and she willed it away. This was no time to think of hot, sweaty sex with a Glock-toting Meta Corps agent. Her inner voice suddenly chimed in.

What's the old adage? Be careful what you wish for? You wanted a man's man, and now you've got one. How do you like him so far?

Sonny shivered at the question, and then she heard the click of a chamber sliding into place. The toad carried a gun. Was he bent on using it? She peered around the edge of the table, studying the surrounding trees.

"Can you tell where he's shooting from?" she asked.

She was slammed back against the wood roughly.

"Stay put, you fool! You want to get yourself killed?"

Startled by the ferocious command, Sonny raised her gaze a few inches. Rotten swine! Why was he pretending to be worried about her now, when it was so obvious before he would enjoy seeing her boiled in oil.

Glancing up, she caught sight of his upturned chin and grimaced. His gaze was scouring the surrounding shrubbery with the same intensive stare he had given her face moments before.

"Perhaps you should fire your gun. Show him we're not defenseless," she said.

The hint of a smile crossed his lips. "Right. Fire my gun against a hi-tech rifle. That's great advice, Miss Blake. Where did you come up with that pearl of wisdom?"

"I do my best thinking when being shot at."

His gaze returned to the surrounding rocks and trees, and then on to the cascading waterfall on their right. "Do me a favor. Let me do the thinking."

Sonny studied the dark shadow kissing his cheekbones and ventured a soft observation. Was there anything he wasn't good at?

"Being nice to women," he muttered, as if reading her thoughts. His head swiveled around to study the drop-off behind them. "I think it's time we go. Get ready to run." The command was so unexpected that Sonny could do no more than stare at him as if he had grown two heads. Talking with him was like taking a roller-coaster ride through a dark tunnel. You could never see the next dip in the tracks. "Get ready to run, I said!"

"Run?" she managed to stammer. "Run where?" She braced her back against the table. "No way; I'm not going out there. We can wait."

She felt a breath of hot air on her right cheek. "Don't argue with me, Miss Blake. It makes me want to leave you under this canopy to face our sniper alone."

"Go ahead and leave then," Sonny sniffed. She poked his chest with her finger. "Just leave me your gun when you go. I'm not afraid to fire at the bastard. Unlike you, I'd enjoy going down with a fight."

Lightning-quick, Sonny found her neck in a viselike grip and the back of her head pinned to the table. Nose to nose, she felt his steely blue eyes bore into hers.

"You *never* want to know what it's like to go down with a fight, Miss Blake. Don't *ever* say anything so stupid again in your life!"

Sonny's mouth went dry, stunned by his sudden attack. Heavens but he had a low boiling point. Did he think she was insinuating he was to blame for getting himself shot last summer? Why couldn't he see she had said it because she was terrified of being shot the same way? She lifted her hands, winding her gloved fingers around his wrist. To her surprise, she felt a stirring of her senses and severed the connection immediately by jerking her fingers away. She couldn't afford to send them both into an unexpected vision. His fingers relaxed as if he knew her thoughts, and she managed to sneak a breath before whispering, "I'm terrified. When I'm scared, I babble."

His face moved away, and she could breathe again. Absently, she rubbed the front of her neck.

"Get ready to run."

The command came again, and Sonny rocked her head. "That part I meant. I'm not leaving the safety of this canopy."

"We can make it to the chapel."

Sonny's gaze shot to the path on their right. The chapel was at least fifty yards away.

"Wake up, Miss Blake. We're out of here."

"I'm not going."

"You're going."

Her brain searched for another excuse. "I can't run in this dress. It's simply too tight."

"Christ but you're an aggravating wench."

To her astonishment, his fingers gripped the hem of her dress and ripped the right-side seam up over her hip. Sonny stared in horror at the shredded fabric.

"I don't believe you did that." She placed a hand over the sheared material and tried to piece it back together. "You've ruined a Michael Kors original. You're going to burn in hell for that."

"The devil will have to stand in line to get me. Now, do you have any other objections as to why we can't leave this canopy?"

"There are still bullets in your gun?" she asked sarcastically.

Again, she found herself stunned by a sudden movement. Only this time, he stood up, moved into the open, and emptied his Glock into a tall line of fruit trees. Ducking her head, Sonny covered her ears, trying to stay out of the way of the back blow. In a flash, he was hunkering back down beside her and fanning the air in front of them. Silence descended with no return gunfire from the trees. Sonny lowered her hands from her ears, giving the man in front of her a sideways squint.

"How long have you been a deranged maniac?" she asked. "And why am I putting my trust in you?"

"Because I'm the best, Miss Blake. Now, since my gun is empty, there is no reason for us to stay under this canopy any longer, is there?"

"None."

Sonny bolted to her feet, and in a flash, she was out in the open, heading for the stone pavers in front of the chapel. An angry curse followed her flight, but she ignored it, concentrating on the ground in front of her. The sound of heavy footsteps soon clumped on the stones behind her.

Gunfire erupted from the trees, splicing the ground in front and behind Sonny's feet. Dodging, she hid her face from the showering debris, expecting to be felled by a stray bullet at any moment. A hefty shove between her shoulder blades kept her from thinking about stopping, though. Rotten toad! What on earth had possessed him to think they could outrun speeding bullets? She was as deranged as he was for buying into that fantasy.

A sharp ping echoed alongside her heel, and Sonny doubled her pace. They were almost there. She just had to keep her eye on the steps. She counted the strides off in her head. Three, two, one ...

She hit the bottom step and dashed into the shadows of the chapel with a heavy pant. Logan raced in behind her, swung around, and slammed the entry door behind them. Hearing the bolt click, Sonny breathed a sigh of relief and headed for the first pew she saw. Once there, she collapsed against the back of the seat, thanking God, the Universe, and any spirit guide who might be listening. They had been oddly lucky. She stole a peek at the man dropping beside her and inhaled sharply.

"My God, you've been hit!"

CHAPTER SEVEN

Logan stared at the bright red stain saturating his left pant leg. Christ, when had he been hit? He heard a rip and then saw gloved fingers wrap a piece of black fabric over the red stain and tie it off. He felt a slight pressure around the wound and tried not to wince as a familiar burning sensation snaked itself up and around his thigh.

"I told you it was the height of stupidity to try to outrun a rifle. But would you listen? No. You had to continue—"

"It's only a scratch," he interrupted.

"It could've hit an artery."

Logan placed his hand over hers. "It didn't. It's a graze, nothing more."

"Still …"

The stained-glass window over the entry door shattered with a horrific blast, and the woman beside him scrambled to the floor beneath the pew.

"Is he following us in here?" she asked, peering over the seat at Logan. "He must really want me dead."

Logan studied the hole, now filled with an expanse of blue sky.

"You would think the bastard realized we got his message after the first round of shots," Logan stated. He caught Sonny's eye. "We *will* be dead, Miss Blake, if you don't tell me there's a back door out of this chapel that doesn't send us hurtling two miles down to the desert floor."

Her lips tilted at the words, and she sprang back up to the pew seat. "You don't think Daddy would build a masterpiece two miles up and not build an emergency exit down, do you?"

"Don't be smug, Miss Blake. If there's an out, lead me to it."

Seizing his hand, she hauled him out of the pew behind her, ignoring his painful intake of breath. She led him down the aisle and then angled to the left, where she dropped to the floor and attempted to lift the handle of a trapdoor. Pretending his thigh didn't hurt like a son of a bitch, Logan helped her lift the door and push it over on its hinges. He glanced down the dark shaft to a ladder bolted to the side of the wall.

"How far down does it go?"

"Not too far," she replied, dropping to a sitting position and dangling her legs into the hole. "The shaft ends at a lighted tunnel, which leads to the private elevator on the south rim of the Loop."

Logan caught her gaze, stifling a fractured groan as he thought of the pressure that would seize his leg the moment he attempted to descend the ladder. His look sent the smile from her face.

"She was ill, you know—the woman who shot you." She saw his eyebrows rise. "She was suffering from a form of mental displacement. It happens after an empath has absorbed too many heavy emotions year after year. Your empath was unable to carry the burden any longer, so she looked for a way out. Unfortunately, she chose you."

"You got all that from a vision that lasted only a few seconds?"

"Well, I am the best," she said with an airy wave.

Logan grinned. "Tit for tat, Miss Blake. Now, we've more urgent things to worry about than old gunshot wounds."

"Why our sniper wants to kill me?" she asked.

"No, why he was toying with you. If he meant to kill you, you'd be dead."

Sonny shivered and then threw off the tremor. "I'll not give the bastard another thought. It gives him power over me."

She started to descend the ladder; however, Logan halted her movements. "Let me go first. This ladder looks like it has seen better days. Can't have you falling to your death so soon after we've met."

She made a face at him. "I know the shaft and tunnel. You don't. I need to go first."

Logan swung onto the ladder quickly, forestalling any chance of her going first. He clung to the top rung of the ladder, sucking in his breath and willing his thigh to stop burning from the sudden exertion. He waited for it to quiet, and when it did, he looked back up at the mouse.

"I promise not to peek up your skirt, Miss Blake, but if I do happen to see anything, it won't be the first time I've seen two gorgeous buttocks."

He started down the ladder, giving her no time to mount a scathing retort. When his foot hit the fifth step, he felt the ladder vibrate beneath his fingers.

"You better keep your eyes front and center, mister," she warned from above. "The shaft is going to get smaller and darker as we go, and you'll need to pay attention to that. I just hope we can open the exit door when we reach the bottom. I don't remember if the latch has a digital lock or not."

Logan couldn't keep a grin from emerging. "Where's your adventurous spirit, Miss Blake?" he mocked her.

"It's back with the whizzing bullets," she muttered.

Logan's grin widened. The wench had a sense of humor, he'd give her that. *Another admirable trait in her favor,* his inner voice advised. As he took each rung, he wondered where the next attack would come from. There would be one. In his line of work, there was always a next one.

. . .

Sonny heard a swift intake of breath and wondered what was wrong with the toad. Was his leg finally giving out? Or had they reached the exit only to find it did have a digital lock? She halted on the ladder and whispered into the darkness below, "Have we gone all this way for nothing?"

She heard a measured grunt, and though she knew she should be reassured by the sound, she wasn't. If it turned out they had reached a dead end, she would begin sobbing like a hysterical teenager who had caught her boyfriend kissing her best friend.

Hearing a light scuffling sound, Sonny dropped two steps, realizing the man below her was stepping off the ladder. She could sense it through her gloves. And then she heard a light bang, followed by hands gripping her hips.

"We've reached the tunnel. Watch your step."

Sonny took the last few rungs quickly, jumping to the floor in relief.

"Thank God Daddy put a string of lights in the tunnel, because I am never going to climb a dark shaft again," she stated. "All I could think was, is he standing over the hole with infra-red goggles, prepared to pick us off as we climb down?"

His voice held amusement as it washed over her. "If we had one of those bullets, you could touch it and we'd have the shooter's identity lickety-split," he said, brushing an open patch of skin on her shoulder.

"Did you just say *lickety-split?*"

"No, of course not. Your hearing must be slipping."

"You better hope not. If I have to use my empathic talents in the dark, there's no telling what might occur. I might end up days ahead, or days behind." She shivered uncontrollably. "I don't relish having to relive this day over again. Do you?"

Ignoring the question, he turned from her, signaling for her to lead the way. She took off, focused on the energy surrounding his body as he followed. She had never imagined her contract with Meta Corps would bring her face to face with one of its agents one day. She had relied on staying in the background, her contract nothing more than an amicable handshake between colleagues. She had helped when she could over the years, declined when she couldn't. That agreement had always worked, so what had changed? The High Priestess Tarot card flashed through her mind. Of course. The packaged Tarot cards Meta Corps had sent her. Their arrival wasn't a coincidence. They weren't just about other victims. They held a message for her as well.

As if reading her thoughts, the man beside her took her elbow. "Penny for your thoughts," he said.

"They're not worth a penny," she replied, "but here's something that is. Nothing that occurs in my world is random. Everything has a place and a meaning. A plus B always equals C. Your being assigned this case is no coincidence. Nor were the Tarot cards you sent me to decipher. My interpreting them will be no coincidence, either, when we get to that place. Spirit never makes mistakes, you see, and it never deviates from the plan it has orchestrated once it starts."

Logan clutched her elbow tighter. "How far is the elevator, did you say?"

"End of the tunnel," Sonny answered, slipping around a corner and heading north. Logan matched his stride to hers.

"Humor me for a moment, Miss Blake. If what you say is true, and nothing is random, then the vision we shared back there was purposely meant to rattle us. And if, as you pointed out, my shooter skidded off the rails, how far can you push your nervous system now and not skid into your own meltdown?"

"Empaths do suffer from bouts of madness from time to time," Sonny said. "And even though you'd like me to, I can't promise you that what lies ahead of us won't push both of us over the edge. However, we have one thing going for us."

"Which is what?"

"Faith. I trust in my talent, and you trust in your logic."

Logan gave a resounding chuckle. "I didn't realize you were such a Pollyanna." He switched subjects. "So why did your father build The Sanctuary in New Mexico?" he queried, picking up the pace.

"Privacy, mostly," Sonny replied, spotting a pinprick of light in the distance. "It was a chance to stay off the paparazzi radar. Since we cater to the rich and famous, it has given our family blissful anonymity."

"Admirable."

"What's not to admire? My father is a genius. He knows quality when he sees it."

"And obviously knows how to sire it, as well."

"Why, thanks for the compliment—I think. You did mean me, didn't you?"

"Don't fish for compliments. You know you have magnificent looks."

She winced at the backhanded compliment. "Ouch," was all she said.

Obviously seeing how fast the bright sunlight was closing in on them, Logan tightened his hold on her elbow. "You talked about learning lessons before. I sense my first lesson is going to be learning how large the security force at the retreat is and who heads it up."

Sonny sighed. Why was he focusing on the practical when she wanted to focus on the personal? Ever since her mind had merged with his, she had fallen under his spell. He was so totally opposite her that a push-pull vibration had been created between them. It had set off a sexual attraction, as well; one that she could sense strongly and he couldn't. What would he do if he knew that she was hoping the Lovers card in her pocket signified a night of hot sex with him?

"Lieutenant Dick Cutter," she said, finally seeing the end of the tunnel. Seconds later, they stepped into the sunlight and onto a cement patio housing an elevator. Sonny shaded her eyes from the bright light. Logan did the same. "After what just happened," she went on, "we have to step up security."

Logan dropped her elbow and then pressed the "down" arrow on a metal panel. When the elevator door slid open quickly, the pair stepped inside.

"I know you don't trust me yet," Logan stated, as Sonny's fingers hit the floor button. "But it would be in your best interest to tell me what the card in your pocket signifies."

"Wasn't being shot at enough to make the card seem pointless?"

"Not when you take into account that nothing is random in your world."

Sonny's mouth tilted at the declaration. "Are you saying that there might be something to my 'spiritual shit' after all?"

A scratchy growl emanated from the man beside her, and Sonny's smile withered under the drawl of his mocking taunt. "I'm hardly a convert yet. I grew up believing logic wins out over faith every time. So far, I've not seen anything to convince me I'm wrong."

Sonny's smile vanished. "Well, I shall just have to try harder to convince you."

"You can start by telling me about that Lovers card in your pocket. Is it a vague reference, or have you been dallying with a naked lover in some exotic garden of the retreat?"

Sonny bit back a scathing retort. She ought to tell him that the picture depicted him and her dallying in the gardens. Naked. What would he say to that interpretation?

Probably attempt to choke you, like before, her inner voice taunted.

Right. Keep the conversation away from erotic lovemaking.

"Cat got your tongue? Or have I discovered one of your naughty little secrets?"

"Change the subject, Mr. Reed," she said, as the elevator cage settled into place and the doors swung open. She stepped out onto another cement patio. "So far, I sense no connection between the

Lovers card and the evidence collected at your crime scenes. Until I do, they are separate entities."

"There is a connection, though."

Sonny smiled. "See there, I *am* making a believer out of you."

His hand suddenly lifted and caressed her hair. "I'd rather make you a believer in the *physical* world. It can be a magnificent place with just two people. You're a stunning wench. A man would be a fool not to let nature take its course and have incredible sex with you."

Stunned by his words, Sonny swallowed a sudden lump in her throat. She wished she had the courage to floor the man and kiss him. She'd love to know what his lips tasted like. *They're delish*, her inner voice chided. *Can't you tell just by looking at them?*

Again, shut up, she told her ego. *We are not kissing any toads today.*

A loud sigh emanated from Logan as he dropped his hand. "I'll take that as a no," he said wryly.

Ignoring his sarcasm, Sonny stepped further out onto the patio and headed towards a pair of intersecting sidewalks. A wolf whistle startled her, and she turned back at once.

"What's wrong?"

"Nothing. Just wanted you to know that I always get what I want—sooner or later." He took her elbow and propelled her forward. "Now, while we're on our way to meet this Lieutenant Cutter of yours, could we finally discuss the Tarot card?"

Sonny gave a weary sigh. Were all Meta Corps agents so one-track minded? Her heart was racing at his offer of sex, and what was his doing? It was pulling her out of a fantasy world and back to reality. Stiffening her spine, she realized there was no reason she should ignore his question.

"It's easy for the Lovers card to be misinterpreted," she said, as they descended some steps. "The image depicted is obvious, of course—the erotic attraction between the male and female;

realistically, there's more to it. An attraction that starts out with a sizzle comes with problems—namely, having to make a choice about the relationship somewhere down the line. Generally, the lovers are tossed into a trial of some kind, which keeps them together or tears them apart for good."

"That sounds an awful lot like a spurned lover's MO to me," Logan replied. "What about the note your father left on the back of the card?"

"What note?"

"Don't test my patience," he told her. "Remember, I have none. Your father left a note on the back of the card for you. Did it warn you were in danger?"

Sonny's eyes widened at his words. How had he managed to see the note? He had barely touched the card.

"Whatever you're about to say—don't," he warned. He threw her a warped grin. "My job calls for an intuitive eye, and everything I perceive is a clue to a bigger piece of the puzzle … "

"And you say you're not psychic," Sonny mocked him. She waved him towards a lavishly decorated but empty pool area. His scowl reappeared as they walked, making her suppress a shiver. If looks could kill, she'd be dead.

"And buried," he said, enigmatically.

"How do you do that?"

"Do what?"

"Read people's thoughts and then pretend there's no such thing as the supernatural world."

"Years of practice," he said. "Plus, I had plenty of time to read up on the Blake family on the airplane. Your father leads a charmed life—beautiful sister, beautiful daughter—and more money than he can possibly spend in two lifetimes. However, there's one glaring fault with the biography."

"Which is?"

"He doesn't appear to protect his daughter's empathic talents. If anything, he appears to use your gift for his own gain. On the other hand, you have almost as much money as your father, but you make substantial donations to a number of worthy charities."

"Those donations were made in private."

His hiss cut her next words off. "Stow your outrage. There isn't anything a Meta Corps agent can't get his hands on these days. I have no intention of revealing your magnanimous donations to anyone."

"Then get to the point," she said. "We're almost at the security offices."

"How are you going to introduce me to Cutter? How you do will change how I approach him."

Sonny met his stony stare. Did he intend to manipulate the lieutenant as he had done with her? She'd love to see him try it. No, on second thought, she knew he would get along famously with Dick. Both were pompously arrogant and proud of the fact.

"United we stand, divided we fall?" she jibed, leading him onto a second veranda decked with outdoor tables and chairs. A crowd of sunbathers stood huddled around a long buffet table, and as the pair zigzagged past the waiting line, a matronly senior waved for Sonny's attention. The pair paused.

"Miss Blake, I can't thank you enough for the reading yesterday," Marilyn Boulder gushed. "I can't believe how much I got out of it. You know what a skeptic I was. But to hear that Thomas is at peace … Well, I cried all the way back to the bungalow."

"You did all the work, Mrs. Boulder," Sonny said. "And, of course, Thomas did his part."

Tears welled within the matron's eyes, and she dug for a tissue. "I'm such a sentimental old bitty," she said, wiping her cheeks. "I don't know how Thomas ever stood me."

"He loved you to pieces."

A grateful sniff came Sonny's way. "Bless you for that, my dear." She blew her nose and then signaled the pair. "Now, don't let me keep you and your young man from enjoying your time together." She dove back into the buffet line and began following the procession.

Sonny's lips tilted. The woman thought she and Logan were an item. *If only*, her inner voice chided.

Logan took her arm, sidestepping the line. "Do you remember all the guests' names?" he queried as they walked.

A mischievous glint surfaced in Sonny's eyes. "Well, I *am* the best."

His mouth twitched with amusement, but he didn't offer a verbal retort. Instead, they strode the portico, coming to a halt at a pair of double swinging doors. Once there, she threw up her hand, signaling him back.

"Give me a minute to speak with Dick. The mess on the mesa needs to be cleaned up stat. The trails open at two on Sunday, and we can't have people seeing broken tables, bullet shells, and shattered glass while they're hiking."

Logan nodded, holding the door open for her. Appreciating the chivalry, Sonny felt compelled to lighten the mood between them.

"Since I didn't say it before, welcome to The Sanctuary. If you keep walking along this corridor, you'll see signs pointing to the registration desk. When you get there, ask for Jessie and tell her to give you the cactus suite, per my orders."

"Is the room next to your suite?"

Sonny gave a sarcastic laugh. "I never allow handsome men to stay in the suite next to mine. If I did, the gossips would have a field day. Not to mention Ned and Uncle Brad would come knocking on your door, asking what your intentions towards me might be."

His lips tilted upwards. "I'm sure I can convince them my intentions are honorable," he spouted.

"I'm sure you could, but we are not going down that rabbit hole anytime soon."

"Too bad. I fancy sleeping next to you, even if there's a brick wall between us."

Sonny laughed. "Sorry. You'll just have to grin and bear it. We'll meet for dinner tonight, though. I'll introduce you to the family then."

"Looking forward to it."

He signaled her inside again, and Sonny went, surprised when he slipped his fingers through her gloved ones. Her heartbeat quickened as she sensed the touch of his fingers through the fabric.

"Don't you ever take a hint?" she asked, as he strolled alongside her.

"About what?"

"About me going *my* way, and you going *yours*."

"I can't protect you unless we're both going the same way."

"You are not sleeping in my suite, Logan."

"Ah, my first name at last," he teased. "I thought you'd never stop thinking of me as Agent Reed."

"It was a slip of the tongue," she countered.

He made no comment, just grinned at her, and she wondered how one man could be so baffling—dripping with arrogance one minute, soft gentleness the next. It was a deadly combination, and she could only hope his stay at the retreat would be extremely short. In fact, she'd leave no stone unturned in her effort to make it so.

Shaking his fingers loose, she led him through the kitchen area, through a crowded dining hall, and then followed the signs marked "Security Offices." A minute later, they stopped at a double glass door with a digital box on the wall beside it. Sonny punched in a passcode, and the doors slid back quickly.

Stepping in, she shivered. She hated how cold this room had to stay. Her gaze swept the massive command center. She also hated all the surveillance cameras, console stations, and monitoring equipment. She didn't like spying on people. She did enough of that when reading clients. This technology was different, though. It was secretive and intrusive, which her father deemed necessary for the safety of the guests. *At least when we spy, we have a client's permission*, her ego advised.

"You could've told me your father owned Fort Knox," Logan said softly in her ear.

"And ruin any chance of earning your respect?" she shot back. Her gaze skimmed the room, searching for the lieutenant.

"You earned that up on the mesa. Now, where the hell is the lieutenant?"

"Good God, Sonny, what happened to you?" The voice was booming, and Sonny whirled, spotting Dick Cutter's giant frame barreling towards them. When he reached her side, he took one look at her disheveled appearance and cursed. "What the hell have you been doing? Rolling around in the mud?"

Sonny started to say, "Dodging bullets," but had no chance as Logan stepped forward, offering his hand.

"Agent Logan Reed—out of Meta Corps, New York City branch. You've a serious problem on your hand, Lieutenant. Someone just tried to kill Sonny up on the mesa."

CHAPTER EIGHT

Standing in front of a computer monitor, David Blake adjusted his headset.

"You're sure Sonny was the target and not this agent fellow?" he asked, glancing at Dick Cutter's face on the screen. "What kind of credentials has he shown?"

The lieutenant made a face. "All the proper ones. Plus, I've spoken with his boss in New York City, who confirms he and Sonny are working on a Meta Corps case together. According to him, the man's a goddamn legend."

"Well, he better be, or I'll see him rot in hell," David said. He flicked a switch and then lowered his sturdy frame onto a standing chair. "Keep me in the loop, Dick. And keep an eye on Sonny and her companion—nothing obvious."

"Her companion won't like it. He notices everything."

"Well, don't rock the boat unless you have to," David said, flicking off the monitor. He sat for a moment, wondering what his next plan of action should be. He checked his watch. Ned was on his way. He didn't have much time to load the stolen disc into the computer and passcode it for Sonny.

Hitting the keyboard, he brought up the "load" icon and began loading the disc. When it finished, he programmed it with a key code and then secured it with a fail-safe subroutine. He'd make damn sure no one could delete the program before Sonny saw it. A series of back loops followed the first loop. It was clear he had seriously miscalculated Ned's ability to hide in plain sight, but he would soon rectify that error.

"You crazy bastard ... Where's the disc?"

The words ripped through the air, startling David. He swung on his chair, spotting the knife in Ned's hand immediately. He grimaced.

"Killing me won't get you the disc, you bastard. I've sent it so far into cyberspace, it'll take ten teams of computer hackers to retrieve it."

Ned's face clouded with a rage that shocked David. "If you think I'm going to let you destroy everything I've built the last ten years, you're a fucking lunatic." In the next instant, he moved, bringing up the knife as he came.

Whirling on his chair, David attempted to flee, but before he could make it to his feet, a sharp, burning pain erupted in the middle of his back and trickled upward. It ended with a blinding explosion across his lower neck. He reached up and back. When his fingers encircled the stem of the knife, he attempted to pull it out; however, Ned reached out and plunged the knife deeper into the confines of his back.

Drained of air, his lungs shut down, and a blinding flash of pinpricks skewered his eyelids. Soon, like a balloon deflating, his head sank onto the keyboard. He struggled for control and forced one last conscious thought. *Touch the knife, Sonny.*

• • •

Leaning against the doorjamb, Logan studied the woman crossing the carpet. She was like a sleek tiger, silently stalking its prey one minute, happily eating it the next. Right now, she was standing on tiptoe, opening a skylight, and her silhouette was so mesmerizing that Logan's blood stirred unexpectedly. He banished the desire to his "don't go there" file.

Sunrays filtered through the room quickly, bouncing off a half-mirrored ceiling. "The cactus suite," she had called it when they had entered. The name suited it. And he was sure she thought it fit his prickly demeanor perfectly. Even now he saw the hint of a smile on her face as she moved back across the room. She glanced at his change in jeans.

"Are you sure you don't want to see a doctor or nurse? We have a working clinic on site."

"I don't do doctors anymore," he said firmly.

"Yes, well then, did you find everything you needed in the bathroom?" she asked. "Neosporin? Bandages? I see the jeans fit."

"Yes," he stated, glancing down at the denim. "Although one wonders whose jeans they are." He glanced up. "An old boyfriend's?"

"Can I offer you something to drink?" she asked, deflecting his question with a question. "Something stronger than tea or coffee?"

He stifled an urge to chuck her nose playfully. "Whiskey?" he queried. He dug a cigarette from his chest pocket with a grin. The match sizzled with a flare, reflecting in baby-blue eyes. The cigarette was immediately snatched from his fingers and put out.

"The Sanctuary is a no-smoking zone," Sonny said. "How about a martini, shaken, not stirred?" she teased. "Isn't that what James Bond drinks when on assignment?"

"Not this Bond," he muttered.

Sonny waved her hand airily. "The bar's over there. Help yourself. I'll be back in about an hour. I have a meeting with Daddy."

"I'll go with you. I'd like to meet the genius."

"It's going to be a boring meeting," Sonny emphasized.

"I like boring; in fact, I thrive on boring."

"I don't need a babysitter, Logan."

"Good, because I loathe babysitting."

A sigh greeted his ears. "I'm not going to get rid of you, am I?"

"Not in this lifetime."

With a sudden bolt, she fled past Logan and out the front door. Left behind, Logan cursed her dashing stride. Just when his thigh showed signs of improvement, she was rushing him around like a bat out of hell. He took off after her racing figure.

Twenty steps later, he caught up to her in the first-floor stairwell. Side by side, they rounded a corner and then dashed across a footbridge into a maze of half-grown fruit trees. From there, they sprinted onto a sidewalk in front of a small-framed bungalow.

Nearing the door, Logan pulled Sonny behind him and took the lead. He needed time to scope things out before they charged in like elephants on a rampage. However, the mouse thwarted him by passing his shoulder and entering a passcode into a panel on the wall. When the door didn't open, her brow furrowed.

"That's odd. It's not taking my passcode."

"No emergency override?"

Her face relaxed. "God, you're right." She pressed a small spot on the wall. A cement panel slid back, revealing a red "emergency" button. She hesitated before pushing it, chewing on her lower lip. "I hate to do this. It will signal Dick and the security team, but after all that's happened today, I think Dick will forgive me." She reached for the button; however, Logan's quick grasp of her elbow forestalled her.

"How many doors to the room?" he queried.

"Only this front one. Daddy's bungalow is a security-based computer complex. If he's in there, he won't leave any other way."

"Let me go first," Logan advised, stepping in front of her and lifting his pant leg. He took his gun from its holster and then withdrew a moon clip from his jacket pocket. Slapping the clip into place, he turned, signaling Sonny. "No heroism once we get inside," he warned.

Her answer was a dubious look. "I'm no hero. Aren't all Meta Corps agents?"

"Hell no," he quipped. He coiled himself, ready to spring as her fingers hit the button, followed by her passcode. The door sliced open with a rapid whoosh, and Logan dove through first. He skidded to a halt, blinded by a flashing strobe light ricocheting across the walls and floor. Its garish hue changed the furniture assembled into eerie spectral goblins. The giant computer screen on the north wall hummed like the ceaseless hum of traffic. Below the screen, draped across the console keyboard, Logan spied an inert figure.

"Dear God!" The mouse's cry was shocked as she pitched herself from behind him. "Daddy!"

Logan jerked her back. "Stay put!"

She squirmed, attempting to break his viselike hold on her wrist. "Let go! I can help him. I can touch the knife."

"Touch a piece of evidence? Not while I'm here to see it, you won't." Logan attempted to haul her back, but she evaded his grasp.

"You don't understand. I can tell who did this!"

"Touching the knife will contaminate the scene, and I can't allow that at the moment."

She ignored him, snatching off her gloves and reaching for the knife. Logan reached for her hand at the same time. Their fingers collided at the same moment she touched the knife.

Familiar shock waves shook his frame, and in one brief instant, she had hurled them into a mysterious ripple of moving images. A sudden vision of two bodies entwined in heated sex washed through his mind; however, as quickly as it appeared, it disappeared. In seconds, he was moving again, whipped into a second vision. The vision took a moment to settle, and when it did, he was once again studying solid images through a plate-glass window.

An eerie feeling stole over him as he spotted a woman in a chair, wearing a green headset, and not much else. She was young and beautiful, with a figure most women dreamed of, and the glow saturating her face was totally mesmerizing. And then the image was yanked from his mind, and he felt himself traveling again. This time, he saw a green door with the word "Pandora" scrawled on it. And then he was moving again.

He came back to reality with a walloping jolt, clutching the mouse's hand, and then, like before, he heard her tortured gasps.

"Sonny!"

"Still here," she said.

He dropped her hand quickly. "What the hell was that?" he asked. "The couple was having amazing sex."

He heard a gasp. "You saw a couple having sex?"

"Yes. Didn't you?"

"No. I saw a young woman participating in some kind of therapy session." She gave him a sideways squint. "Are you sure you saw a couple?"

"I know what I saw. I saw the couple first, the therapy session next, and then a green door with 'Pandora' plastered on it last."

She gave him an enigmatic stare, and he returned her look with a grunt. And then she was lifting her hand to her nose. When she found it free of blood, she commented, "No nosebleed this time."

Logan ignored her words, his mind jumping back to the figure at the console. "How long before your security team arrives?" he asked.

"Couple of minutes."

Logan gazed at the motionless figure. "Can you connect the images? Or what the word Pandora might mean?"

"N-no."

"If you touch the knife again, would we see the same progression of images?"

"What?" Her squawk was horror-stricken. "My father's been stabbed, and you're wondering whether we can go back in and look at the images more closely? Don't be such a bastard!"

"Humor me. Can the same images be recreated at a different moment in time? Or is it one per customer?

"Depending on how important they are, they'll resurface, but maybe not in the same order as before."

"Good." Logan leaned over and inspected the body. He felt for a pulse and found none.

"The killer's close by," Sonny stated, shivering. "I can feel it."

"Man or woman?"

"Unclear. The energy's fading."

Logan swung from the console. "Do you trust me, Sonny?"

"I think so …Yes, I do."

"The less the police know about your vision, the better—at least for the time being."

Sonny shivered at his pronouncement. "We can't keep the knife a secret from Dick. We've contaminated the crime scene. Besides, our fingerprints are all over the handle."

"Right now, honesty is not the best policy."

Her second shiver had him suppressing one of his own. "What is the meaning of the green door?" she asked. "I didn't see it."

"Good question," Logan said. "A better one is why did I see it and you didn't?"

Their gazes locked as she donned her gloves again. Logan took a step towards her.

"Promise me you'll do as I say and stay mum on the vision," he said. He saw her nod with a resigned sigh. His sigh matched hers. "Thank God your security staff knows you. They'll accept any story you present them with."

"I don't lie to my security staff," Sonny said tartly. "And they don't jump to conclusions until they've investigated every incident thoroughly."

Logan's mouth dipped into a lopsided grin, but before he could offer his retort, she added, "Would this be a good time to tell you that the note on the back of the Lovers card warned me that my life was in danger?"

Logan's head whipped around. "Christ! I ought to kill you myself for withholding that piece of information from me." He came to life, taking hold of her arm. She balked at the manhandling.

"Daddy's note said to trust no one. And 'no one' included you. For all I knew, you could've been sent to kill me!"

"If I was sent to kill you, you would've been dead ten seconds after we met."

"I believe you."

Her quiet remark deflated his anger; however, in the next instant, a booming voice brought it back up.

"Don't move, or I'll shoot!"

CHAPTER NINE

Gun outstretched, Lieutenant Cutter ducked through the front door and then into the room.

"Don't shoot us, Dick."

Sonny stepped forward, and seeing her distraught expression, he lowered his gun.

"Dammit, Sonny! I could've killed you. What the hell is going on now?"

His eagle eye canvassed the room, lighting on Logan Reed first and then the body at the console. The hair on the back of his neck prickled, and he gave a heated curse. "What the hell?"

The expletive bounced off the walls, startling even him. And then, his security instincts kicked in, and he headed for the console. Logan followed on his heels. A second later, the lieutenant was turning to the man.

"Tell me neither of you touched the body or the knife."

"We just got here," Logan answered. "Sonny had a meeting with her father. When her passcode wouldn't trip the door, she got worried. We pulled the emergency switch."

Dick turned to the woman hovering behind them. "Any discrepancy with that story, Sonny?"

"No, and it's not a story. Daddy asked to see me after my aura class. But as you know, I got waylaid on the mesa."

She shivered, and Dick realized she was recalling the incident. Shifting focus, he snatched a two-way radio from his security belt and barked for immediate assistance. Hearing the request being relayed, he pocketed the radio. Once again, his eagle eye took in the scene. There was no sign of tampering by the pair, but then he didn't know Logan Reed well enough to know whether he would fudge the truth to save his ass. Dick snatched some gloves from his inside coat pocket and donned them quickly.

Bending, he studied the knife. *Damn effective*, he thought. He observed the red stain fanning out from the knife and shifted his focus back to Logan.

"What do you think, Reed? I could use some Meta Corps insight."

What the man thought was lost, as arguing voices suddenly erupted at the front door. A second later, a scuffle took place, and before he could call for everybody to stay put, three figures attempted to gain entry to the room.

"Don't you dare keep us out of here, Peter Hammond!" Charlotte Blake railed at the uniformed officer blocking the door with outstretched arms. Manicured fingers poked him in the chest for emphasis, but he stood his ground.

"Get out of the way, Peter! We're going in!" Brad Fletcher's voice demanded.

"Stand aside, Hammond! That's an order!" The third demand was blistering, and this time the young man had no choice. A gargantuan hand lifted him off the floor and tossed him aside.

"What the hell is going on?" Ned Chambers snarled, catching sight of them standing by the console. His gaze swept over the slumped body behind them, and he frowned. "What the hell is going on?" He started forward, halting when the lieutenant waved him back.

"Stay put, Ned. You're of no use here. You're too late."

A tortured cry sounded behind Ned. "My God! David!"

Ned whirled, catching the woman behind him as her knees buckled and she headed for the floor. In the next instant, her husband scooped her up and shuffled her to the sofa. Propping her there, he hovered, fanning her face while he took her pulse.

Ignoring the gesture, Dick lifted his radio and barked a new order to the dispatcher. When finished, he turned and fed orders to the uniformed officers hanging about the bungalow door.

"Get your asses out of here," he ordered. "Set up a perimeter north and south. I want anything that breathes stopped and interrogated. We might have a chance to get the murderous bastard."

A flurry of blue uniforms fled from the door, and Dick could hear distant shouts as his orders were relayed down the line. He went back to examining the body, signaling the remaining two officers at the door to join him. They inspected David briefly, taking cell phone photos, and then Dick radioed for a sheet to cover the body. As soon as he did, muffled sobs came from the couch.

"I need you clearheaded," Dick stated, approaching the sofa. "You know how this works. I've got to get sensible answers, and fast."

"I can't," Charlotte muttered. "Seeing him like that ... so still ... " She broke off, covering her mouth. "Don't ask me to be strong—not now." She tugged on the silk ties of the filmy caftan she wore and attempted to pull herself together.

Snatching a pen and notepad from his shirt pocket, Dick addressed the trio. "You first, Ned. Where were you in the last hour?"

The large figure stiffened, obviously offended; however, Brad was determined to ask questions.

"Who the hell set off the alarm?" Brad asked. He stepped forward, and Dick raised his hand in irritation.

"Hold on, Brad. I'm asking the questions here. I'll get to that later."

Brad's mouth twisted in annoyance. He spotted Logan's figure. "Who the hell is this?" he asked. "And what's he doing with his arm around Sonny?"

"He's a Meta Corps agent out of New York City, and he's obviously comforting Sonny," Dick replied calmly. "Now back off, Brad, and let me do my job."

Brad retreated to a high, wing-backed chair and flung himself into it. "I don't need to lecture you on retreat security, Dick," he chided. "Not when David is ... " He broke off mid-sentence, stealing a quick glance at the covered body and then looking back at Dick. "Well, I don't need to lecture you about opening our doors to strangers," he finished abruptly.

Seeing his strained expression, Dick made note of it in the back of his mind. Was Brad's annoyance real or fake?

"Brad's right," Ned muttered. "Our company protocol is straightforward; we don't invite other agencies into our business without a formal request and approval."

Sonny stepped forward. "I approved Mr. Reed being here. I'm currently working a case with him."

"And without the board's approval, I might add," Ned stated.

"I don't need company approval. This isn't Sanctuary business. And what I do on my own time is none of your business, Ned."

The room's atmosphere charged up as three sets of eyes targeted Sonny's face. Dick hid a smile. Trying to intimidate Sonny by staring her down wouldn't work. Not with her ability to sense what everyone in the room was feeling—and thinking. The silence became pronounced, and wanting to defuse the situation, Dick shifted the topic back to his questioning.

"I'll ask again, Ned. Where were you in the last hour?"

"Where were *you* in the last hour?" Ned asked sarcastically.

The lieutenant fired up. "Answer the question, or I'll assume you had something to do with David's murder. Where *were* you?"

"Driving over from Serenity," Ned responded quickly.

Brad seconded the info, his expression mellowing. "We drove over together; we each had therapy sessions in the lab this morning."

"Did you leave the facility between sessions?"

Charlotte's head lifted. "How could he? I had the car."

"And none of you talked to David in the last hour?"

"We haven't seen or talked to him since breakfast," Charlotte stated.

Dick nodded and then wheeled around, returning his attention to Brad. "Anything troubling David lately? Any change in routine? Arguments?"

"We run a tight ship here, Dick," Brad responded. "Just ask your staff. We try to keep any arguments for the Monday Morning Coffee Klatch."

"And you, Charlotte? Have you noticed David acting differently?"

Charlotte twisted her wedding ring. "He's been edgy, but then he always is when meeting with our lawyers. Arguments? He always had them. With Ned, with Brad, it was normal."

Dick shifted his stance. "Ned?"

"This is ridiculous," Ned scoffed. He tugged his black vest down with a jerk. His smile did not indicate compliance. "I own part of the retreat. There's bound to be friction now and then. David and I didn't always see eye to eye on company policy."

"You had words recently?"

"A few."

"What about?"

"He received a complaint that I had treated several clients badly during their session. He felt they deserved a personal apology. We exchanged words."

"There have been more than a few complaints," Brad mocked him.

"*Your* history with clients is not so squeaky clean, either," Ned shot back. "There was that lawsuit last year, claiming you touched a client inappropriately."

Brad stiffened at the slur, but it was Sonny who lashed out.

"Don't you dare accuse Uncle Brad of touching young girls! You know the girl lied. It was proven in a court of law."

"We're getting off topic here, don't you think?" Logan asked, pulling Sonny back. He stepped around her frame. "Is there a way to track David's whereabouts over the last week, Fletcher? Who he saw, what meetings he attended?" His gaze shifted to Ned. "Did he have a datebook the lieutenant might look at? It would help to know who he met with before his meeting with Sonny."

"Surely you don't suspect one of us killed David," Ned said. "His death will ruin our personal and professional reputations."

"How much of The Sanctuary do you own?" Logan asked.

"Enough," Ned replied evasively.

"The same as Brad?"

"Hardly," Ned scoffed. "David rewarded hard work. He abhorred slackers. Brad hasn't quite gotten the hang of the hard work part yet."

"Fuck you, Ned!" Brad yelled. "I do own shares in the retreat."

Ned hid a smirk, his eyes openly amused. "We all know how you obtained *your* shares," he said

Charlotte, still slumped on the couch, came to life, bristling at the slur. "That kind of slander is uncalled for. Brad has never asked anything from David—not shares or favors." Her gaze bounced to Dick. "You know quite well that David hired Brad to oversee the investment portfolios long before we married." Her gaze jumped back to Ned. "Brad deserves your respect, not your contempt."

Ned managed an apologetic stare. "Sorry."

Tossing her head, Charlotte refocused on Logan Reed. "I'm sure Meta Corps knows our history well. David and I founded The Sanctuary together; however, over the years, I found it necessary to sell my shares back to him. Brad holds only ten percent of the company."

Brad rose from his chair suddenly, cutting into his wife's explanation. His stare impaled Dick. "Once the press hounds get wind of David's death, they'll camp outside the front gates. Can you guarantee additional protection? We're not equipped for a worldwide paparazzi descent, you know."

"Our security team is more than equipped to handle overzealous paparazzi," Dick responded.

Ned tugged his vest down again. "We all want the same thing here—a very discreet handling of the matter."

Dick grimaced. He would have loved to use the press hounds to his advantage, though. The Sanctuary was bigger than life, and keeping David's murder on the down-low wouldn't produce glaring headlines unless he unleashed the details of David's demise to the World Wide Web.

"A feeding frenzy is not the answer," Sonny said firmly. "If there's any hint of scandal, The Sanctuary will crash and burn."

"Besides," Logan offered, "David Blake was killed for personal reasons. By someone he knew very well."

The group winced at the bald statement.

"What makes you say that, Mr. Reed?" Charlotte asked.

"Don't listen to him," Brad fumed. "He's been here for … what? A couple of hours? He can't possibly know whether one of us is capable of murder."

"He's right, though. It *is* a possibility," Dick stated.

Every face showed outrage. Only Brad had the audacity to complain out loud.

"I suggest you investigate a little more before labeling one of us a killer. Your job is to remain impartial."

"And thorough," Ned added.

"You do work for us, after all," Charlotte threw in. "Our safety is your number-one priority—and the guests', of course." She rose from the couch. "We must prepare a statement for the press as soon as possible—one that's carefully worded." She signaled to Ned. "Help me devise a statement that doesn't backfire on us, Ned. You always know the right way to word things." He took her arm, and Dick listened to their voices as they exited the bungalow. To his surprise, his elbow was grasped tightly.

"Send Reed packing, Dick," Brad said quietly. "He has no right to imply David was murdered by one of us."

"If you have something to say to me," Logan interrupted, "say it to me, not the lieutenant."

"I'm merely pointing out that, for only knowing us for an hour, you're overly fixated on us—and Sonny."

"If I don't mind his attention, Uncle Brad, why should you?" Sonny asked.

"Sonny's right," Dick said. "She's certainly capable of sensing who is dangerous and who isn't."

"Stow the lecture, Dick," Brad chided. "I get enough lectures from Ned." He left the bungalow quickly, slipping out the door without a backward glance.

Silence descended in the room for a moment, and then Logan broke the quiet. "Who wins if The Sanctuary goes bust?"

"Aunt Charlotte would," Sonny replied, and then, to the men's horror, she burst into tears.

Logan was the first to move, wrapping his arm around her shoulders and listening to her distraught sobs. "You're not going to fling yourself into one of your visions, are you?" he asked. "Remember, I can't go where you go unless you take me."

Her tears intensified, which made Dick panic. "Take her out of here, Reed."

"Where the hell to?"

"She likes Saddleback Ridge."

"Where the hell is that?"

"It's my favorite place," Sonny said between sobs. "It's peaceful and quiet, and doesn't have dead bodies." Her sobs intensified again, and this time, Dick saw Logan panic. Dick reached into his pocket and threw Logan the keys to his truck.

"My truck's out back. Use the GPS to find the ridge."

Logan moved quickly, propelling Sonny out the door ahead of him. Watching them disappear, Dick grimaced. Who the hell had murdered David?

His thoughts fell on the men who had just left. Brad Fletcher was shrewd, but would he murder his brother-in-law to take control of the Blake empire? On the other hand, Ned was prone to hot outbursts that ended as quickly as they started. Both spent day and night working at Serenity, and they seldom, if ever, drew attention to themselves. In Dick's mind, it was more likely that Brad's low-key demeanor hid the desire to take out an enemy.

He turned and studied David's body. Thank God Sonny hadn't had time to use her empathic skills to reprise the moment of David's death. If she had, the news would've spread like wildfire—right to her unknown stalker.

Hearing his name called sharply, Dick spotted Charlotte Fletcher re-entering the bungalow. He saw her tear-stained cheeks at once and realized she, like Sonny, was attempting to push David's death to an "I'll deal with it later" file. Stopping in the center of the room, she glanced around, avoiding the covered sheet.

"Has Sonny left?" she asked.

"Just did. She had a meltdown. Logan took her for a ride to calm her nerves."

Charlotte gave a strained laugh. "I suppose it's her turn now, to be thought of as a murder suspect."

"Guilty till proven innocent, right?" He quickly changed the subject. "What's between Ned and Brad? Some petty work grievance, or does it go deeper than that?"

Charlotte's head shot up. "It's a continuance of a childhood rivalry, if you must know," she stated. "They grew up together, and they have always tried to outdo each other in everything. As men, they're still fixated on besting each other, except now Ned uses Sonny as a weapon to needle Brad."

Dick's head whipped around. "Are you implying Ned has made romantic overtures towards Sonny?"

"Hardly that." Charlotte laughed. "It's her talent he secretly wants. He's said several times over the years that he wishes he could fling himself in and out of worlds like she does; however, I suspect that what he really means is that he wants to create a perfect world where he's master and the rest of us are his adoring slaves."

"God help us if he ever finds a way to accomplish that task," Dick said.

"We all lived different lives before coming to The Sanctuary," Charlotte added. "Some of us may have a black skeleton or two in our closet."

"I've already probed your life histories before coming to New Mexico." Dick laughed. "But, with your permission, I'll take a closer look. My gut agrees with Logan Reed. David's murder was personal, not professional."

Charlotte said no more and left Dick's side, making him wonder why she'd made a point to return and throw Ned under the bus. And why had she stressed Ned's relationship with Sonny? Her hints were casual, but he suspected something more lay behind them. He'd take another peek into Ned's background when he got back to the office. A second look might uncover some massive secret that got David killed.

"We're ready, Lieutenant."

Dick turned, nodding to the EMS techs rolling a gurney into the room. He stepped aside as they collected David's body, wondering why Ned hadn't stayed to toss Brad or Charlotte under the bus. Was he deflecting suspicion from himself by flying under the radar? For what reason? Dick didn't know yet, but he'd bet his next month's paycheck that it was to keep from being grilled about where he spent his time when he wasn't conducting therapy sessions. Dick frowned at the thought. Was it possible to skip out on a therapy session, kill David Blake, and then be back in time for your next therapy session?

Dick shuddered at the thought. No, he'd not start suspecting Brad or Ned of murder just yet. Right now, he had to concentrate on their loyalty. Besides, if they really wanted to hurt David Blake, wouldn't bankrupting him be a much better ploy? After all, David prized money above all else. No, Dick's gut instinct was right. David had pissed someone off—the wrong someone. And it was Dick's job in the next few hours to find out who that someone was.

His thoughts took a sudden nosedive. Perhaps he *should* involve Sonny in the investigation. Her uncanny insight into people and things might just be the thing he needed to jump-start his investigation. But could he rely on her focusing her talent while grieving for her father? He didn't think he could ask that of her. For once, he wished he had the talent to touch an object and know the truth of its essence. And for once, he wished he had another cop's mind to brainstorm with.

"Don't forget to collect the surveillance footage here and along the walkway," he said, seeing a new set of blue uniforms taking up residence inside the door. "Send them all to my office stat." The officers nodded, heading for the cameras.

Sidestepping the EMS gurney as it passed, Dick followed their exit and then headed back to his office. Once again, he wished he had a magic lamp with a powerful genie. What he couldn't do with a spirit that had the ability to see both the past and the future at the same time.

• • •

Sonny wiped her drenched cheeks, surveying the canyon floor below her. She was a mess, her emotions all over the place, but coming to Saddleback Ridge had quickly calmed her down. It was her designated "safe place"—for when her inside world overpowered the outside one. The cactus flowers always lifted her spirits, and the vast landscape always put her talent into prospective.

Her glance drifted left, back towards the retreat hugging the hillside in the distance. She hadn't been aware that Dick knew of her secret hideaway, but then, as Head of Security, where she went and what she did was of paramount importance to him. *It's the one place he knew you'd be safe from gunfire*, her inner voice advised. She frowned at the thought. Was any place really that safe in today's world?

A hand touched her shoulder, and Sonny jumped, almost slipping off the scenic overlook.

"Sorry," Logan said, gripping her arm to steady her. He followed her perusal of the landscape. "When Cutter said to bring you here, I didn't think he meant driving into the wilderness."

"We're really quite close to the retreat," Sonny said. "We came by car, which is the long way. You can walk the trail in less than fifteen minutes."

"No, *you* can walk the trail," he remarked. "I prefer a faster and more comfortable mode of transportation."

His words rankled, making Sonny wish she could leave him to walk the trails back.

Her glance latched on to a two-story cabin nestled a couple of miles below the overlook. If only she had her briefcase. She could take a quiet moment to look at the Tarot cards and determine why a serial killer would use them as the focal point of his killings. She was sure his identity was amongst the cards—if she could figure out how to arrange them. And then, of course, her path would be clear after that. She would link them to her father's death, then do everything in her power to bring the despicable bastard out in the open, and have him arrested.

Was it a "he" they were looking for? She couldn't be sure without a point of reference. Women tended to be drawn to metaphysics more than men. Though eighty percent of her clients were women, the scattered twenty percent of men that came met with her out of curiosity, desperation, or flat-out hatred.

A vision of her father's slumped figure had her biting her lip. Was Logan right? Had a friend killed him? Ned and her uncle certainly fought enough with her father to put them at the top of any suspect list, but her aunt had been at odds with her father for the last month, too. Perhaps she had just gotten tired of his incessant need to put money above family responsibilities and snapped.

A jerk on her arm made Sonny stumble to a nearby bench. She sank down, surprised to find Logan slipping into the seat beside her.

"Has the crisis been averted?" he asked. "You look like you're feeling better."

"I'm calmer," Sonny told him. "But I won't be better until I know who killed Daddy and why."

"First things first. We need to find out who wants *you* dead and why. Once we know that, we'll know why your father was killed. The two incidents are related."

"There's a third related incident," Sonny said.

"Which is?"

"The serial killings. Ever since I looked at the images, I've sensed they are connected to The Sanctuary."

"Are you sure? Your life seems to have been a roller coaster for the past week. You could be off your game." He started to elaborate, but the cell phone in Sonny's pocket set off with a rousing rendition of "Hail to the Chief."

Sonny glanced down at the screen. "It's Ned," she said. "Should I answer it?"

"By all means," he replied. "Put it on speaker, though. I want to hear the tone of his voice." He lifted a finger in her direction. "Talk to him the way you normally talk to him."

Sonny chewed on her lower lip. Talking with Ned was like walking barefoot over a bed of hot coals.

"Buck up," Logan added. "You can do this."

Forcing her mind to take his words as a compliment, Sonny hit the speaker button. "Hello, Ned."

"Charlotte says you're in distress."

"I was for a while, but I'm feeling better now."

A pause descended, and for a moment Sonny thought the line had gone dead. But then Ned's voice came on the line again.

"I owe you an apology, Sonny. I crossed the line in mentioning the lawsuit earlier."

"You owe Uncle Brad the apology, not me."

Another pause originated.

"I apologized to your uncle an hour ago, so that fence is mended … We've prepared a statement for you to read before we release it to the press. How soon can you get here to go over it with me?"

Sonny glanced at Logan, who held up three fingers.

"We'll be there in about thirty minutes."

"We?" Ned asked. "Can't you park Logan Reed at Serenity until we've finished company business?"

Sonny gave a broken laugh. "I can't just *park* him, Ned. He's my guest."

"With all that's happened, he'll understand. You can conduct whatever business you have with him tomorrow. Right now, your focus should be on assuring our guests they are in no danger. Rumors are already circulating, thanks to the heightened security. You must come home stat."

"Is that an order?"

"It's a polite request."

"I'll be there in thirty minutes, I promise."

"Don't argue—"

Sonny disconnected the call, cutting Ned off mid-sentence. She saw Logan's lips pursed in a frown.

"Relax," she said. "You told me to act naturally with him, and I did. He is used to my hanging up on him."

"He's a marvel, if he takes that kind of abuse from you without retaliation."

"Forget him. What's our next move? I've bought us thirty minutes." Sonny slipped the phone back into her pocket.

The man beside her began to study the canyon floor, and Sonny knew his mind was sifting through all their options. *Are there any?* her inner voice rallied. *Besides making a reservation for two at the local psychiatric hospital?*

"Returning to The Sanctuary is best," Logan said, coming out of his trance. He shot to his feet. "I think it's time to reveal the incident on the mesa to your family."

"For heaven's sake, why? They'll go ballistic."

"Good. People make mistakes when they're angry."

"We should discuss it with Dick first," Sonny said. "We owe him that much, don't you think? After all, we're keeping a whopper of a secret from him."

"As always, you're right. We'll run it by Cutter first and then spill the news."

"And if Dick says no?"

"You don't solve murders by hoping the killer will have a sudden attack of conscience and turn himself in. You push his buttons."

Sonny shivered. "This killer will push back. He's cunning, devious, and without conscience."

"Again, you're right. He's not going to stop what he's doing until we *make* him stop." Logan reached for her hand. "All set to re-enter the lion's den?"

Sonny took his hand, hopping to her feet and pulling him towards the exit sign. As they descended the trail and cut back through the trees, she wondered why Logan was taking her suggestions. Surely, his crackerjack mind didn't need her input.

But then, he doesn't know the family dynamics, her inner voice prompted.

"Sonny?"

She brought her mind back to Logan as they reached the end of the trail and stepped onto a black asphalt path.

"The company calendar will have no record of Daddy's appointments, by the way," she said, stepping off the path. "He keeps his agendas on his computer, locked with a passcode that has umpteen subroutines."

"Is that a recent thing?" Logan asked. "The paranoia?"

"No, he's done it for years. He claims building loops within loops is like solving a challenging brain-teaser."

They crossed two more vacant parking spaces and then, reaching the pickup, Logan jerked the driver's door open. He slipped behind the wheel quickly, waiting for Sonny to slip into the passenger seat.

A moment later, he fired up the engine and shoved the vehicle into drive. In seconds, the truck was sailing out of the parking lot and onto the local state road. Noticing the truck's alarming speed, Sonny chided him, "You do remember this is the lieutenant's personal vehicle you're driving, don't you?"

Logan tapped the brakes with a grin. The truck settled into a decent speed, and Sonny picked up their conversation again.

"I think, if I can keep Uncle Brad and Ned focused elsewhere, I can access Daddy's computer. He's left a message in it for me."

Logan's foot shot from the gas pedal. "How the hell do you know that?"

"From experience. When I'm hurled into a vortex, all kinds of images are swimming in the abyss. My mind has only a split second before it centers on the relevant one, but that doesn't mean the other images disappear. They just pull back, so I can *see* a specific moment in time. When I touched the knife earlier, I didn't see the couple making love, but you did. We both saw the therapy session. You saw the word Pandora last; however, coming out of the vortex, I saw a computer screen with Daddy's name on it last. Since you obviously didn't mention seeing that, you didn't see it. That means Daddy left me a 'for your eyes only' in his computer."

"You're starting to make a spirit-world believer out of me," Logan said, braking at a stop sign. Seeing no traffic, he turned the car onto a secondary roadway. They were soon cruising past a billboard announcing: "The Sanctuary" and then seeing a familiar television van parked alongside the road. Sonny realized Ned was right. It was best to park Logan in a suite and come back for him later. The news hounds would be chomping at the bit, vying to one-up the other for a new spin on her father's death. The appearance of a Meta Corps agent might be a temptation too hard to resist. The security teams would definitely be in force, too, and she was sure the paparazzi would notice that. From then on, life would become miserable for all the retreat guests.

"You're thinking of ditching me," Logan said, reading her thoughts.

"How did you know?" Sonny asked, turning to him in surprise.

"If I've learned anything from being around you in the last couple of hours, it's that you can't abide chaos."

"Who's chaos?" Sonny asked.

"Don't joke. I assure you I saw that news crew by the side of the road. They're gearing up for a firestorm, and since I'm no stranger to glaring headlines, nothing they could say or print about me means a damn thing. But they can hurt you and the retreat. And that, I won't allow, so tap that beautiful brain of yours and tell me how to get in the front door without bringing my Meta Corps credentials into the limelight."

"There is no way."

"Will a personal way work?" Logan asked.

Sonny's heart skipped a beat. "You're not suggesting I pretend we're dating?" Her eyes came up to study his face.

"Hardly. We need something more serious than that. Will an engagement work?" His eyes roamed over her face and figure, and Sonny knew instantly what he was thinking. Her cheeks colored under the heat of his gaze, and she cleared her throat, pretending not to be affected by the thought of a romantic liaison between them.

"Certainly not," she scoffed. She schooled her features into a blank television stare, determined not to let him see how much the idea appealed to her.

"You're right," Logan said. "The family would never believe I took one look at you and fell madly in love with you."

This time, Sonny laughed. "Do you know how many lies you'd have to tell to pretend you fell in love with me at first sight? You'd never be able to keep a straight face when you uttered them. No, the best angle is for you to take on the persona of one of our guests. Should they discover you're part of Meta Corps, you can say you're on holiday. No one will question that."

"Very well," Logan said, grudgingly. "I'll defer to your wisdom. Although, I promise you, if there's any sign you're about to be crucified by the press, I'll step in and shake things up."

Sonny heard the determination in his voice and suppressed a shudder. She'd hate to be on the wrong side of Logan's determination. If she had learned anything since meeting him, it was that he was a man with a driving need to win. He obviously ran his own cases and brooked no interference while investigating them.

She wished she could agree to his suggestion, though. He was a perfect candidate for a lover—handsome, witty, smart, and she was sure he knew what to do with a woman when he got her in bed. His touch would be oddly soft and caressing … Sonny halted the erotic thought. It was ridiculous to be fantasizing about Logan Reed's body flexing rhythmically against hers. They were strangers, bound together by a maniacal serial killer. *That's it; think of Logan as a business associate*, her inner voice suggested, *and remember that mixing business with pleasure never works.*

Sonny frowned. Why did her ego choose to throw her aunt's favorite adage at her? *You know why.* Yes, she did. She was teetering on the edge of a cliff. She would have no problem pretending she and Logan were more than business associates; however, having the information splashed across headlines for the world to see would be devastating for her family and the retreat. She had never had a steady boyfriend, and the paparazzi knew it. They'd pounce on an engagement like fleas on a dog.

Never mix business with pleasure, her inner voice cautioned again. *Pleasure will always win out.*

Sonny brought her mind back to the roadway. The turnoff to the retreat was only a few miles away, and she would need to decide whether to let Logan continue to serve as her shadow. She peeked at his profile. She wished she could've met him under different circumstances. In a different space and time, they might've become friends, and the friendship might've led to romance, and the romance to a hot marriage bed of gratifying sex.

"Wake up, Sonny," Logan said. "We're at the turnoff."

Sonny shook off her reverie, resorting to sarcasm as the truck sailed off the state road and turned onto the tarred street leading to the main building. "Yes, dear," she mocked him.

Emitting a chuckle, Logan wheeled the vehicle past the large outdoor sign announcing the retreat. He then turned the car onto a second roadway, angling behind the hotel building and towards a row of bungalows nestled behind the hotel. Seconds later, the truck was slowing down and braking behind a terra-cotta cottage. Turning off the engine, Logan spun to face her.

"Are you going to allow me the privilege of your company for a few more hours?" he asked. "Or are you going to listen to that insane voice of yours saying to ditch me?"

"Ditching you would be rude," Sonny said. "And I'm never rude to handsome agents, especially those who fall madly in love with me at first sight."

"I see you've found your sense of humor again." Logan grinned.

Sonny sobered quickly. "What else can I do? Sobbing hysterically didn't work; it sent me into a tailspin." She threw open the passenger door and slid out of the car. Following her lead, Logan slipped from behind the wheel and then came around the front bumper. With matching strides, they struck off for the front of the cottage.

"I intend this meeting with Ned to be in and out and gone," Sonny said. "And please, don't get caught up in Ned or Brad's macho crap if they start. Ned is prone to outbursts, and we ignore them. Besides, the sooner we take a look at the cards you sent, the sooner we'll know who has it in for me and lure them out of hiding ... What, no comeback?"

"None. As always, your reasoning is superior to mine."

"What a nasty thing to say—given the fact that I've bent over backwards to keep you from being ousted from the retreat."

His voice was resigned. "And you'll go on doing so, because we both know you don't have a chance in hell of getting through the next hour without me by your side."

To her dismay, Sonny's voice broke. "Never say never."

He made no further comment, but Sonny saw a dangerous glint enter his eyes. What was he really planning on doing when they got inside? She was sure he had already decided on a course of action. Would she be agreeable to it, if she knew? The question hammered at her, but Logan gave her no time to think it out. He grabbed her shoulder, whirled her around, and marched her up the front steps.

"Be a good little mouse," he said. "Don't rock the boat unless we have to. And if at all possible, let me do all the talking."

Sonny started to object but then thought better of it. What good would it do to argue with him? He never listened to anything but his own counsel. He was an odious, arrogant toad ... She halted the slur, suddenly comforted by the thought that there was no one better to probe her father's murder than an obnoxious, arrogant toad.

Taking a deep breath, Sonny turned the doorknob and pushed the front door open. The foyer was deserted as they entered, and she craned her head, listening for the sound of muted voices.

"They're in the living room," she finally said. "I hear Uncle Brad's voice." She headed towards an open archway, a stirring of fear suddenly exploding in her heart. Five steps later, she placed a hand on her throat and slowed her steps. "Not now," she breathed. She glanced at Logan. "I think an unwanted vision's coming through." She swayed on her feet, and Logan grabbed her shoulders.

"Can't you halt the vision?"

"Not unless I ground myself," Sonny said, gasping.

"Well, ground yourself, dammit!"

The thought was so preposterous that Sonny laughed. The action sent her senses spinning in a new direction. To her dismay, she found her hand snatched and her body hauled into Logan's arms. She had no time to think of anything as his mouth descended on hers. Nothing could've prepared her for the explosion of pleasure that suddenly rocked her body, throbbed through her ears, and short-circuited her pulse.

Unable to stop herself, and uncaring whether she initiated a vision from the pressure of his lips on hers, she threw her arms around Logan's neck and parted her lips. His tongue slid into her mouth, sending new shock waves coursing through the pit of her stomach. To her delight, she remained rooted to reality, enjoying the kiss immensely and molding her body to Logan's. The kiss soon became surprisingly gentle, and her body quivered at the sweet tenderness of it. All too quickly, his mouth lifted, hovering inches from hers.

"How's that for grounding?" he asked.

Stunned, Sonny opened her eyes and met his stare. He winked broadly at her, and to her surprise, her eyes suddenly misted with tears. The kiss had only been a ploy to short-circuit the vision and realign her brainwaves. It had been a means to an end, and it had worked thoroughly. The thought left her sadly disappointed, and her heart dropped like a lead balloon. And then Logan surprised her by raining a series of light kisses on her face. The first skimmed the tip of her nose, the second caressed her right cheek, and the last ended in a sensual nibbling of her right earlobe.

"Sonia Madeline Blake! What is the meaning of this?"

The couple sprang apart, her aunt's disapproving voice breaking the romantic moment. Sonny lifted her head, scrutinizing Logan's wry grin.

"Now see what you've done," she declared. She glanced around Logan's shoulder and faced her aunt's frigid expression with a bright smile. "Hello, Aunt Charlotte. Is my thirty minutes up?"

Annoyed, her aunt whirled on her toes. "We've been waiting an hour for you," she threw over her shoulder, disappearing back into the living room.

"She's furious, and it's your fault."

"You needed grounding; I obliged."

"And what next? You'll pour water over my head and plant me like a flower?"

"Don't tempt me."

Her aunt's blistering tone shattered the air. "We are waiting, Sonny."

Sonny's hackles rose immediately, and she followed the voice. "For heaven's sake, Aunt Charlotte, if the press release is done, it calls for no further discussion."

As if suddenly hit by a bolt of lightning, her aunt sprang from her chair. Sonny could see her barely contained fury; however, Logan forestalled her venom by stepping forward.

"I assure you that I meant no disrespect by kissing Sonny. I was attempting to divert her from falling into one of her damn visions. Kissing her seemed better than dealing with her nosebleeds."

"You kissed Sonny?" Brad Fletcher bolted from his chair, and seeing the fire behind his eyes, Sonny stepped in front of Logan.

"Yes, he did, and I enjoyed every second of it," she stated.

Flabbergasted, her aunt sank back down into her chair, while her uncle came to a screeching halt in the middle of the room.

"Are you insane?" he demanded. "You met the man only an hour ago."

Sonny's posture changed rapidly. "Don't you dare lecture me as if I were still sixteen years old, Uncle Brad. I'll kiss whomever I please, whenever I please, and that's the end of this discussion. Now, where is the press statement we're releasing?"

No one answered the question, and Sonny realized she had stunned them with her attack. *But at what cost?* her inner voice asked. An answer came a moment later. *The loss of our life?*

CHAPTER TEN

"That could've gone better," the lieutenant said a few moments later.

Logan eyed the group gathering around the table. "Her temper certainly matches her hair," he remarked.

"With good reason. Her aunt smothers her, her uncle patronizes her, and as for her father, he idolized her while secretly wishing her talent would go away."

"And Ned?"

"Smoke and mirrors. The guests either love him or hate him."

"Any baggage?" Logan asked.

"None that I can find. Outside of parking tickets, he's a model citizen."

Logan reached into his jacket pocket and removed a business card. He handed it to the lieutenant. "Call this number and ask for Monica. Give her Ned's name and tell her I said she should go where no man has gone before."

The lieutenant studied the card. "Is it ethical for you to intervene like this?"

"I'm offering a suggestion, nothing more. You do want to solve David's murder, don't you? This might help."

The lieutenant's glance narrowed. "I see now why you're such a legend in Meta Corps. You manipulate a case where you want it to go—without getting any blood on your hands, I might add."

"They're bloody—"

"Don't start with me, Ned," Sonny said, springing from her chair. "I said no."

The men twisted their heads, startled by Sonny's angry tone.

"I'm not starting anything," Ned declared, "I don't understand why you refuse to speak with the press on behalf of the retreat."

"It's not my place. I don't own the retreat."

"You're its star attraction, though."

"What? So now The Sanctuary is a zoo, and I'm its trained monkey?"

"Don't twist my words. You are the most qualified to speak on your father's behalf."

"I won't do it," Sonny exclaimed. "You're asking too much of me."

"Why do you always have to be such a contrary bitch?" Ned railed.

"Why do you always insinuate that I owe the retreat an undying loyalty?"

"Because you do," Ned responded. "The Sanctuary has made you a very rich woman over the years."

"I earned that money on my own—without Sanctuary backing. And if you don't believe me, I'll take my gloves off and prove it to you." She began pulling her right glove off, and Logan moved from the window. Sonny's temper had gotten the better of her. He needed to power it down.

Seeing him come, Ned waved him back. "Stay where you are, Agent Reed. Sonny doesn't need your protection."

"Then change your tone," Logan said, reaching Sonny. He took one look at her angry stare and grabbed her chin with his hand. "Put your glove back on. An empath should always pick their battles. This is not the right one. There's too much testosterone flying around."

She studied his face, and he saw the fire go out of her eyes. His grin surfaced.

"Do you need another grounding?" he teased.

She laughed, the fire completely extinguished. "I'm good for now. Maybe later."

Logan chucked her nose. "I look forward to it. Now, apologize to Ned for being a bitch."

She made a face at him but turned towards Ned. "You win. I'll do it."

The tension in the room evaporated, as if sucked through a black hole and out the other side. Sonny returned to the table and took a seat. A second later, a hand descended on Logan's shoulder.

"When I'm right, I'm right," the lieutenant said. "You're a master manipulator. You shifted that argument exactly where you wanted it to go."

"Quit it, Lieutenant. You're making me blush," Logan said.

The lieutenant chuckled, smacking the business card against his pant leg. "I'll go make that call—unless you need me to stay and keep you from kissing Sonny again."

"I make no promises since she enjoyed the kiss thoroughly," Logan remarked.

"Tread lightly, my friend. Sonny has the ability to look into a person's soul and decimate it if she doesn't like what she finds there."

The lieutenant strode off, leaving Logan to ponder his words. Would Sonny exact payback for the kiss? No way. She had been tempted to return the kiss. He had felt it in the subtle shift of her body weight against his. And then he had powered down the kiss, just as surprised as her when he didn't end it outright. He had caressed her lips with feather-light touch, letting the soft union of their mouths communicate an unexpected, radiating pleasure between their bodies. And then her aunt had ruined the moment.

Feeling eyes boring into his back, Logan knew it would take an intelligent handling of the group to earn their trust. The family was tight-knit, and they didn't welcome strangers into the fold easily. He replayed the last few minutes in his mind. How did one proceed after defusing Sonny's anger? The matter was taken out of his hands by Brad Fletcher.

"That was a nifty piece of work," he said, crossing the room. "Sonny doesn't take kindly to being bossed around."

Logan whirled about. "I sensed she didn't really want to make a scene."

"No, I didn't," Sonny said, joining the men. She rubbed her forehead vigorously. "Daddy's death has put me in a tailspin. My thoughts are disjointed, and I can't concentrate. It's as if I am being warned. I'm struggling to sift through the emotions and get out of the whirlpool."

The room went quiet, and Logan saw the swift change in postures. Noting her faint smile, Logan realized that, in meeting Sonny Blake, he had met a new breed of woman—an elegant wench with class and brains. She was the first mouse he knew with that intriguing combination, and he didn't know why, but the knowledge upset him. Before he knew it, Sonny was surprising him even more.

"You said before that Daddy's death was personal. My inability to locate any smudges of his energy proves that point."

"Perhaps you should let your uncle take you through a session," her aunt offered. "You've been conducting so many classes, your energy has run dry. You need an overhaul. Your uncle can put you under and realign your chakras in less than an hour. He excels at hypnosis, you know."

Sonny's hand clutched her throat, and Logan silently congratulated her on manipulating the conversation exactly where he wanted it to go next. Seeing her ashen face, her uncle stepped forward, grabbed her gloved hand, and led her to a chair.

"I'd consider it an honor if you'd let me lighten your load, Sonny. You never turn down requests for readings, and your body and mind are now paying for it. I can ease the stress with just a few words."

Logan crossed to Sonny's chair, perching on its wide arm. He slung his hand across its back, as if protecting her. He hid a wry grin at the action. He was acting like a horse's ass. Sonny didn't need protection from him, or anyone. With just a touch of her hand, she could fling a bystander into an unwanted vision and leave them there.

His thoughts flew to his rib cage suddenly. He could still feel the moment his scar had gone painless. It had been a moment of clarity, as if somehow, in transferring the pain from him, Sonny had left some of God's innate goodness behind in its place. He cringed at the thought. He should've been the last person to equate his life with God's goodness. Not after the secrets he and Sonny were keeping.

The tantalizing perfume of Sonny's hair wafted to his nose, and Logan felt Sonny's shoulders tense up. Her mind was back on her father's murder, when he wished her mind was on his kiss. Did she realize that since their kiss, her face had radiated an outer and inner glow? And did she know that glow made him want to forget serial killers and Tarot cards, drag her off to the nearest room, and make love to her for the rest of the day and into the night?

Logan heard the clearing of a throat and glanced up to find Brad rocking on the balls of his feet, waiting for an answer. *Back to reality, Reed*, his inner voice advised.

"Well, if you don't want Brad to ease your stress, go have a massage in the spa," her aunt finally declared. "Hattie works miracles with her fingers."

"The massage will have to wait," Sonny said. "I've got to call a press conference and, of course, alert our overseas partners to Daddy's death." She turned to Ned. "I'll need Daddy's key card and password to access his computer."

Ned looked stymied by her request. "Where's your key card? he asked.

"At home in the vault."

He pulled down his vest. "Well, go home and get it. I haven't the foggiest idea where David keeps his cards."

Sonny tensed up again. Her gaze switched between her uncle and Ned.

"You both lied to Dick earlier," she stated suddenly. "You each had a major row with Daddy—a knock-down, drag-out—I can almost see it."

Hearing the insinuation, Ned's face froze, but her uncle's didn't.

"What do you mean by that?" he demanded. "Do you honestly think one of us used our key cards to enter the bungalow and kill David?"

"You had an ugly confrontation with him, Uncle Brad."

"And I apologized to him," he replied. "He forgave me."

"So you say."

Her aunt intervened swiftly. "You also had an argument with him, Sonny."

"Which I forgave him for."

"What was the argument about?" her uncle interrupted, suddenly all cop.

Hearing his good-cop, bad-cop tone, Logan stirred. "David called Meta Corps, complaining that Sonny had too much on her plate and requesting the serial killings be assigned to another empath. When they refused, David confronted Sonny."

"He demanded I drop the case," Sonny cut in. "When I refused, reminding him that no one decides my agendas but me, he apologized and dropped the matter. I forgave him."

She sent Logan a sideways squint, and he hid a grin. The mouse was maneuvering them into a new set of lies. As if reading his thoughts, she blushed, and then, remembering they were discussing her father's computer, she returned her attention to the trio.

"Perhaps it's not too late for me to touch Daddy's keyboard and see if there is still a trail of smudged energy."

Put off by the thought of mystical powers at work behind the scenes, Logan rose. "Perhaps you should ask the lieutenant's permission before you start contaminating his crime scene."

"A second eye couldn't hurt."

Her uncle balked at the offer immediately. "Dick is more than capable of handling the investigation. No need for you to become involved."

"I've worked a homicide case before," Sonny told him.

"Not one that hits this close to home, you haven't," her uncle said. He eyed Logan. "Agent Reed must certainly agree. Amateur sleuths only manage to cloud an investigation."

"Your uncle's right," Logan said. "The bungalow is still in flux. Aren't there any other computer terminals you can use?"

"She could use the mainframe at Serenity," Ned said. "It's safest—less chatter."

Her aunt jumped on the suggestion. "Ned's right. But first, you need to go home and recharge your batteries. Consuela can fix you something to eat while you nap. I'll show Mr. Reed to his suite."

Logan grinned immediately. Charlotte Fletcher was relentless. She wanted him out of here.

"I'm famished too, Mrs. Fletcher," he said. "This Consuela sounds like she wouldn't mind feeding an extra mouth while Sonny naps."

"Are you always this stubborn?" Charlotte asked.

Logan ignored the scorn in her voice. "Do cats have nine lives?" he drawled.

Sonny stirred in her chair. "If we hide Daddy's death any longer, we'll take a giant hit in the stock market by morning. And then we'll be facing headlines on CNBC."

"Very well, I see your point," her aunt said. "We've always been brutally honest with our branch managers." She rose from her chair, her glance bouncing to Logan. "Meta Corps is not to hear of David's death until I say so. Is that clear? As far as the public is concerned, he had a heart attack."

"Nothing will be leaked to the press on Meta Corps' end."

"See that it isn't, because I promise you, if Blake Industries takes a financial hit due to wild rumors about David, we will file the appropriate charges against the perpetrator."

She left the room rapidly, not bothering to offer a formal good-bye to anyone. Watching her disappear, Logan frowned. He had made an enemy of Charlotte Fletcher, and he didn't know why. *She knows a secret you don't*, his inner voice mused. *Pandora?*

The mysterious word flitted through his brain like sand through an hourglass. The sooner he and Sonny traced its origin, the sooner he could offer a solution.

"We need to go," Sonny said. She stepped over to Ned, intending to hug him. He balked at her approach, waving her back.

"I'm sweating like a hog. I'll stain your clothes."

Sonny stepped away, but not before Logan saw her give Ned a puzzled look. She turned back to her uncle, giving him the farewell hug instead. In seconds, she had spun and exited the room. Crossing into the foyer, she snatched her briefcase and purse from the side table and stormed out of the cottage.

Logan's lips twitched as he followed her outside. The mouse was pissed; he could feel her angry energy radiating out into the ozone and beyond. But who was she pissed at? She rounded the cottage, away from the truck, towards a light gray Kia.

"You drive," she said, flinging open the passenger door and sliding along the leather seat. She slammed the door shut, not bothering to ask whether he wanted to drive or not.

Grinning, Logan circled the front bumper and opened the driver's door. Sometime during the drive he would have to apologize to Sonny for blindsiding her with the kiss. Of course, he wasn't going to apologize for the kiss itself. He had enjoyed the taste of her lips too much to make that apology. But he would apologize for the blindside.

And then what? his inner voice prompted, as he slipped behind the wheel and fired up the engine. He answered his own question. He didn't know what the hell he was going to do next.

• • •

Sonny took a moment to glance at the passing villas. At each marked signpost, Logan turned the car and followed the road signs. She knew she was being rude to him in the most obvious way a woman could be. Outside of barking directions, she was refusing to carry on a conversation with him.

She raised her gaze to his profile. This was not the time to alienate herself from that smart brain of his. They had to work together to get to the bottom of her father's murder. But did she have enough courage to forgive him for throwing her into a series of lies that she'd never extricate herself from?

Only one way to know, her inner voice chided. *Talk to him.* She swung around on the seat and addressed his profile.

"Have you had a chance to think about what the word Pandora might mean?" she asked. "In Greek mythology, Pandora opened a forbidden chest and released all the ills of the world, *on* the world." She pulled the Lovers card from her pocket. "I wonder if that's what the Lovers card might mean? If I access Daddy's computer, are we releasing something that will come back to bite us in the butt, or are we meant to halt a conspiracy in the early stages of its life?"

"Neither choice is appealing," Logan replied.

Sonny picked up her briefcase from the floorboard and hauled out the Tarot cards she had placed there this morning. She flashed the cards at Logan.

"I think the answer to the puzzle is hidden somewhere in these images. Even though I'm wearing gloves, I can feel vibrations through them—as if no piece of fabric can hold back the truth."

"How reliable is that feeling at the moment, though?" Logan asked, finally taking his eyes off the road to scan her face. "How accurate can you be when you're emotionally disturbed?"

Sudden anger washed through Sonny. The odious toad thought she was on the verge of an emotional meltdown. Well, wasn't she? A vision of his soft lips devouring hers had her heart slamming against her rib cage.

"You can't think a simple kiss can throw me off my game?" she said. "I've been kissed plenty of times before, and I've not gone insane. If anything, being kissed heightens my talent."

Sarcasm laced his response. "If that's the case, when I'm stuck for answers, I'll just kiss you."

Sonny laughed unexpectedly. "Or you could just let me use my ability to get the answer."

"But kissing you is so much more pleasurable," he teased.

Sonny gave a bright laugh, wondering how she could be amused when his kiss had sent them down a dangerous rabbit hole of deception and lies.

"You've only seen me in action in small spurts," she added. "If given enough time, I can see and feel incidents in their entirety. Why do you think people are so skittish around me? Take Ned, for example. He wouldn't even hug me good-bye back there. It's going to get harder and harder for you to keep your deep, dark secrets from me the longer we're together."

"Well, now that I know that, perhaps you'll be a good wench and promise to keep whatever you learn to yourself."

"I wish it were that simple," she said, flexing her fingers. "My talents didn't come with a set of instructions. Sometimes the message is remarkably clear; sometimes, it's shrouded in guesses."

"From what I've seen so far, you've hit nothing but home runs."

He went back to studying a new signpost, tapping on the brakes as soon as he saw the street sign marked "Serenity." The car veered sharply, and the action had Sonny clutching the door handle. The man beside her was becoming the only solid reality in a shifting world. She was already half in love with him, she knew, and that was a dangerous place to be. He was here to solve a case, and once the killer had been caught, he'd return to New York City. Besides, hadn't her father drilled into her head time and time again the stupidity of trusting strangers at first glance?

Dropping the briefcase back to the floorboard, she sighed loudly. "I wish there was a pill you could take, like the one Alice found in Wonderland. It would save us so much time and energy if we could just swallow a pill labeled: 'To solve David Blake's murder, eat me.'"

Sonny heard a grunt. "Where's the fun in that?"

"It's better than having an emotional meltdown every hour."

"We both know after you get some food in your belly and a good night's sleep in your own bed, you'll see things in their proper perspectives again."

"And that's when we'll go back to being two strangers attempting to solve a series of murders together?" Sonny asked.

"I'm afraid so."

Sonny faced the front windshield again. "I don't like that scenario one bit," she said. "I'd rather pretend we are friends attempting to give sixteen families closure. It's what the families deserve. Besides, we've been thrown together for a reason."

"What reason?"

"How should I know? You're the James Bond. I'm simply one of the bikini-clad girls Albert Broccoli liked to people his James Bond films with," she said. "Turn right at the next intersection, and watch out for joggers crossing on the trail. When you reach a gated entrance, turn into it."

Reaching the designated intersection a few moments later, the Kia veered right and then braked as a lone jogger breezed past the front of the car with a wave. Slowly, the car rolled across the trail and coasted down a circular driveway. Closing her eyes, Sonny wished sleep wasn't so far in the future. *Forget sleep*, her inner voice nudged. *Remember the kiss.*

She smiled at the memory. She could still feel the kiss as if it had happened just a moment ago—the heady sensation, the swirls in the pit of her stomach, her blood racing through her heart and lungs like a runaway train. *His heart raced, too,* her ego added. *He might deny it, but he felt the connection.*

Sonny's lips twitched at the thought. If nothing else, the kiss proved Logan Reed was a man who knew exactly what to do with a woman when he got her in bed. It was such a delicious thought that she sighed. Seconds later, the car braked to a halt in front of a rambling hacienda, and Logan addressed her.

"Do I have time to have a smoke before we go in?"

"Do cats have nine lives?" Sonny asked.

"Is the Pope Catholic?" he retorted.

"Do bears hibernate?" she queried.

"Does James Bond like his martinis shaken, not stirred?"

Sonny held up her hand. "Okay, okay, I give up. You win. You have time for a smoke."

• • •

Grinning, Logan slid out of the car and fished in his shirt pocket. He hauled out his lighter and then a cigarette. Lighting the stick, he sent a perfect smoke ring wafting in the air. Being around the mouse was becoming habit-forming, and her tantalizing perfume was making it hell for him to keep her at arm's length. He put a brake on that thought at once. He couldn't, and wouldn't, allow himself to kiss the mouse again. If he kissed her, he'd start liking her, and no matter how good her lips tasted, mice spelled trouble with a capital "T."

Lounging against the hood of the car, Logan studied the sidewalk leading away from the hacienda and down a hill. He caught sight of sparkling water and three colorful buildings. His gaze shifted to the joggers and power-walkers circling the lake's hiking path.

"Remind you of anything?" Sonny asked, lounging beside him.

"Disney World?"

"Very good." A pointing finger obscured his vision. "Like parts of Epcot, the metaphysical complex is color-coded to help the guests," Sonny said. "The north complex is Amethyst. It's purple. It houses the dream laboratory and classrooms. The west complex is Tranquility. It's blue and contains an open-air yoga stage, and reiki and massage therapy centers." Her hand swung left. "The south complex is Green Arbor. It's green and contains the hypnotherapy lab and chambers. It's where Uncle Brad and Ned spend most of their time."

Using his thumb, Logan signaled behind them. "And the path heading east?"

"It circles back to the hotel, which, as you know, is nestled against the mesa's hiking trails."

"The hotel isn't The Sanctuary?" Logan asked in surprise.

"No, the entire five hundred acres is The Sanctuary. The hotel, villas, and time-share condos are designated as Casita Suites— each with their own décor and charm. It's where the guests reside. If they want to indulge in any of the New Age sessions, they come here to Serenity."

Logan's gaze swung to the second-story balconies on their right. "And the terraces above us?"

"You'll see," Sonny said, hoisting her frame from the hood and signaling him to follow her.

Logan dropped his cigarette and ground it beneath the heel of his boot. "Lead the way, Your Highness. Show me this Cinderella castle of yours."

"It's not a castle. It's an office complex."

"Still don't want me to see where you live, eh?" he said, trailing her to a set of steps. "Don't worry. I'll figure it out. After all, I am a detective."

"You forgot obnoxious. You're an obnoxious detective," Sonny stated.

"Whatever," he drawled.

CHAPTER ELEVEN

"I could use a two-hour nap," Sonny said, as they climbed the hacienda steps side by side. Her fingers massaged her scalp. "It's been a long day. Out west, we always take an afternoon snooze."

"I'm game if you are," Logan responded, dodging her raised elbow. Her eyes widened as he grasped her arm and turned her towards him. Was the toad about to kiss her again? He was staring at her lips in a most alluring way, as if he found them the most fascinating thing since the creation of the world. *If he kisses you, you're a goner*, she thought.

He lowered his head, and Sonny ducked away quickly. Her wrist was suddenly snatched, and she was jerked back in front of him. He made no comment, just stared as if she had suddenly sprouted two horns on the top of her head. Annoyed, she counterattacked.

"What now? Is it time to kiss me again? I don't see the point since we have no audience."

The hint of a smile teased his lips as he grabbed the back of her head and slowly drew her towards him. Before she knew it, his mouth was on hers, shattering her calm with a moist, sensual kiss.

Shock waves shook both their frames simultaneously, and to her horror, she tossed them into a colorful vortex, where, to her dismay, the see-through window effect swam into view. As if in a dream, the window took on a rosy hue, and Sonny saw two swaying bodies on a bed. The pair was engaged in hot sex, their lips moving across each other in sensuous exploration.

And then the image ramped up, sending her and Logan into a new, distorted vision. This time, Logan lay atop her, her hips lifting in unison with his steady, possessive thrusts. When the sex powered up, heading for a climax, Sonny tore her lips from Logan. The vision severed at once, leaving Sonny dizzy and Logan staring perplexedly at her.

"What the hell was that?" he asked. "And don't tell me you didn't see a couple having sex this time."

"I saw it," she answered, clutching her stomach. Her hand suddenly shot to her nose, expecting the usual nosebleed. When her hand came away dry, she frowned, glancing at her gloves. "I've never been thrown into a vision that wasn't initiated through my hands." Her fingers shot to her dress pocket. "I suppose the Lovers card could've triggered the vision. Many authors of Tarot believe the cards are doorways, and if you meditate on them properly, you can enter the images. It's more likely that my system's so compromised it's caused my skills to go haywire."

"This was an erotic image, not some replay of a damn shooting."

"Well, I can't explain it at the moment," Sonny said, exasperated by his tone. "I told you. Empathic abilities have a life of their own. It could be that kissing heightens them in a way I've never encountered before."

"I thought you said you've been kissed plenty of times before."

"I have. But I wasn't emotionally compromised then."

His fingers took her chin, forcing her to look at him.

"Do you think you're the only one emotionally compromised? Your kiss has put *me* into a tailspin." He ran his fingers across her lower lip. "I wish I had time to take you to bed, but … " He dropped her chin. "We have a job to do and little time to do it in."

Sonny let out a reluctant sigh. Why was he making her think about reality instead of the euphoria coursing through her veins? He wanted to sleep with her; she wanted it too. *Later,* her ego advised, *when the stars align*. Sighing again, she reached around him and entered a key code in the door panel.

"We forgot to spill the sniper attack to the family," she said, waiting for the tumblers to roll.

"I didn't forget. I changed my mind. I don't want them to know."

Sonny made a face he couldn't see. "You really do think one of them killed Daddy, don't you?"

"Yes."

She heard the tumblers roll. "I've known Ned and Uncle Brad all my life," she said. "They're insensitive to the point of rudeness, but they just don't have it in them to kill anyone."

"You're forgetting Pandora," Logan reminded her, as the front door finally whooshed open.

"They don't know what it means," Sonny said, hesitating on the threshold.

"Don't be so quick to assume. Many murders are family driven."

"Ned isn't family," Sonny remarked. "Besides, we aren't even sure whether the killer is male or female yet. Women have vicious streaks as well as men. Just pick up any newspaper and read the headlines." She swiped the air. "'Woman kills best friend in fit of jealousy.' We need to worry about handling the press. I've seen what can happen when they rework a story into a nightmare of blistering headlines."

Logan's expression darkened. "I know that feeling as well," he said. He fell silent, and Sonny knew he was focused on something unsettling in his past. Was he remembering the cause of his bullet wound? Had there been glaring headlines surrounding the incident? She was sure there must've been, but she had no desire to learn what those headlines were. "Your aunt's reaction to my being here is flat-out hostile," Logan continued. "As if my arrival has thrown her for a loop."

"You're from Meta Corps," Sonny told him, crossing the threshold. "And you've come without warning. There's nothing that pisses her and Uncle Brad off more than being left out of security matters."

"Too easy," Logan countered, following her into the alcove on the other side of the door. "She's protecting you like a mother hen. And don't say you haven't guessed that already."

Sonny reached into her dress pocket and fingered the Tarot cards. How were the cards really related? Since Spirit tended to work in threes, it was possible the cards held one meaning in one scenario, a different in a second.

Out of the blue, Sonny heard a familiar voice. *"Buenas tardes, querida Bienvenido a casa."*

Sonny stepped out of the alcove into a foyer decked out with an ornate side table and two vases of colorful roses. Two matching, ornate pots of plastic greenery peppered the rest of the foyer. Home, sweet home.

"Ay, *querida,* what have you done to yourself?" The pleasant voice was closing in. "You look like you haven't eaten in weeks. *No es bueno.*"

Sonny smiled at the chubby figure bustling towards them. "Don't fuss, Consuela," she said, stepping down into the great room. She gave the woman a bear hug when she reached her. "I had breakfast at Rosita this morning."

"Yogurt *no es* proper *desayuno,*" Consuela sniffed. "I fix you a dinner with *pollo … Madre Dios …* Who is the handsome *diablo* you've brought with you?"

Sonny winced at the question. Who *was* this handsome devil? She whirled, assessing Logan's face. Outside of his intimidating Meta Corps badge, she hadn't a clue.

CHAPTER TWELVE

Sonny studied Logan's face, surprised to find him surveying the room in front of him with a quizzical eye. Her lips twitched.

"Did I forget to mention Serenity is my home?"

"I think you mean the U.S. Treasury," Logan drawled, finally coming down the steps into the spacious room. He studied the wall paintings, spotting a movie poster advertising *The Twilight Zone*. Amusement flickered in the eyes that met Sonny's. "A *Twilight Zone* poster? Really? An empath who loves science fiction?"

"I love Rod Serling, and watching *Twilight Zone* marathons on Syfy helps me to not take myself so seriously."

Logan chuckled. "You continue to amaze me, Sonny."

"Is that a good thing?" she queried.

"I don't know yet," he said, then cut off the rest of his sentence as the housekeeper bustled towards him, clucking in half English, half Spanish.

"*Como se llama, mi querido?*" she asked when she reached him.

"Logan," he answered quickly, surprising Sonny with his understanding of the question.

"*Aye, querido, you es my bebé's enamorado.*" Her gaze found Sonny. "The hotel deliver *su enamorado*'s luggage a few minutes ago. I put him in the suite next to yours. I fix you both nice, romantic dinner tonight, *sí?*"

Sonny hedged quickly. "We won't have time for dinner, Consuela. Some of your delicious chicken tortilla wraps will do." She headed towards a carpeted staircase. "We'll eat them in the computer room while we're working."

"*No es bueno* that you work so hard," Consuela chided. Her look latched on to Logan. "You *hacer el amor con este hombre* and have *muchos bebés, no?* He *es muy atractivo.* You have many *bella bebés con él.*"

Sonny blushed at the housekeeper's words. "Mr. Reed is a detective, *no es mi enamorado*."

The housekeeper clucked loudly. "*Lo siento mucho, querida*," she said. "He look like he *hacer el amor muy bien*."

Sonny's cheeks turned scarlet. It was bad enough when her own mind thought Logan probably knew how to make love really well, but to hear her housekeeper voice such an erotic thought was, well, embarrassing.

Signaling Logan, she finished crossing to the staircase and began climbing rapidly to the second floor. Reaching the top of the steps, she made a beeline for a set of French doors and threw them open. Her thoughts switched quickly to business mode, as a familiar, cool breeze hit her face. She studied the giant TV screen covering the west wall.

"The afternoon financials are already in. Tokyo took a whopper of a hit today. No cause yet."

Sonny intended to peruse the data but halted mid-stride when she realized Logan hadn't followed her into the room. Whirling, she saw his eagle eye was at work again—raking in the enormity of the room and all its marvelous gadgets.

"You could've told me you own half the stock exchange and all of Wall Street," he drawled.

"I thought you did your homework on me before coming," Sonny said, unfazed by his sarcasm. She waved at the mammoth ticker-tape machine flashing numbers and percentages across its banner on the far wall. "Surely Meta Corps knows how rich the Blake family is. We have spiritual retreats all around the world, and we've spent millions building a financial network that rivals CNBC."

"It turns out the Meta Corps files are seriously lacking," Logan said, lounging against the doorframe. "I intend to rectify that when I get back to the home office."

Smiling, Sonny returned her attention to the console. "A little hiccup like Tokyo will fix itself overnight," she said, stretching her arms above her head. "It always does."

"Again, your talents are impressive," Logan said, closing the French doors.

Pleased by the compliment, Sonny slipped the Tarot cards from her pocket. "As I said in the car, I think if we arrange the Tarot cards in a specific order, we'll have the first part of the puzzle solved." She headed for a burgundy sofa and placed the five cards on the table in random order. "Once I skim the cards, we'll know why everyone is telling lies."

"Who is lying, besides us?" Logan asked, taking a seat beside her.

"Aunt Charlotte. She has had several arguments with Daddy in the last month. She didn't confess that to Dick when he asked. And what's worse, the rest of us didn't tell. We all let it slide by. Dick is going to find out."

"Not if we decipher these cards," Logan declared, studying the images before them. "I'll need a crash course in Tarot, though." He touched her knee. "And remember, I can't go where you go."

"But you did. When you accidentally touched my hand your energy piggybacked on mine. That's why, once inside, we saw different things … Remember earlier, I said when I tap in, the images pull back, allowing the relevant one to take center stage?" She saw his nod. "It took me a long, long time to understand that, like the images, I could pull back my energy, skim the outskirts of the vision, and still come away with the truth. I intend to do that now."

Sonny tapped the plastic sheets one by one. "The Fool. Judgment. The High Priestess. Death. And The Tower. I'm going to disregard their spiritual meaning for the moment and focus on what they might mean in your world of logic and facts." She tapped the first card. "If we say what we see, this image depicts a jester carrying a backpack, unaware he's about to walk off a cliff. If we equate that to a victim, we could assume the victim was backpacking in the mountains and went over a cliff."

"Or was pushed over," Logan said. He caught Sonny's eye. "And the second?"

Sonny tapped the baggie. "Judgment is about a wake-up call. I haven't read the report, but I sense through the plastic that the victim was killed and then buried in a churchyard. Looking at the card, it's Judgment Day and the Angel Gabriel is blowing his horn. As you can see, the card has a whole spiritual, religious feel to it. Figures rising from their coffins."

"I'd say finding the victim's body was a fluke, but in truth, an anonymous call came into the police station regarding the grave. Does Gabriel's horn represent the phone call? Or is the horn the killer's way of thumbing his nose at the police? Either way, finding the body wasn't such a fluke, after all."

"Now you're getting the hang of everything connected to everything." Sonny smiled. "Nothing is random." She tapped the third card.

"The High Priestess is about secrets—known and unknown, seen and unseen."

"That's rather vague."

"Purposely vague. As you can see, our High Priestess is seated between two columns, with a diaphanous veil stretched between them. What lies behind the veil, only she knows, and she's not willing to give up the secrets yet. In some decks, she's seated before a doorway—considered to be the doorway of *all* knowledge." Sonny turned to Logan. "With the card being so secretive, I bet the report says the police are baffled by this death. In fact, they probably don't consider it part of the other murders."

"Is it?" Logan asked.

"I won't know until I skim the card."

"And the fourth card?" Logan asked, tapping it.

"The Death card is pretty obvious—a brutal killing with a beheading. Mr. Death is astride his steed, mowing down everything in his path with a giant scythe. And as you can see, he plays no favorites. Priests, slaves, and regular middle-class folks—no one is immune from his visit."

"And the fifth?"

"The Tower hints at the total destruction of a way of life—or thinking. Every Tarot deck portrays that destruction differently, however. Sometimes, lightning strikes The Tower, hurling the figures out the window and crashing into the sea. Some decks show The Tower dissolving out from under the figures' feet. No matter the image, the meaning is the same: something is about to rock your world."

"The police have determined the victim died from a fall over a balcony."

"So why are you frowning?" Sonny asked.

"Because I deal in facts—not fiction. I've read the victims' files; I know the circumstances of the deaths. Knowing that, isn't it possible you're picking up my thoughts and making the images fit the facts? If your mind is such a vast wasteland, manipulating the cards to match the reports would be easy for you."

Sonny frowned. "I don't need to cheat." She tapped the cards. "Remember when I said I sensed the cards, the sniper, and Daddy's death were all related?"

"I remember."

"Well, then, take a look at this." She reached beneath the table and pulled two Tarot cards from a purple bag. She then pulled the Lovers card from her pocket and placed the three cards side by side. "These are all Lovers cards, but they all have very different images." She lifted the first card and flashed it at Logan. "This one shows a man having to choose from three beautiful women. One is young and fair, the other two older, but each with their own unique charms." She picked up the card her father left for her.

"This card hints at Adam and Eve in the Garden of Eden, naked and making love." She picked up the third card. "This card shows a naked couple holding hands, with an angel watching them from above.

But how do we interpret these cards? Does the first represent the killer having to make a choice of what empath to kill? Or do we use the second image to surmise that the killer may have had sex with each of the victims before killing them? Or is the third card the relevant one? The killer spies on his victims, worms his way into their lives, and then, when they least expect it, he kills them. Three completely different scenarios. Is one right, and the other two wrong?" She shook her head. "Not if they are all happening at the same time. Our killer scopes out who he's going to kill, then worms his way into her life, has sex with her, and then kills her, and never kills in the same way. The cards now show the different levels of a killer's journey, and all the pieces are connected." She lifted the center card. "If we match the victims' cards to Daddy's Lovers card, we see an alternate reality. Did Daddy risk his life to warn me that something was about to rock my world—a secret that could get me killed? Or is he hinting that I am going to have to risk my life—face death to reveal a secret that will rock the world? Or—"

"How many interpretations can be deduced from these five cards?"

"An awful lot."

"Well, we're not going to sift through that many, so let's go with the first thing that came out of your mouth. Because my gut tells me doubting your instincts at this stage would be suicide on my part."

"And you say you don't believe in the supernatural?" Sonny smiled. "Going with your gut is the same thing as listening to a spirit guide." She tapped the third card again. "The High Priestess is about seeking the answers from inside your own mind rather than in the outside world. If that isn't going with your gut, I don't know what is."

"Don't be smug. It makes me want to kiss you again. Now, let's assume your father *was* taking a risk in leaving you information that could get you killed. It seems to me that The Tower exploding alludes to the entire Blake Empire crashing down around your ears."

"But generally the destruction has a more positive meaning," Sonny responded. "It hints that once destroyed, the person becomes enlightened." She shoved the packets to Logan. "Take the cards out and place them side by side. It's time for me to skim the energy and see how far off the mark I am."

Logan took the plastic, withdrew the cards, and then arranged them as Sonny indicated. When they were in place, Sonny removed her right glove, quickly prayed for guidance, and then let her fingers hover over the top of each card. "The arrangement is wrong. Judgment should be first, The Fool second, The High Priestess third, The Tower fourth, and lastly, the Death card."

Logan rearranged the pattern. "So your father sends a wake-up call, taking a risk by revealing a secret that personally rocks your world, and then what? You kill yourself?"

"No. Remember, The Tower enlightens a person, so that a transformation can occur." She skimmed the Death card. "People see this card and think automatically, 'Oh, I'm going to die,' but that isn't its meaning at all. It's about letting go of the old, to make way for the new. The Death card signals that we must stop hanging on to ideas that are outdated, as well as people who are no longer essential to our spiritual growth. Figuratively, we must kill our old life, so that we can be reborn again to a new and better one."

"Is that what the killer has done? Changed his identity and reinvented his life?"

"I sense my father thought so," Sonny said. "I know him. He'd never use this card to refer to a spiritual death; he means the card to represent a total physical transformation." She waved her hand. "Put the Lovers card above the group … No, in the center, above The High Priestess." He shifted the card a few inches.

"This one's easy to decipher, thanks to your runaway visions," Logan stated. "We're The Lovers; though, I must say, my anatomy doesn't resemble this guy's in any way." He tapped on the image. "I'm not built *that* well."

Sonny laughed at where his fingers were resting. "What a pity. I had high hopes for a night of unbelievable sex from you. Now you've dashed my hopes thoroughly."

He ignored her sarcasm. "You said earlier the card stands for a choice. Is it an amicable one between the lovers, or painful?"

"Hold on." She ran her fingers above the card. "The energy's blocked. With The High Priestess below it, it's clear she's not ready to reveal the answer. The only thing for certain is that the choice is going to come."

"From your father, I'll wager."

Sonny's gaze shot to the TV screen. "I don't know why, but, after skimming the cards, I feel compelled to prove that Ned and Brad aren't capable of murder," she stated. She donned her glove again. "Thank God I had the brains to listen to my father when it came to computers. He was a full-fledged hacker, and he taught me to be just as proficient."

"Taught you to evade cyber mousetraps, eh?"

"Exactly," Sonny responded.

Logan snatched her hand and sprang off the sofa, bringing her to the console with him. When they reached the computer chair, his knuckles rapped the edge of the desk.

"Hop to, Miss Blake. Make the connections."

"And if they're more spiritual than logical?"

"I'll take you to Paris on our honeymoon."

The statement sounded so sincere, Sonny almost believed it. She didn't voice the thought aloud, though, knowing it would sever his current overture of friendship towards her. And his friendship was something she wasn't quite willing to lose yet—even though she was nothing more than an irritating mouse to him.

Noting his thoughtful countenance, she asked, "What if I'm wrong and we find the connections are unrelated? I'm not my effervescent self at the moment."

His forehead crinkled. "Stop being a doubting Thomas. If the clues don't match, we'll deal with it." His gaze scanned her face. "You do understand that there will be no going back once we go into the computer. Whatever we find may rock your world in ways you can't begin to imagine."

"My life has already been rocked, so that point is moot. We need to find out what Pandora is and, more importantly, how safe I really am, if murder is the goal of this insane game."

"Where do we start?"

Sonny reached under the desk and slid a keyboard out. Locking it in place, she pressed a button. A row of synchronized lights flashed on, and the TV-screen wall shifted to a blue haze. Across the console, Logan's eyes met hers. His lips twitched with a brief smile.

"Care for a snack, Miss Blake? Say, a piece of cheese?"

Sonny gave a brief shiver. "Ugh, don't even go there."

CHAPTER THIRTEEN

Biting her lower lip, Sonny pulled off her gloves and set them aside. She needed to *feel* the keys with her fingers. It was the only way she could discern if Pandora was real or imagined. Obviously alarmed by the gesture, the man beside her bent down and touched her shoulder.

"What the hell do you think you're doing? I need you to stay in the real world, not in some damn vision."

Sonny laughed at the concern in his voice. "Relax. These keys are Sonny-proofed."

He straightened. "They better be."

The computer hummed with the sound of booting discs, and Sonny returned her attention to the keyboard. She only hoped that the next few minutes would prove she and Logan were on the right track. The console hummed with another strange whir, and it settled into its familiar password process. Out of the corner of her eye, she saw movement and waved Logan back.

"You'll be better off watching the big screen," she advised.

He nodded, falling back to his original position. Seconds later, he hauled a red-cushioned bar stool under his butt and settled atop it. Sonny waited for him to notice her again. When he didn't, she drawled, "Whenever you're ready, Detective ... And no smoking!" Her sharp command had his right eyebrow jerking up, and his hand halting in its path to his shirt pocket. He dropped his fingers and leaned back, assuming a bored expression.

Sonny swung back to the computer, tapping two keys. "It's a cinch Daddy used his subroutines in the least obvious place. Hopefully, I can trigger the main program with a password and slip in behind it."

"I'm all eyes," Logan teased. He hooked his feet around the stool legs, finally giving both her and the TV screen his full attention.

The steady clicking of Sonny's fingers became the only audible sound in the room for the next two minutes, and it took all of Sonny's concentration to keep her mind from floating into a dreamless mind fugue. Soon, however, a crackling thump echoed from inside the machine, and the huge screen flashed seven letters.

PANDORA

"Good girl," Logan said. "We're in the front door."

"We're in the front door," Sonny agreed, an idiotic euphoria sweeping over her at his praise. *Come on, brain,* she nudged, *find the trap door.* To her surprise, it complied, sending her fingers into a steady conversation with the keyboard and supplying a new sequence of numbers. The disc drive thrummed, erasing the word "Pandora" from the screen; however, it substituted no new word in its place. It just remained a bright blue background with a white, blinking cursor.

Shifting thoughts again, Sonny added a new sequence of numbers, but to no avail. She tried again with the same result. She tried a third tack, using her social security number as the trigger.

PANDORA cropped up again.

"Damn!"

Hearing her annoyed hiss, Logan shifted on the stool. "It doesn't refer to a piece of jewelry, does it?" he asked sarcastically.

Sonny swiveled on her chair, giving him an amused smirk. "Daddy abhors jewelry—used to, I mean." She felt her throat start to constrict and forced her mind back to the computer screen. She let her fingers hover inches from the monitor, casting off any smudged energy. "I sense Daddy *does* mean for us to look at the mythical Pandora and her chest of ills; although, if we use Tarot-speak, Pandora would come from the mythic Tarot deck. The Star card, in fact."

"And its meaning?" Logan asked.

"Hope. You see, after Pandora opened the chest, the Spites, who had somehow gotten trapped in the box, flew out and infected all of humankind, except for Hope. When the chest was opened, he didn't fly away. It was a sign that if one never loses hope, salvation is possible."

"Well, we won't lose hope. Your father obviously didn't."

"But I don't feel the word resonating with my skills, outside of the thought that whatever it is, it should be left in the box, unleashed." She added a new set of numbers, hoping for an immediate response. The screen shimmered and then illuminated a new sentence:

YOUR PASSWORD IS?

Sonny smiled, tapping the keys. Keep it simple, Daddy. A plus B equals C. She typed in the word "Sonny." The screen darkened momentarily and then radiated light again.

INACCESSIBLE CODE. TRY AGAIN?

Sonny plucked at a strand of her hair. "Using that word would have been *too* easy," she declared. She erased the sentence and fed in a new set of numbers. The screen produced PANDORA again. She erased it and tried twice more. No success.

Annoyed, Sonny lifted her fingers from the keys. You couldn't sift through sawdust without a shovel, could you?

Free-float, her inner voice advised. *Think about the character, Pandora.* She opened something she shouldn't have, like Eve taking the apple from the snake in the Garden of Eden. Could it be that simple?

Her gaze drifted to Logan Reed. If the Lovers card represented the two of them, how did Logan Reed fit in? Her father had no knowledge of his existence. So how could he fit her father's elaborate chest of ills? And who in the mythical story did he represent? Prometheus or Theseus?

"Pride goeth before a fall," Logan murmured

Sonny caught his meaning at once. "You can say it. I'm not as smart as I thought. I can't make the password work."

"It's simply not the password then," he replied. He tucked his thumbs into his belt loops and studied her face.

Damn, why did he have to be so laid-back and patient now, just when she had finally gotten used to his overbearing sarcasm? It was unsettling for her concentration for him to give her time to sort it out. Idly, she began drumming her fingers along the side of the console, replaying the sequence of numbers in her head.

"Let's go about this with a procedural eye," Logan said. He scanned the screen above them. "Let's assume your father is here in the room with us, typing the word. What would he be saying to you as he typed?"

Nibbling on her lower lip, Sonny digested the thought.

"He'd be reminding me that everything has its place in the universe. Nothing is random. One plus one equals two; two plus two equals four … " She broke off, giving the cards on the coffee table a quick look. "Of course, that's it." She flew to the sofa, bending over the cards. She studied the engraved numbers at the top of each card. "The Fool equals zero; The High Priestess two." She studied the remaining numbers as Logan stopped beside her. "Judgment equals twenty, which equals two plus zero equals two. Death equals … "

"Thirteen," Logan supplied.

"No, it's one plus three equals four," she said quickly. Her gaze found the Tower card. "One plus six equals seven." Her contemplation stretched back across the cards. "0-2-2-4-7." Her gaze shot to the TV screen, and she bolted from the sofa. "Pandora's card is seventeen; one plus seven equals eight." She sank back onto the computer chair, inputting the sequence of numbers. 0-2-2-4-7-8.

The computer suddenly flickered blue and white and then produced a new sentence:

YOU'RE A CHIP OFF THE OLD BLOCK!

Sonny smiled at the compliment. *I'm better than good, Daddy. Even though you never knew these cards existed, your spirit guides did and they routed them into your mind as messages for me.* In seconds, sentences began to ripple rapidly across the screen, halting her rambling mind and forcing her to focus on the words. She left the console, joining Logan at the bar stool again. Together, they read the missive rolling across the screen.

IF YOU ARE READING THIS, SONNY, I AM DEAD—MURDERED BY A SADISTIC PREDATOR WHO MAKES THE SANCTUARY HIS HUNTING GROUND. I HAVE LEFT CLUES HERE—AND A DVD OFF-SITE. BOTH WILL LEAD YOU TO 'PANDORA.' USE YOUR TALENTS TO DESTROY IT. PANDORA MUST NEVER SEE THE LIGHT OF DAY. I LOVE YOU MORE THAN YOU KNOW.

The computer paused, awaiting new instructions, and Sonny's mind reeled under the words. A sadistic predator? She felt warm hands descend on her shoulders.

"Now we know for certain Pandora exists. Next, we need to learn what it is."

Sonny's stomach turned nauseous. "The hand of Spirit is moving things into place," she said, clutching her stomach. "I can feel the shift."

"When the student's ready, the teacher always comes," Logan stated.

"But who's the student, and who's the teacher?"

"For the time being, your father is doing the teaching," Logan said.

"What do you suppose he meant by 'Pandora must never see the light of day'?"

"We won't know that until we see the clues he left."

Sonny suppressed a shiver. She'd rather not see any clues ever. Just hearing that someone hated her enough to kill her was enough to shake her confidence. She didn't need every detail spelled out.

"Snap out of it, Sonny. We're wasting precious time."

Sonny jerked to attention. "Sorry." Leaning over, she typed a new command into the program and stood back. The drive whirred and finally fed up a new set of items: two Tarot cards and a photograph.

The photo was adorable—a young, petite face wreathed in an animated, carefree smile. Under the picture, a caption read:

AMANDA

"Amanda who?" Logan asked.

Studying the pigtails and heart-shaped face, Sonny felt a surge of inexplicable connection to the girl in the photo. She clutched her stomach again.

"I don't recognize her, but I can almost see her aura connecting with mine," she stated. "I wish Daddy wasn't being so mysterious."

"Perhaps the truth would've gotten him killed sooner. The predator may have discovered his secret was out. Besides, not all mysteries start out that way. Most times they are truths turned upside down by the passage of dark minds," Logan advised. "At any rate, we have our first clue. And once we match it with the others, we'll be one step closer to solving the mystery."

"And where on the predator's hit list I am," Sonny muttered. "First, second?"

"One step at a time," Logan cautioned. His fingers gave her shoulders a final squeeze. He studied the card on the screen. "Another damn Tarot card," he chided. "I wish your father had added some variety to this game." He sighed. "Alright, I give up. Who's The Hermit?"

His question had Sonny moving to the screen with a subtle lift of her fingers. She closed her eyes, drinking in the card's energy. Her eyes popped open a moment later.

"It's Foster Sykes," she said in surprise. She dropped her hands.

"And who is Sykes?"

"He's a hypnotherapist. He ran my dream laboratory until a car accident left him paralyzed a year ago. He's wheelchair-bound now and very rarely comes out of his house. Hence, The Hermit."

A long pause descended, and Sonny sensed Logan was trying to figure out how this information fit a logical solution to their dilemma. And then, as quickly as he fell silent, he rallied.

"Perhaps he became an invalid because of what he knows about Pandora," Logan said. "If you sense a connection with the photo, then my first thought was right. This mystery revolves around something secretive from your past. Your father obviously learned the secret, and it scared him enough to resort to hiding clues in a computer."

"But murder!" Sonny stressed. "What secret could be so important that people would kill to keep it safe?" She broke off, covering her trembling lips. She saw Logan's arms snake out to her in sympathy, and she shook her head, warding him off with a raised hand. "I'm not having a meltdown," she said.

"Good girl. We can't get the right answer until we ask the right question. Right now, the connections are vague, but I admit they are connected." He gave her one of his arrogant grins. "I promise you, as good as you are with interpreting Tarot cards and initiating visions, I am just as good at solving my cases."

Sonny attempted a smile, but she knew it lacked force. "That's the spirit," he chirped, seeing the tilt of her chin. "Now, what does The Ten of Swords mean?" He ran his fingers along the image depicting ten swords embedded in a slain figure's back. "Not a happy card, by the looks of things."

Sonny suppressed a shiver. "My least favorite card in the deck," she remarked. "It represents being s-s-stabbed in the back."

"Tell me something I can't see for myself."

"It's a card of despair; however, it also represents the ending of unimaginable mental pain. See the sun coming over the horizon in the background? All is not lost."

"That's encouraging," Logan said, throwing her an admirable look over his shoulder. "Why are you frowning? We're getting better at connecting the dots."

Sonny shrugged off the compliment. "I'm confused by its appearance. So far, all the cards I've been sent have been part of the Major Arcana … No, don't hiss. I know you don't know major from minor in Tarot-speak, but believe me when I tell you, this last card is far removed from the others."

He studied her stymied expression. "Though these all appear to be separate clues, each one is really part of the whole," he told her. He began rocking on the balls of his feet. "Which one do we need to know first, I wonder?"

Sonny wondered, too, but not out loud. Her thoughts centered on what the final outcome would be once all their questions were answered. Would The Ten of Swords signal her being stabbed in the back like her father?

The smell of smoke interrupted her sour thoughts, and Sonny looked up at the red warning light flashing across the monitor. On the giant screen, a visual and vocal countdown began.

"Thirty, twenty-nine … " Sonny issued a halt command; however, the countdown continued. "Twenty-seven … twenty-six …"

"What's it doing?" she asked, issuing a second termination command. She felt Logan at her side. "I've never seen a program do this before."

"You should be asking what it's counting down to," Logan supplied quickly.

"I don't want to know," Sonny said, hitting the reset button and then exhaling loudly when the computer squealed like fingernails down a chalkboard. The screen flicked off, and relieved, Sonny tumbled back into her chair, her legs buckling. "I don't ever want to know how close that was."

"You can say that ... What the hell?"

The glass of the monitor in front of Sonny cracked, spewing smoke and emitting an acrid smell of fried wires. Rolling her chair out of the way, she saw small puffs of smoke curling up from the back of the monitor, heading for her chair. The heat bouncing off was an omen that a larger fire was about to erupt. She recognized the danger at the same time Logan did.

"Fire extinguisher," they said simultaneously.

Logan whirled around first, his glance surveying the walls. When it lit on the red canister, he dashed towards it and ripped it from its holder. He was back in a flash, spraying the back of the monitor with its foam contents and ordering Sonny to get out of the way.

She complied, but not before snatching up her gloves from the console and donning them. Mesmerized, she watched the foam saturate her keyboard and the sides of the console. *So much for priding yourself on knowing things before they happen*, her inner voice mused. Sonny immediately dammed her ego for pointing out the obvious, and then she nearly jumped out of her skin when a fail-safe shutdown set off every electronic gadget in the room. One by one, each fizzled out and went dark.

Though surprised by the sudden quiet, Logan's fingers continued to wield the twisted knob of the canister, making sure that no fried wires had a chance of reigniting. It only took a scant ten seconds for the small fire to be totally put out, and another five seconds for Sonny to realize that her father's killer, a skillful hunter, had made sure the mice didn't come away with any of the cheese.

Smoke teased her nostrils a few seconds longer, and then, hearing the canister hit the floor with a crash, Sonny sank into her chair again. All remnants of her computer had been turned to melted mush. The clues inside were now nothing, at least nothing that could be traced from this location. Their hunter had put them back at square one.

On the other side of the console, Logan shoved the fire extinguisher with his toe. It scraped loudly, a perfect mirror to Sonny's thoughts.

"The bastard should be shot," Logan said. "Preferably twice."

She heard a sudden, rapid tapping on the door.

"Your sandwiches, querida," Consuela called through the glass panes. Sonny started to send her away, but Logan's growl brought her attention back to him. A second rap sounded on the door. "*Señorita*, I bring food."

"The computer was triggered with a shut-down," Logan said, ignoring Consuela's third hammering. "Who has access to this room?"

"No one," Sonny said tartly. "This is my home. Besides, the shutdown was done remotely."

"How the hell did you discern that?"

She waved her gloved fingers at him. "This is how." She ripped off her glove and skimmed the fried wires. "I can sense the shutdown didn't come from this computer." She donned her glove again. "And now, thanks to our hit man, we haven't a chance in hell of proving who murdered Daddy today. We'll have to wait and use the main bungalow somputer when Dick releases it."

Even as she said the words, Consuela pounded on the door again, this time yelling in a voice laced with panic. "*Señorita* Sonny, mi querida!"

The shaking of the doorknob vibrated through the floor beneath their feet; however, neither of them moved to let the housekeeper in.

"I wish to hell we'd thought to print out the clues right away," Logan said.

Hearing his heartfelt declaration, a lump rose in Sonny's throat. She was the one who was sorry. Her problems had put his life in danger. He forestalled any comment from her by chanting ominously:

"Three blind mice, three blind mice, see how they run, see how they run … "

"That isn't funny," Sonny chided, shivering.

"Neither is burning to death," Logan said, finally moving to the French doors to let the housekeeper in. Consuela's pounding became intense, and to Sonny's horror, a fire alarm activated. *Good grief!* Consuela had hit the police emergency button.

CHAPTER FOURTEEN

Frowning, Ned entered the hypnotherapy chamber, his focus on Logan Reed's sudden arrival. The man was a stupid bastard if he thought he could protect Sonny from her destiny. No one could stop the hands of time or the plan in motion—especially not a Meta Corps agent. Ned snickered, and the sound bounced off the walls of the empty room. It would be a pleasure to abduct Sonny from under Reed's nose. He'd never find her in the dark abyss Ned would be sending her to. In fact, when he was finished scrambling her brain, he'd focus on her body. She'd give him weeks of pleasure before he killed her, and he'd make sure he didn't leave a trail a bastard like Logan Reed could follow. The timing would have to be perfect, though. One false step and his abduction plans would come crashing down.

Sinking into his console chair, Ned continued to fuel his anger. Logan Reed was an unexpected complication. He had already managed to impress Cutter with his Meta Corps badge and credentials. And if he actually had managed to impress Sonny, well, it would be hell to short-circuit their partnership.

Remembering Sonny's declaration that she enjoyed being kissed by the bastard, Ned's jealousy flared anew. It didn't matter how many times the pair kissed. His lips would be the last she tasted. Love wasn't in the cards for her—only a brief life as his plaything.

Shifting his attention to the console, Ned booted up the machines in front of him, and then, rising, he removed a headpiece from a robotic crane arm. He set the piece down on the seat of the room's client chair. Too bad he'd had to kill David so soon. The man had been good to him over the years. But the wily bastard had brought his own demise. He had found Ned's Pandora tape, been appalled by what he had seen on the disc, and then threatened to reveal everything to Sonny first—then to the world. Well, now he wouldn't have a chance to breathe a word of what he knew to anyone. The secret had gone with him to his grave.

In the distance, Ned heard a police siren wail, followed by the shrill whine of a fire engine. It was obvious the shutdown at the hacienda had occurred. The security team was en route.

Lifting his wrist, Ned checked the time. His last appointment of the day would be here in less than ten minutes. No time to seize Sonny today. Lady Luck had chosen to delay her capture for another day. There'd be another chance to abduct her, though. All one had to do was wait for it. Carpe diem! Seize the day!

Swinging about, Ned headed back to the console; however, before he reached it, the lab door swung open. Margie Hunt shuffled through the door, dressed in a strapless tank top and jean shorts. The energy surrounding her frame sizzled with her apparent excitement.

"I know I'm early, Dr. Chalmers, but this morning's session was so invigorating, I couldn't wait to feel that way again."

Ned signaled her to the chair. "Then why wait? Let's get right to it."

She climbed into the chair rapidly, and then, settling into a comfortable posture, she donned the green headpiece and matching headphones.

In seconds, Ned had ramped up the power system and taken his place at the console.

"Close your eyes, and breathe deeply. We'll start by counting backward from twenty."

She complied, and soon, she was answering a taped question. "And where are you now?"

"I'm in your bedroom. We're about to make love." She gave a breathless pant. "You're slipping off my clothes."

Ned flipped off the tape, rose from the console, and approached Margie's chair. The woman was completely under, with no conscious thought of her surroundings.

"And now what are we doing?" he asked, studying her glowing face.

"We're naked. We're kissing." Her breathing revved up, and Ned reached out and tugged her tank top down. Her large breasts bounced free, the material sliding under and catching. Seeing a pair of large, dusky nipples, Ned inhaled sharply. The woman had breasts to give any man a raging hard-on. Luckily, today, he was that man.

"And where are we now?" he asked, hitting the "recline" button on the chair.

"We're on the bed."

The chair slid back, and Ned lowered the arms, locking them into place under the seat. "And what do you want?" he asked.

Her voice became euphoric. "I want you to make love to me."

"Done," Ned said.

He began unzipping his pants.

• • •

Standing in the doorway, Sonny watched the security team rummage through the melted debris.

"You cold?"

She jumped, startled to find a lacy shawl being dropped across her shoulders. Tucking it around her, Sonny glanced up at Logan's face. "I'm freezing."

"And fighting off the urge to go in there and touch the wires so you can see who wants you dead, I bet," Logan added.

"It's too late for that. Nobody could possibly sense anything but smoke and charred ash." Sonny pulled the shawl tighter around her shoulders. An unexpected heat washed across her face, and she bit down the urge to prove Logan right. She would have liked nothing better than to shove the evidence team aside and sift through the embers of the fire with her fingers. She had the overwhelming sense that the Tower card lying on the coffee table signaled the total destruction of the hacienda, not just one little computer.

"You're shivering," Logan remarked. "Are you getting some kind of supernatural message I need to know about?"

Whipping her head around, Sonny smiled at him. "No, I was thinking how lucky we were that he doesn't want me dead yet."

"He'll be back," Logan countered. "He's already made the card with the Tower image come to pass. I hope this is the only thing designed to rock your world." He let his gaze graze his slacks and then brushed at a foam stain near his groin. "He's a wily bastard, I'll give him that."

Flashbulbs lit up the room, startling them both. They shifted their gazes, spotting the lieutenant's tall figure motioning to them from the bottom of the staircase. Descending, Sonny was the first to greet him. "Anything?"

He gave her a brief hug. "Are you hurt?"

"No. We're fine."

The lieutenant's gaze found Logan. "What the hell is going on with you two?" he asked, turning back to Sonny. "It's as if, together, you are a magnet for trouble."

Sonny shivered at his words. If only Dick knew what they knew. He would not only think they were magnets for trouble, he would *swear* to it. Her gaze found Logan's, and she saw the clear, almost imperceptible, shake of his head. He knew she was thinking of spilling every detail of Pandora. And he didn't want her to. Why? No answer came, thanks to her uncle's voice shattering the air.

"What the bloody hell is going on here?" He strode into the room. Reaching the middle of the carpet, he took one look at the cluster of uniforms upstairs and gave a fractured growl. Here it was again, that growl Sonny knew so well. It indicated an explosion was on the way. She braced herself for the worst as he took a step towards her.

"You know bloody well that when something goes wrong here, you are to call me first, Sonny."

"Lighten up, Fletcher," Logan commented, stepping in front of Sonny. "And change your tone. I don't like it." Hearing the rebuke, Sonny moved away, dropping onto the nearby sofa. It was best to retreat when men resorted to high levels of testosterone. Why couldn't they just bypass the macho crap and talk to one another?

To her amazement, no explosion came from either man. Instead, her uncle appeared baffled by Logan's complete shift of attention to the lieutenant.

"Sonny was in the middle of checking the daily financials, when the computer caught fire. We managed to hose down the wires and halt any major damage to the room, but Consuela panicked and hit the fire alarm button."

The lieutenant eased his stance, but not the bite in his tone. "You're lucky the entire hacienda didn't burn down with you three in it."

"It was a minor fire, Dick," Sonny advised. "Easily handled. However, Consuela did the right thing in hitting the alarm."

The lieutenant studied her face, attempting to read it for any hint of a lie.

"Was it an attempt on Sonny's life this time?" he asked Logan.

"Most likely—or a damn fine scare tactic," Logan replied.

"Bloody hell, Reed, you're out of line," Brad snarled. He ignored the immediate glare sent his way, and Sonny winced as he turned and joined her on the sofa. He took her hand and raised it to his lips. "How are you really feeling?"

"Shaky. But you should thank Logan, Uncle Brad, not growl at him. He acted quickly in putting out the fire. If it had spread to the other computers, it could've been a lot worse."

Schooling his features, her uncle made a weak apology to the man now standing alongside the couch. "Sorry, Reed. When it comes to anyone harming Sonny, I see red."

Logan ignored the apology, turning back to the lieutenant, who was in the midst of jotting something on his notepad.

"The killer must think David told something to Sonny before he was killed," Logan said. "It must've been pretty damn important." He jerked his head towards the computer room. "Your men aren't going to find any evidence up there. Sonny sensed the fire was detonated remotely."

The lieutenant's gaze canvassed the second floor overhang. "What the hell was he looking to cover up?"

Sonny started to say, "Pandora," but stopped her runaway tongue. No one but she and Logan knew about Pandora. Should they confide in Dick? Legally, she knew they should. They were withholding pertinent information in a murder investigation, and if found out, they could be held liable themselves. She glanced at Logan. Why had he chosen to mention her sensing the detonation? It made no sense.

Seeing the strained expression clouding his face, she decided it was important to do everything in her power to convince him to give up Pandora to the police. She couldn't let him sacrifice his life or career for Blake Industries, especially since she was coming to depend on him so much. She had to convince him to let her reveal her disturbing vision of the mysterious therapy session. Of course, they'd leave out the vision of them having sex.

She glanced towards the terrace window. It went against the grain of things to give Logan an order when she knew he couldn't abide being told what to do. But it had to be done. So, how did she get him to see it? She thought deeply for a moment, realizing their talk had better be soon. There was a cold chill stealing over her bones again, plus an overwhelming fatigue. Both were clear signs that her empathic skills were about to reach behind the fabric of her gloves in an effort to detect the truth behind things.

Another angry voice erupted in the foyer, and all eyes swung to the pair entering the front door.

"Don't you dare tell me to calm down, Ned. I am perfectly *calm!*"

Ned's flat, inflectionless voice made an autocratic reply, but to no avail. In seconds, Charlotte Fletcher was standing in front of the lieutenant, her voice laced with contempt. "Are you going to wait until we're all murdered in our beds before you take my brother's death seriously?"

Her aunt always attracted attention when fired up, and right now Sonny realized her heaving breasts and stiff posture were garnering a lot of attention from the male officers on standby. Her turquoise eyes, sharp and assessing, finally took in the activity on the second floor and then impaled the lieutenant again.

"Well, what do you have to say for yourself?" Her voice arced to a high-sonic falsetto, and hearing it, she broke off, obviously afraid to continue. At her look of consternation, Sonny rose from the sofa.

"Calm down, Aunt Charlotte; we're fine. Not even Dick could've imagined a second attack coming so soon."

Charlotte touched her cheek, her expression softening. "Are you alright? No dizziness or sudden headaches?"

"I'm fine." Her aunt's smile made Sonny pat her fingers with a stilted laugh. "Don't go reading anything into this episode. I'm not dizzy, at least not in the way you mean."

"Now, Char, don't be an alarmist," her uncle scolded. He popped up from the sofa and threw an arm around his wife's shoulder, attempting to draw her back to the couch. Irritated by his overt mothering, she smacked his hands away.

"Don't patronize me, Brad. I hate it when you do."

As if stung, he dropped his fingers and stalked back to the sofa. "I'm not so fond of you, either, at the moment."

Seeing her aunt's mutinous glare, Sonny changed the subject. She had to ward off the ugly confrontation brewing between the pair. "We really are fine—all of us."

Hearing Sonny's words, the lieutenant cleared his throat and gave Logan a long, unfeeling stare. "Just what do you think happened, Reed? Cop to cop, I mean."

"A definite arson—which was set off when Sonny used her personal keyboard. It triggered a full-scale meltdown of the computer. We could hear the static as the wires crackled." He whirled about, glancing at Sonny. "Do you remember anything different, Sonny? Something your mind might've recorded?"

"No. It all happened too fast."

Her aunt shivered, tossing the lieutenant an anguished look. "See, Dick? The bastard knows how to circumvent computer systems. We'll all be murdered in our beds before the night is out. Do something!"

"Calm down. I'm working on it," the lieutenant replied.

She took his answer in stride, but not without a loud sigh. He then turned to Ned, slipping his notepad into his back pocket.

"Could David have fallen into partnership with some unsavory characters, Ned? Someone with the knowledge to crash an entire network of enterprises?"

Brad interrupted with a frivolous toss of his hand. "Our security system cannot be overridden by outside forces," he declared. His wiry fingers shot up, raking his dark hair and then dropping to pull a crumpled Salem cigarette pack from his shirt pocket. He surveyed Sonny's outraged face just as he lit up. A second later, he had pocketed the cigarette pack and stamped the cigarette tip out. "Sorry, Sonny. I forgot what a bitch you are about smoking in the hacienda." He stuffed the unsmoked stick into his pocket and then continued with his soliloquy. "I'm not saying this wasn't arson, but an electrical short in the walls is certainly possible, too."

"I pay big bucks to keep this room's security tight," Sonny said. "Brad's right. No hacker gets in, period."

The lieutenant cut in. "But a meltdown did occur, preprogrammed or not."

Sonny turned her irritation on him. "Hackers worm their way into mainframes all over the world daily. However, I pay big bucks for a system that can't be hacked." She rubbed her arms briskly to warm the goose bumps suddenly rising. Why did her head feel like it was stuffed with musty cobwebs all of a sudden? She glanced at Logan, wishing he would look at her. She longed to tell him her senses were kicking in with an unwanted vision.

And then it happened: a vision that took her breath away and sent her senses spinning. She flew through the white vortex, as if shot from a cannon. By the time she hit solid ground, she was standing in a small, cramped room, where she heard a male voice droning monotonously.

"You're safe; nothing can harm you. Where are you now?"

A melodic voice answered, "I'm in Venice on my honeymoon. Matthew and I are riding a gondola to our hotel. Check-in is at four."

"And where are you now?" the voice asked, inflectionless.

"Umm." The melodic voice turned breathless. "Matthew and I are having sex. His hands are all over me … We're climaxing … "

The vision shattered into a thousand pieces, and Sonny was hurled back into reality, like a dart winging its way to a marked target. She came awake with a start, finding herself on the floor, in Logan's arms. Their eyes met sand held, and Sonny saw the panic written on his face. He was wiping blood from beneath her nose, and her hands covered his.

"How long was I out?"

"About forty-five seconds." He knocked her gloved fingers out of the way as she tried to wipe her upper lip. "Put your head back," he ordered. "The bleeding's stopped, but let's be sure."

Sonny did as instructed but found the motion nauseating. When a sea of upside-down faces swam into view, she closed her eyes. She had been thrown into a vision of another hypnotherapy session in progress, but who had been the participants? Definitely one male and one female.

"Can you sit up?" Logan asked, slipping his hand behind her neck. He offered his other hand to her, and Sonny took it. In seconds, she was sitting upright. "What the hell happened?" he asked once she sat staring out at the sea of legs surrounding her.

"Too much smoke," she lied.

"Too much excitement, you mean," Logan said. "Can you stand?"

"Is the Pope Catholic?"

"Every damn day," Logan replied, scrambling to his feet. He then hauled Sonny up from the floor, whirled her around, and captured her shoulders. He tucked her into his chest, glancing at the group watching the action.

"Show's over," he stated firmly. He glanced over his shoulder, signaling to Conseula, who stood in the kitchen doorway, wringing her hands. She bustled forward, making clucking noises as she walked.

"*Sí, señor?*" she asked when she reached him.

Logan palmed Sonny's hand off to her. "Take Sonny to her room and see that she lies down. I'll be along later to tuck her in." His glance found Sonny's surprised one. "I mean it, Sonny. Lie down and get some sleep, or else."

Consuela tugged on Sonny's hand, but Sonny held her off. Instead, she tapped Logan's chest with her free hand. "What are you going to do?" she queried softly.

"Talk to Cutter and then get some shut-eye myself," Logan replied. He signaled to Consuela again, who clucked at Sonny affectionately.

"*No es bueno* to go without sleep, querida," she said. "I shall bring you warm milk to sleep. And then I shall make a bed for *su enamorodo* in the guest room. He is, how you say, 'done in'?" Sonny's eyes crinkled at the corners. Consuela clucked again. "He no make love to you tonight, I think."

"Especially if I wear those dreaded pajamas you hate so much," Sonny said, lowering her voice so only Consuela could hear. "Any thoughts of *mi enamorodo* making advances while I'm wearing them are nonexistent."

Consuela clucked disapprovingly.

"Don't worry, Consuela; I like a woman in PJ's," Logan said, overhearing Sonny's last comment. "It makes the sexual adventure so much more fun."

"Don't be a smart-ass," Sonny chided, dragging Consuela away. However, when they reached her bedroom door, she whirled around, surprised to find Logan right behind her. "I don't need a babysitter," she exclaimed, pushing him back.

His grin surfaced, but no comment. Instead, he gave her a mocking bow and rejoined the group. *Damn toad!* Sonny thought. She wanted him to stay and discuss her vision.

The bedroom door closed in front of her, blocking out the living room and its occupants.

"You must rest, querida, Consuela said. "It is the *señor*'s wish."

Sonny sighed. Even Consuela had fallen under the man's spell. She headed for bed, shedding her clothes as she went. In minutes, Consuela was snatching up Sonny's clothes from the floor and hanging them over a chair.

"I check on you, querida, before I leave—in case you need me to stay." She continued to the door, and then Sonny heard it close softly. Tuning in to the quiet, Sonny quickly drifted off to sleep.

CHAPTER FIFTEEN

Logan held his stance, waiting for the bedroom door to close behind Sonny. He realized he must look like a lovesick fool to the group around him. *An absolute idiot*, his inner voice agreed. *You're acting as if the woman's welfare is a personal matter.*

The truth was not that kind, Logan knew. His concern was simply ego-driven. He hated not being in control of an investigation from start to finish. And more than that, he hated feeling like he had been thrown into the middle of a hungry pack of wolves. A feeding frenzy was coming; he just didn't know from which family member it would come.

Whirling around with a sigh, he found Charlotte Fletcher standing close behind him. She was staring at him as if she couldn't quite fathom what kind of meal he would make.

"I don't approve of you and Sonny working together," she stated rudely. "She has a full schedule of clients on her calendar already. To ignore them, and concentrate on solving a case of serial killings, can only jeopardize her health, as well as her reputation."

The attack took Logan by surprise, but he didn't show it. He smiled at her instead. "Sonny assures me that my time here will be brief. She's already studied the case files and evidence. I'm waiting for her to render a verdict, and then I'll be out of your hair."

No answering smile came his way, just an icy retort. "I've seen the way you look at Sonny. And I saw the way she molded herself against you when you kissed her. Sonny's extremely impressionable. It's easy for her to misinterpret a cavalier kiss as something binding."

Logan suppressed a sudden urge to strangle the woman in front of him. He had wondered how long it would be before someone took potshots at the kiss he and Sonny had shared in the cottage. Charlotte Fletcher was the first, and hopefully she'd be the last.

"If I've learned anything since meeting Sonny, it's that she never misinterprets her feelings for anyone. She's too bright, too articulate, and too in tune to her talent to make that mistake. The kiss was spur-of-the-moment on my part, and Sonny shut me down quite thoroughly after it."

"Did she indeed? Perhaps I've misjudged her."

Logan heard the mocking sarcasm in the words and knew the woman was not pleased with his explanation. She gave him a last stony glare, and then, as if he was nothing more than a lowly amoeba on the scale of evolution, she shifted her attention to the activity going on in the computer room above.

Logan let his grin surface. "No need to freeze me out, Mrs. Fletcher. I already got the message loud and clear."

"And what message is that?" she asked, not bothering to glance his way.

"That men looking for a marriage partner are unwelcome in Sonny's life."

"Well, as long as you know it, we needn't spend any more time discussing it."

She left him then, moving up the staircase towards the activity beyond the French doors.

"Touché," he mumbled softly, shifting his torso to relieve a growing kink. And then, like Charlotte, he turned and focused his attention on the police techs vacating the upstairs room. Watching them shuffle through the door, dragging their equipment down the stairs behind them, Logan's mind slid into an uneasy game of brain tag. What was the next tack to try when it came to dealing with the family? Background checks were a must, he knew.

His gaze sought the lieutenant's tall frame. He would need to utilize Cutter's clout to get the info he needed. He could call Meta Corps himself, of course, but then he'd have to sell Dresden a pack of lies about Sonny. Not seeing Cutter, Logan's gaze turned to Ned and Brad, who were standing just inside the French doors. Their resentful stares were aimed at him, which made him realize the pair disliked him as much, if not more, than Charlotte Fletcher. He schooled his features into an impassive stare, wondering which one of them had killed Blake. He was sure one of them had. *Better yet,* his ego nudged, *which one of them is trying to kill Sonny now?*

Lieutenant Cutter's large frame finally appeared in the doorway, shooing the pair out of the room. They hustled down the stairs, allowing the lieutenant to dismiss the blue uniforms standing about. The room emptied fast, except for the family. And then, to Logan's surprise, the lieutenant ordered everyone out of the room, including himself.

The family went reluctantly; however, Logan was not about to be dismissed so easily. He shored up his Meta Corps persona.

"A word with you, Lieutenant," he muttered, seeing the man about to vacate the room behind Ned and Brad.

The lieutenant paused, giving Logan his undivided attention. "I recognize that look from this morning," he said. "You want something from me." He moved back into the room. "Access to the crime scene, maybe?"

"It's too late for that," Logan replied. "What I need is information." He pulled his ID wallet from his back pocket and headed for the kitchen counter. Once there, he plucked a business card from the wallet and then pulled a pencil out of a glass jar. He scribbled on the back of the card and then handed it off to the lieutenant. "I need you to call this number, but ask for Dresden Charles this time. Tell him it pertains to the serial killings. Ask him to do a code-one background check on Ned Chalmers and Brad and Charlotte Fletcher. Ask him to go back at least thirty years. And while you're at it, have him search the files for any project that might be labeled 'Pandora.'"

The lieutenant studied the number on the back of the card. "Why the hell don't *you* call the number? It's your office. I have my own calls to make."

"Humor me, Lieutenant. Talk to Dresden."

The lieutenant pocketed the card. "What the hell is Pandora?"

"I'm not sure yet," Logan replied. "Maybe a secret project the trio is involved with."

"Where did you get the name from? Sonny?"

Logan emitted a crusty growl. "Stop asking for explanations I can't give right now. I'll explain when I can. Until then, call Dresden."

"You're a relentless bastard," Cutter muttered. "I'm warning you, though, when I call the number, I'm going to ask for a thorough background check on *you*. My gut tells me you were sent to The Sanctuary as some form of punishment—probably for doing something illegal."

"Let me ease your mind and save you the trouble of bothering Internal Affairs," Logan responded. "My last assignment ended badly; however, I don't intend to see Sonny go down that road."

"Neither do I; so whatever I can do to help, I'll do it."

"Good. Tell me what you know about Foster Sykes."

"Good God, where did you hear that name from?"

"I'll tell you later. Right now, I need to know whether this Sykes fellow might have a grudge against David Blake—enough to kill him." The lieutenant's expression changed rapidly, and Logan hoped he wouldn't suddenly clam up and treat him like a leper. He needed the lieutenant as a sounding board. "I have a good reason for asking the question, Lieutenant," he pushed.

The lieutenant's expression mellowed. "Sykes is a local therapist. He ran Sonny's dream laboratory. He lost the use of his legs in an accident last year; however, if you're thinking he killed David, you're barking up the wrong tree. He's a recluse that never ventures more than ten feet out his front door. And if you're thinking of visiting him and testing the waters, let me caution you that he's a gnarly, stubborn bloodworm."

"I have no intention of accusing anyone of Blake's murder yet." Logan frowned. "One needs proof to do that."

"You won't find proof in that quarter," the lieutenant responded. "David and Foster have been friends since college. After graduation, they stayed in touch. They eventually pooled their monies to buy a hundred acres of land, which in turn led to buying more land—about five hundred acres."

"They built The Sanctuary together?" Logan asked. "I thought Charlotte Fletcher was David's partner."

"She is. But Foster was a silent partner—might still be. Once The Sanctuary got on its feet, Foster opted to go back to school. He earned three degrees in parapsychology and hypnotherapy, disappeared off the grid for a while, and then returned to The Sanctuary to work with Sonny. So, you see, the man is simply not capable of killing anyone." He halted mid-sentence, and Logan sensed he was remembering something unpleasant. "There was that thing years ago with his sister," he said. "Her name was Gail. She died at the same time Sonny's mother did. Now that I think of it, it's possible the pair had a falling out over the deaths."

"Don't jump the gun," Logan advised. He studied the lieutenant's expression, which was once again easy to read. "Let's go with your gut feeling that he'd never kill anyone, until we prove differently."

The lieutenant shook his head. "I can't believe David's dead, although I can well imagine someone wanting to murder him. I've had the thought myself over the years."

"I could use a name, if you'd care to share."

"Brad and Ned are on the top of the list," the lieutenant said. "They each run their own therapy labs, and they tolerate no interference from anyone. As you heard earlier today, David was taking an avid interest in their appointment schedules and demanding a complete accounting of their travel itineraries and expenses."

"Anyone else?"

"Sy Belvin, the retreat's attorney, had a grudge. He was recently fired by David for misappropriating funds. He claimed innocence, but a thorough investigation revealed he was knee-deep in insider trading. And then there's Charlotte," Dick added. "She and David had some wicked rows over the last few months."

"And then there's Sonny," Logan stated.

"You can't possibly suspect her. She was David's biggest fan."

"Everyone's a suspect until they're not. Isn't that what you said?"

"I did, but I didn't mean Sonny. Besides, she has an alibi—*you*—unless of course you killed David before meeting her."

"Why don't you do something productive, like making that phone call?" Logan snarled.

"Before I do, tell me why you felt compelled to piss Charlotte Fletcher off?"

"She dislikes me for no apparent reason," Logan said.

The lieutenant grinned at him. "It was that damn bombshell she witnessed in the foyer. That kiss you and Sonny engaged in was smoking hot. And I do mean *smoking*."

"How do *you* know?" Logan asked. "I don't remember you in the foyer."

"You were too busy playing kissy-face to notice you had an audience."

Logan growled peevishly. Would they never get past that damnable kiss?

Voices rose behind them, and Logan whirled around. The security team was settling into place. He headed towards the voices, not surprised to find the lieutenant matching his stride. As they walked, he reminded his brain that playing mind tag served no purpose. To protect Sonny, he needed concrete answers. *That don't get us killed*, his inner voice added. Was it time to reveal David's obsession with Pandora? The longer he held back the information, the better chance there was that the lieutenant would believe David Blake had become paranoiac in recent months, rather than focused on a real threat.

He frowned. He should have put two and two together on the mesa, but he had been gulled by the mouse's tits and legs. And that was dangerous. An agent who didn't attend to business got people hurt. *Or ended up in hospital beds,* his inner voice reminded him. The thought set his teeth on edge so much that he began plucking at his shirt collar. *We need a shower badly,* he told his alter ego. *Sleep wouldn't hurt, either.* Reaching the foyer, the lieutenant finally spoke.

"Because of the knife embedded in David's back, his autopsy should be quick and easy. But I wonder if there'll be a surprise we aren't expecting?"

"In my line of work, there's always one more surprise, Lieutenant." Logan saw the lieutenant's frown and purposely changed the subject. "How important is Sonny to The Sanctuary if she doesn't hold shares?"

The lieutenant wrinkled his brow, unperturbed by the sudden change of thought. "She has no proxy, can't vote. Doesn't seem likely she's a threat."

"Is it possible she might inherit the retreat now that her father's dead?"

"Good Lord; that would make her a sitting duck."

"Relax. Blake was silenced for what he wanted to reveal to her. It's possible our killer thinks he's already revealed it to Sonny."

"Then why not set the entire hacienda on fire, instead of burning out one small computer?"

Logan sucked in his bottom lip. It was time to reveal David's suspicions.

"I haven't been entirely honest with you, Lieutenant," he remarked. "David left Sonny a note on the mesa warning he was in danger and so was she."

The lieutenant blanched at the news. "How long were you going to withhold *that* piece of information from me?"

"Until it was time to give it up," Logan answered calmly.

"What did the note say?" the lieutenant prodded.

"That Sonny should access his computer as soon as possible."

The lieutenant's head whipped around. "That's why she was so anxious to return to Serenity. She accessed David's files."

"And almost got fried in the process," Logan said. "My instincts tell me there's something in Sonny's past that people will do anything to keep buried."

"Perhaps Sykes' accident last year wasn't really an accident, either."

"I'm working on that connection."

"What else are you keeping from me?"

"Sonny insists that David's death is related to the murders I'm currently investigating. When she touched the knife—"

The lieutenant cut him off, his anger palpable. "You let Sonny contaminate a crime scene—taint evidence?

"Not on purpose. She reached for the knife. I tried to stop her. Her skill set off, and we were flung into a vision of some damn therapy session."

"You entered one of her visions?"

"Yes, but don't ask how or why because no explanation would be believable."

The lieutenant raked his fingers through his hair, and by the look on his face, Logan knew he was battling a war with his conscience.

"I oughta haul your ass off to jail," he finally muttered. "If you're the best that Meta Corps has to offer, this country is in serious trouble."

Logan laughed at the slur. "I'm the best of the best, Lieutenant," he countered. "You'd do well to remember that when you find yourself having to play outside the law to solve this case."

"I'm an honest, hard-working employee, Reed." The lieutenant smirked. "A rent-a-cop with scruples."

"Good for you. Now, besides calling Meta Corps, do you think you can finagle Sonny's medical records for me? I've read her Meta Corps file, of course, but as you know, the agency is only interested in her empathic skills. They could care less how they first started." Logan reached for a cigarette and pulled the stick out. He tapped the tip on the back of his hand, hearing Sonny's voice suddenly tripping through his head. *No smoking!* He pocketed the stub again and threw the lieutenant a lopsided grin. "Sonny's a bitch about smoking inside."

"Outside, too. You can't preach a healthy lifestyle to your guests if they run outside every hour to have a smoke. It defeats the purpose of living well."

Logan grunted and then eyed the lieutenant. "I have every intention of marrying Sonny when this fiasco is through," he stated. The lieutenant's expression switched to shock, which had Logan hiding a grin. "Just thought you should know."

"Love at first sight, eh?"

"Followed by lust at first sight." The earlier image of the pair having sex flitted through Logan's mind. He pushed the empathic memory away rapidly. He'd not go there just yet. However, when this debacle was over, he would make putting his life together a number-one priority. He couldn't ask Sonny to marry a broken-down screw-up. She deserved better than that. For a brief moment, Logan wished he had Sonny's power to touch a person and view the contents of their mind. He'd love to know whether the vision of them having sex was pleasing to her. The lieutenant's voice cut through his thoughts.

"Now that we're in a confession mode, you should know that I was personally hired by Blake to keep an eye on Sonny. He feared some lunatic would attempt to use her skills for something unsavory."

A smile crossed Logan's face. "Do I detect a threat in that statement?"

The lieutenant shrugged. "Men have always found Sonny attractive; however, up to this point, she has made sure the attraction goes no further than the front door, and never into the bedroom."

Logan gave a crusty laugh. "I'll see what I can do to alter that."

The lieutenant chuckled. He pointed left. "So how come you're out here, and she's in there?"

"Because the sooner I find the bastard who wants to kill her, the sooner I can focus entirely on getting her to fall in love with me." The remark produced a smirk from Cutter.

"Subtlety is certainly not your style, Reed."

"So, you'll give me access to her records?"

"I'll see what I can do. I'll call Sonny in the morning, though, to verify that she's okay with the release."

"She'll agree," Logan said arrogantly.

Another laugh echoed, and a hand descended on Logan's shoulder.

"Watch out, my friend. Sonny's a tiger when riled. If you toy with her emotions and then end up screwing her over, she'll have your balls for dinner."

Logan let a tired grin escape. "Though it pains me to say it, Lieutenant, I love the damn wench."

The hand lifted from his shoulder. "What's your next move?"

Logan brushed his stubbly chin. "A shower and sleep—in that order."

"In your own bed, I hope."

"Can it, Lieutenant. You're making me blush."

The lieutenant clapped Logan on the shoulder again. "I'll make that call for you as soon as I get back to the security office."

Logan nodded, glad to let Cutter do all the legwork for him. When the door closed behind him, he whirled around and headed for the room next to Sonny's. Five minutes later, he was enjoying a scalding hot shower and tamping down the urge to dash next door and have sex with the most gorgeous mouse he had ever met.

CHAPTER SIXTEEN

Taking a quick sip of coffee, Sonny's gaze swept the landscape beyond the terrace. It was almost sunrise, and the sky was draped in gorgeous yellow and orange streaks. Most days, she loved watching the rays cascade over the mountaintops, but this morning the sight had an eerie quality to it, as if the streaks were strands of unwanted ectoplasm heading her way.

She shivered at the thought. What had the obnoxious toad done after she left the room last night? Obviously he wasn't worried about anything happening to her. Only one security guard lounged in the foyer. He had also left her in Consuela's capable hands, which proved what she already knew. Toads and mice never mixed; they simply coexisted.

She took another sip of coffee, her gaze softening as she realized the toad's luggage had been delivered to her home. Who had authorized the transfer? The toad himself? She wouldn't put it past him. Had a good night's sleep in her guest bedroom recharged his Meta Corps skills and readied him for whatever battle awaited them today?

"How long have you been up?"

The question startled Sonny so much that she almost dropped the mug in her hand. She whirled around, spotting Logan walking out onto the terrace. She studied his appearance as he came. He had shaved, showered, and donned clean clothes, and like the first time they'd met, she could smell the manly scent of his aftershave. He walked quietly, too; in fact, everything about his demeanor was quiet—except for his ego.

"I've just finished dressing," Sonny answered. "Did you find everything to your liking in the guest suite? A comfortable bed? Fluffy towels? Bath soap?" Her words were dripping with sarcasm, and she didn't know why she was taunting him. *You're mad that he didn't come to our room, buck naked,* her inner voice supplied.

"Soften your tone," he said, reaching her. "I haven't had my morning coffee yet." He took the mug from her gloved fingers and drained the contents. He handed the mug back with a grin. "That hit the spot."

"What happened after you sent me to my room?" Sonny asked, getting right to the point.

He chucked her nose. "I stayed and filled Lieutenant Cutter in on our touching the knife *and* your father's suspicions."

Sonny bristled. "You told him about Pandora, too, I suppose," she groused. When he didn't deny it, she suppressed the urge to box his ears. "Are you insane? I thought we agreed to tell him together."

He gave a fractured growl in return. "I dropped hints, nothing more. Besides, we were treading on dangerous ground by keeping pertinent information from him."

Hearing the censure, an army of snakes began to coil in Sonny's stomach. "I suppose he threatened to jail us," she said.

"You suppose wrong. He threatened to jail *me*. He's too fond of you to upset you in that way."

Sonny whirled back to the landscape, her gaze grazing the desert scrub below. She ran her fingers around the rim of the mug. "He will blame me for the tampering, though," she stated. "We're friends, and friends should always be honest with each other."

"Relax. He knows I'm to blame for our staying quiet."

Sonny's heart did a flip-flop. Why had the toad taken the blame?

"What happened last night?" he queried, his breath teasing her hair. "Your collapse, I mean."

Sonny brushed her temple, unable to keep her voice from trembling. "I think my talent is unraveling," she said. "I got thrown into that same therapy session again, but this time, it felt off."

"Off, like how?"

"The young girl was excited, but at the same time afraid. It was as if she was experiencing both at the same time. The man kept asking her where she was, and each time she answered, I felt my skin crawl, which means the girl's was too. She was waffling between delight and disgust, and I can't explain how she could be enjoying the session and hating it at the same time. An ambivalence like that has never come up before."

"What about the nosebleeds? How recent are they?"

"They started about a year ago, sporadic at first, but getting progressively worse."

He rounded her shoulders and lounged against the balcony wall. "I can see why you might be reluctant to discuss this, but I need to know what could throw your talent off like this."

"I have no way of knowing, since I was born empathic," Sonny replied. "It's not as if being empathic has a time limit." She frowned. "I suppose it could, though. The mind is an unfathomable world really, and you can't explain spiritual gifts in human terms."

"It's possible the nosebleeds are separate from the talent," Logan remarked. "They might be a warning from those spirit guides of yours—for taking on too much."

Her hand flew up quickly. "Spirit guides don't issue warnings. They flat-out say what they mean and mean what they say. Besides, I can feel when I'm overdoing it. It's usually thanks to Ned and Uncle Brad; they make it very hard to ignore their demands."

Logan grabbed Sonny's gloved hand and pulled her towards the living-room couch. Once there, he took a seat beside her.

"Brainstorm with me for a moment. Do you remember hearing about any lawsuits being leveled against The Sanctuary when you were young?"

"No," Sonny remarked quickly. "A lawsuit would've made headlines, which in turn, would've sunk the retreat, especially since it was just gaining financial momentum. Besides, a father wouldn't discuss those kinds of things with a young daughter."

"I'm asking because Lieutenant Cutter told me Foster Sykes and your father pooled their money and bought the land The Sanctuary sits on."

"What?" Sonny went pale at the news. "Foster and Daddy were business partners?"

"According to Cutter, they met in college, and the friendship stuck. It's possible Sykes was, and still is, a silent partner in the retreat."

"Well, that would tick Aunt Charlotte off big time," Sonny said, "but I can sense you think she didn't know. If that's true, and she recently found out, it would make a pretty powerful incentive for murder. Even twenty years after the fact."

Logan sank back, raking his hair feverishly. "God, if only I could manage to connect the dots faster."

"We'll figure it out together," Sonny said emphatically. "With my talent and your firecracker brain, we can't lose." She saw his scowl and spoke up. "You are not going to leave me out of the investigation."

His head shot up. "Simmer down. No one's leaving you out of anything. In fact, from here on out, you won't be staying anywhere alone. You've acquired a heavy-duty bodyguard, whether you like it or not!" He dipped his head in emphasis.

Sonny's lips tilted in amusement. Rotten toad. Arrogance was certainly his middle name.

"What time do you think Sykes rises?" Logan asked. "I'd like to catch him off guard—the earlier, the better."

Sonny cleared her throat. "I refuse to visit him until we've had one of Consuela's delectable Mexican omelets. They cure early-morning grouchiness."

He grinned at her jibe. "And if I say I hate eggs?"

"You'll eat them and like it, or face Consuela's nagging persistence that *no es bueno* for *mi enamorodo* to skip breakfast."

"Would this be a good time to tell you that I minored in Spanish in college?"

The front door opened suddenly, preventing Sonny from telling Logan what she already knew: he had a deceitful nature. She turned to find Consuela bustling over the threshold, grocery bags in hand. Spotting the pair, she clucked her approval, heading for the kitchen counter.

"I cook you *bueno* breakfast," she said, plopping the bags on the counter. She gave them a toothy smile. "I make fine Western omelet, the best in Mex-hee-co." She began pulling bread, eggs, and milk from the bags. "You see, I good cook." She glanced at them quickly again. "You make love tonight." She went back to fussing with the groceries. "You make fine *bebés*. I take care, and we all live happily ever after, *sí*?"

The pair on the couch exchanged grins. "*Sí*," they said simultaneously.

•••

Two hours later, they were on the road. The highway was a sheet of blinding light as the SUV sailed through Echo Underpass and continued its northward trek up the Double S Highway. Each mile brought them closer to a towering series of mountain ranges. Forked saguaros crowded the lengthy roadway, and the blacktop sizzled from the rotation of the tires crackling across its surface.

From her vantage point in the passenger seat, Sonny could see the morning sun being covered by a darkening skyline. In a few moments they'd be at the Adobe Lakes turnoff and five miles closer to their goal. What kind of reception would Foster Sykes give them? Perhaps not cordial. Ever since Logan had shared the possibility of Foster and her father being partners, her senses had shored up. She knew what that meant. Foster and Pandora were connected. Had her father given Foster the Pandora DVD for safekeeping? If not, why else throw his name in the ring?

The car lurched as it began its final descent through the last of the mountain underpasses. They were now four miles closer to their goal, and she hoped Logan wouldn't go all Meta Corps badass when they reached the Sykes hacienda. She should have dissuaded him from coming altogether, convinced him that Foster would be more agreeable to speaking with a friend rather than a stranger.

Stealing a peek at Logan's profile, she realized he had been overly silent during the ride, and she could see why. His brain was in solve-the-puzzle mode. He was so in the Meta Corps zone that he hadn't noticed the care she had taken with her appearance. Dressed in a yellow-gray blouse, with a gray pleated skirt and matching jacket, she looked like the latest corporate CEO fashionista. She had chosen steel hoop earrings that dangled and spun, and on her feet, she wore the latest in fashion footwear. Her gaze drifted from Logan's profile. It wouldn't have killed the toad to notice how pulled together she looked.

"Do I look presentable?" she finally asked.

His gaze scanned her face. "Don't be coy. You have a mirror."

A rush of color stained Sonny's cheeks; however, before she could offer any kind of retort, she caught sight of a gated row of buildings and the sign adjacent to the turnoff.

"We're here. Turn left at the first street after the entrance. We'll circle the lake and come in behind the hacienda. That way we'll miss the guest traffic."

Following her instructions, Logan slowed the car to a crawl and waved at the security guard who responded with a quick lift of the barricade arm. Soon they were traversing two yellow speed bumps and turning left at the first intersection. In a matter of minutes, they were skirting the lake and heading towards the residential area of the complex.

"How shall we play this?" Logan asked, slowing the car to allow a young couple to jaywalk across the street.

"No good cop, bad cop," Sonny said, pinching her lower lip with her fingers. "If Dick's info is right, Sykes may take one look at us and slam the door in our faces."

"Did you ever talk to him after his injury? Offer your condolences?"

"Of course I did. How could you even ask such a question? We were colleagues. I was heartbroken when he got hurt."

"I meant no criticism of you," Logan said. "I just want to be in control of this interview, not the other way around."

"Foster's body may be crippled, but his mind is as sharp as a tack," Sonny relayed. "Or at least it was six months ago. I'm ashamed to say I let my classes and client appointments take precedence over visiting him. Turn left at the next gate."

The car veered around the designated corner, and before another minute elapsed, the Kia was braking in front of a hacienda covered in clinging vines.

The pair studied the rambling structure in front of the car. A sudden chill swept over Sonny, and she inhaled sharply.

"What?" Logan asked, picking up on the noise.

"Something bad's coming. I can sense it."

"Too much caffeine," Logan stated, opening the car door and slipping out. Hearing the door click, Sonny sighed. Logan was right. Three cups of coffee in an hour was *way* too many.

• • •

Ned slowed the van, watching the Kia turn into the front gates of Adobe Lakes. His instincts had been right when he woke this morning. Sonny and her companion were up to something. But what did Sykes have to do with it? He pulled the van to the shoulder of the road and let it idle. He watched the Kia crawl through the barricade and then turn left towards the row of cottages encircling the lake. When the back of the car disappeared around a row of hedges, he pulled onto the road and into the left-turn lane.

Braking at the guard shack, he greeted the guard pleasantly, and then, given the wave-through, he rolled the van through the rising arm and followed the arrow pointing right, opposite the route the Kia had taken. In seconds, he was circling the lake from the east and pulling into an empty parking spot not far from the parked Kia.

He sat for a moment, thinking over the events of the last couple days. Had he made any mistakes in murdering David? Left any evidence that could be traced back to him? He couldn't imagine what. As soon as he realized David had videotaped one of his late-night sessions, he had attempted to find the damming tape and destroy it. But David had been in the power seat. He hid the tape and demanded Ned's resignation. Ned had refused, of course. He had no intention of leaving such a perfect hunting ground. Not when it was so easy for him to move the blame to someone else.

He saw movement by the Kia and saw Sonny and Logan traversing the front walkway. As quietly as he could, he slipped from the van, rounded the front bumper, and slid the side door of the van open. Reaching in, he snatched a duffel bag from the floorboard and closed the door. In seconds, he was darting around the side of a yellow cottage and out of sight.

•••

"We should've called first," Sonny remarked, as she pressed the doorbell.

"Surprise has its advantages," Logan told her, as a bell pealed deep inside the house. Unnerved by the sound, Sonny shifted her weight, warning her ego to hang tough during the upcoming confrontation. No matter how badly Foster treated them, they couldn't leave without learning the truth. If he held the Pandora DVD, they had to convince him to give it up.

The door swung open with a sudden jerk, and Sonny had her first good look at Foster Sykes in six months. The emaciated face staring up at her from the wheelchair was a shock. He had grown old so fast. And worse, it wasn't fair to come to his home and grill him as if he were a hardened criminal. He sat staring at her for a moment, as if he didn't have the foggiest idea of who she was, and then his eyes fired up in recognition, and his mumble was frigid.

"Out slumming today, Sonny? Or are you just making your yearly charity visit to crippled shut-ins?" His gaze traveled to the man standing on her right. "No, this must be for the paparazzi. I see you've brought an entourage."

Logan's hand flew out. "I'm no reporter, Sykes. I'm a colleague of Sonny's—Logan Reed."

"Can we come in and talk, Foster?" Sonny asked. "It's important."

"Nothing a Blake could ever say to me would be important," he stated. He grabbed the doorknob, attempting to shut the door in their faces. However, he found Logan's foot lodged firmly against the bottom edge. A sour grimace gripped his lips, and he rolled the chair back a few paces. "You've appeased your conscience for the year by coming here, Sonny. Now tell your young man to get his foot out from my door, or I'll call the security gate and have you ejected!"

When Logan's foot remained against the doorjamb, Sykes swung the wheelchair around, rolling himself down the hallway away from them. Logan stepped across the threshold, following the rolling chair and issuing a statement of his own.

"We've come to talk about David Blake's murder."

The wheelchair whirled around, banging into the wall and almost toppling the old man. His gaze stabbed Logan's as he clutched the wall.

"David Blake has been murdered?"

"Yesterday morning."

The wheelchair swung about again, continuing its trek towards the back of the house. "I warned David he'd never get away with it."

Stunned by the pronouncement, Sonny could only stare at the disappearing shadow.

"Get away with what?" Logan asked, following the chair.

Sonny's gaze latched on to Logan's retreating form, and she stepped inside, using the short walk down the hallway to calm her rattled nerves. Entering the back patio area, she tuned in to the raised voices.

"Your history with David Blake means nothing to me, Sykes."

"Good," he retorted. "For you couldn't begin to understand what my history with him was."

Sonny stepped out onto the patio, eager to halt the confrontation. "I never knew you and Daddy attended college together. Why didn't you tell me?"

"It served no purpose. We were young and stupid then. Besides, I don't discuss those days anymore. The past is the past, and it needs to stay there."

"But it isn't staying there," Sonny said. "Daddy is dead, and no one knows why. If there's any chance you know who killed him, you must give us the name."

"And be the one killed this time? In my own house?" Sykes shot back. "I'm smarter than that."

"Lieutenant Cutter can send officers to protect you," Sonny said. "There won't be any more accidents."

He looked at her hard, a twisted smile curving his lips, and Sonny sank down in the nearest chair, her legs giving out beneath her. "My God, you think I had something to do with your accident! For heaven's sake, why have you kept silent all these months instead of confronting me? Why?"

"If I had divulged what I knew, you'd be visiting my grave instead of my house. But then again, perhaps you have an ulterior motive for coming here today. To silence me at last?" His gaze swung to Logan. "You don't look like a hit man, but then again, I didn't look like that kind of man, either, when I was your age."

"I'm no assassin, Sykes," Logan stated. "Sonny and I have come about Pandora."

"Did you now? What an interesting notion."

"Stow the old-man-in-a-wheelchair crap. I don't like it," Logan said.

Foster gave a gleeful chuckle at the threat, fussing with the brake on his chair. "Don't like it much myself, either." He swiveled in his chair to face Sonny, who attempted to put her best game face on. "So, you found out about Pandora. David must've been in dire straits to involve you. Must have been a shock to learn your whole life has been nothing but a pack of lies, eh?"

Sonny barely managed to stifle a choking gasp. What the hell was he talking about? Her life, a lie?

Logan didn't seem to be stunned by the question. "Her face is a dead giveaway, Sykes. Surely you see that? She hasn't quite gotten used to the idea yet."

"She will—once the attempts on her life start."

"They already ha-have," Sonny stuttered.

Sykes chuckled again, rolling his chair to within inches of her own. His gaze scoured her face as if under a microscope. "At first there'll be nosebleeds. It's meant to prepare your brain for the worst kind of pain."

Sonny's breath evaporated quickly. "My God, what are you saying? That I've been poisoned?"

He didn't answer, turning back to Logan instead. "You've obviously seen the nosebleeds."

"I would be a poor friend if I didn't."

His cackle came again, but more twisted this time. "You've got the look of Meta Corps about you. I can tell a Meta Corps bastard a mile away." His gaze wandered back to Sonny. "I've always admired your talent, Sonny, always hoped I'd experience it in person." His gaze drifted back to Logan. "Who sent you here?"

"David Blake did."

Sonny's gaze tripped from Foster to Logan. He made it sound as if her father had ordered them to come and quiz Foster. Would Foster take the bait? She studied the wizened face. No, he was smarter than that, and extremely bitter. He'd go on toying with them.

"How much is the information worth to you?" he asked, sending a searing glance Logan's way. Sonny sucked in her breath. Good Lord, he intended to extort payment from them. Logan's hand hit his back pocket, and Sonny saw a checkbook appear a second later.

"Name your price, Sykes."

Sonny bolted from her chair. "Stop this! You can't seriously think I'm going to let you buy the Pandora DVD from him, do you?" She clutched Logan's wrist. "We'll find it some other way. I'll endure ten nosebleeds at a time if I have to. We've gotten this far. We'll get the rest of the way on our own." She swiveled on her toes, facing Foster head-on. "I'll not pay you a dime, do you hear? You'll have to sell the DVD to some other fool!" She spun on her heels. "We are leaving right now, Logan, and it's not up for discussion!"

An autocratic growl sliced the air. "Sit down, dammit!"

Intimidated by the command, Sonny dropped into the nearest chair and fixed her gaze on Foster.

"How much do you really know?" he asked.

The question was thrown at Logan, and Sonny wished it had been thrown at her. That way, she could've thrown it back in his face with an ugly "go to hell" rebuttal.

"That something catastrophic happened to Sonny when she was nine or ten."

Floored, Sonny's head whipped around. How had Logan deduced something so bizarre from such a simple question? Another silence descended, and then the wheelchair returned to its original position.

"I congratulate you, Detective. You've figured out in a few short days what no one has discovered in twenty years. How did you figure it out?"

"From Sonny. She's been envisioning the same therapy session over and over in the last day. She can't tell me whether the session is from the past or the present, but I'm guessing it's a combination of both, since Sonny assures me that it's possible for her to see both at the same time. Besides, criminals aren't very original when it comes to committing crimes. They figure if it works once and they didn't get caught, why not keep trying it."

"What tipped you off to me?"

"Before he died, David Blake programmed the word 'Pandora' into his computer and left it for Sonny. Once we accessed the program, we found three clues linked to Pandora. You were second on the list."

"And the first?"

"A photo of a young girl, which, in my humble opinion, puts the time frame back when Sonny was ten—at the time her mother took her own life."

"A lucky guess," Foster stated.

"Hardly a guess, especially since the young girl's photo bears a striking resemblance to Sonny. It made me wonder whether the puzzle could be that simple. Your sister was killed the same day, wasn't she?"

The wheelchair rocked on its frame. "You've aroused my curiosity, Detective, but we both know that question isn't the one that needs answering. So what do you really want to know?"

"Why David Blake had to be murdered."

Foster gave a fractured snort. "Ask Sonny. She knows."

"Me?" Sonny squeaked. "I don't know a thing."

"And you don't have empathic powers, either, do you? Don't use that Blake snobbery on me."

"But I don't know anything," Sonny stressed. "I'm in the dark, I swear it."

Foster snickered at Logan. "She pretends she doesn't know who she really is, but she has to know. Her empathic powers are so unique that she must've caught a glimpse of the truth during one of her visions. She's chosen to repress it—like all the others."

"What *others*?" Logan asked.

"The first patients used in The Pandora Project. There were twelve in all."

Sonny's eyes suddenly welled with tears. "Dear God! That's the link," she said, glancing at Logan. "The twelve girls belong to the Tarot cards we've been looking at. They're all dead—except for me." Her glance returned to Foster. "I've never 'seen' anything at all from that time. What am I supposed to have seen?"

Seeing her tears, Logan crossed the small space between them and placed a comforting hand on her shoulder. "Have a heart, Sykes. Can't you see Sonny has no recollection of Pandora? Tell us what you know. Let me be the one to put the pieces together. If you help, I can find the person who really put you in that chair."

The old man's gaze flew to the wall over Sonny's left shoulder, and she knew he was deciding whether to put his faith in Logan's words. Could he be convinced her shock and dismay were real? She didn't know. She only hoped he'd give her a chance to prove it.

His gaze finally swung her way, and Sonny felt her stomach do a rapid somersault. He was going to divulge the truth, and it was going to be bad. She bit her lower lip, trying to maintain a stoic face; however, she found herself glancing up at Logan with an anxious look instead. His return glance was as comforting as the hand that lightly squeezed her shoulder.

"Who's your mother, girl?"

The question startled Sonny, and her gaze shot back to the wheelchair.

"M-m-marion Blake," she stammered. "Everyone knows that."

"Everyone knows the lie," Foster corrected her. "You've been Sonny Blake only since you were ten."

"Ten?"

He ignored her blackened scowl. "There is no Sonny Blake, at least not in human form. She exists only on paper."

"Pa-paper?"

Logan ignored her stammer, focusing on Foster. "Why? And how?"

"The why should be obvious, but the how? The how was cleverly done." Foster gave them his full attention. "Imagine twelve orphans, bought and paid for in the name of science—"

"This is nonsense," Sonny interrupted. "I remember my childhood—where the family went on vacations, birthday parties … How could I remember all that and not have been born Sonny Blake?"

The wheelchair rolled closer to her, and Sonny pulled back in alarm. It took all her strength to keep a choking sob at bay as Foster muttered softly, "Enter Pandora—a hypnotherapy program so radical that to simply call it 'brainwashing' is to insult its very nature."

Sonny studied the frail hands caressing the chair handles and marveled at how natural he made his explanation sound. As if altering the memories of children was a common, everyday occurrence.

"If I'm not Sonny Blake, who am I?"

"You're Amanda King. Your real birth certificate was destroyed long ago."

"I have a birth certificate in my vault—Sonia Blake is in my vault," Sonny whispered. Foster's lips pursed tighter. "Why destroy my birth certificate?" Sonny asked.

"To keep anyone from ever discovering that The Pandora Project worked. You see, the therapy was remarkable. It was done with nothing more than the use of a green-colored door."

"Green door?" The question was uttered by Logan and Sonny simultaneously, and Foster gave them a suspicious squint.

"Yes. This small trigger sent the patient through the door and into a full-scale opening of the memory pathways. New memories were then laid inside, and when the patient woke, there was no memory of the shift. Each therapy session instilled more of the new memories and less of the old. By the time the shift was completed, the memory sensors were in place and could not be reversed. Or so we thought."

"We?"

"You don't think I thought this up all by myself?" Foster said. "I was hired. I hold degrees in psychiatry, psychology, and hypnotherapy, and, like those evil little sprites Pandora let loose in the world, I have the ability and know-how to reprogram the human mind and take it places it's never been."

"You learned the technique when you disappeared from The Sanctuary and remained off the grid for years," Logan guessed. "That's what got left off your resume when Lieutenant Cutter did a background check on you. He could never put his finger on why the background facts felt off, but I can. The Meta Corps Agency was built on the backs of an elite team of paranormal scientists called Para-Corps."

"Three teams—to be exact," Foster corrected him.

"Which were you?"

"Research." He paused, and Sonny sensed he wasn't going to divulge any more information to them without assurance that they would stay mum on what they heard.

"Come clean, Sykes," Logan demanded. "This may be the only chance you get to tell your side of the story."

Foster settled back against the chair and sighed. His gaze scoured Sonny's face again. "I want you to know that I never guessed the memory switch would give birth to empathic talents. If I had, I would've fought like hell to decimate the project."

Sonny shuddered, suppressing a wild desire to strip off her gloves and touch Foster's gnarled fingers. She'd learn soon enough if he was lying about her heritage.

"So, you're saying that David Blake backed a reckless, mind-altering program and blackmailed you to keep you silent?" Logan asked.

"Hell, no. Blake had no idea of the project until a year ago. Seacoast Trust sent him notification of a languishing safe-deposit box. Curious, he had it opened and was floored to find adoption papers inside that named Amanda King as his adopted daughter."

A pool of tears stained Sonny's lower eyelashes. "You worked alongside me day after day, and you never said a word. You had plenty of chances to tell me my real identity. Don't say you didn't!"

"Blake Industries has eyes and ears everywhere. Not to mention hidden cameras. For all I knew, you were in on the deception."

"Well, I wasn't. And as for hidden cameras in my labs—that's ridiculous." Sonny shot him a quelling stare. If he thought she was going to believe someone had planted cameras to spy on her and her staff, he was mistaken. She opened her mouth to tell him so but found her words cut off by Logan's dour tones.

"If your accident was meant to silence you permanently, why aren't you dead?"

"I had a well-oiled backup plan—something that guaranteed my survival."

"You filmed the sessions," Logan said quickly. "That's why David said the video was off-site."

A sly smirk spread across Foster's lips. "Of course, if I had to do it over again, I would've used a different plan. Survival wasn't worth the loss of my legs."

"Where is the tape?" Logan asked.

"Safely tucked away."

"I want that tape," Sonny declared, swiveling in her chair. "I'm not about to believe any of this absurd story without proof. And if you refuse to give it to me, I will sue you for extortion, defamation of character, and any other damaging charge I can think of."

He looked up at her with a sideways squint, and Sonny knew he wasn't intimidated by her threats. However, in the next instant, the whistle of a speeding bullet sizzled past her ear, and the man before her pitched forward and slammed back, pummeled by the blow of a gunshot.

A spray of blood showered Sonny's blouse, freezing her in place. Lightning-quick, Logan snatched her out of her chair and slammed her to the ground. She gripped the chest hovering over hers, an uncanny sense of déjà vu stealing over her. Once again, their sniper had found them, and once again, her face was inches from a raised pistol.

"Are you hit?"

"N-no. It's Foster." She tried to take a peek around Logan's chest but found her gaze blurring. She mustn't cry. Not now, not ever. Her mind and body couldn't take it. A few more bouts of abuse and she'd fall into a mind fugue she'd be unable to bounce back from.

She blinked back the tears and saw Foster's slumped figure in the chair. No sign of life was apparent in his broken body. "I th-think he's dead," she stuttered. Logan shifted sideways, and Sonny clutched his shirt. "Don't leave me!" His chest came back into view, along with a pat on her shoulder.

"Relax. I have no intention of leaving you. The sniper got what he came for, and it wasn't us."

"Foster?"

"Yes." He gripped her shoulder. "I need to examine him. You're not going to space out on me, are you?" His gaze impaled hers, searching for signs of a breakdown. Sonny shook her head, and he gave her shoulder a reassuring pat as he holstered his gun. "Good girl." Seconds later, he was crawling along the stucco tiles to the wheelchair.

Not about to be left alone, Sonny crawled after him, stripping off her gloves as she went. It might not be too late. She might be able to touch Foster and secure the truth of his words. When she reached the left side of the chair, she heard a stuttered wheeze and forgot about getting answers.

Scooting to his haunches, Logan assessed Foster's bloodied shirtfront. He lifted the shirt up and studied the gaping wound. Sonny winced as she spotted the trail of seeping blood. The bullet had been dead on.

Sonny saw a scowl appear in the middle of Logan's brow and knew the news was bad. A gnarled hand batted at his probing.

"I'm ... beyond help."

Ignoring Foster's words, Logan reached into his pocket and withdrew a hankie. He stuffed it over the red stain. "It's never over till the fat lady sings," he declared.

Foster gave a muffled laugh, stilling Logan's fingers. "Get the bas ... tard."

"You can count on it."

Foster seemed buoyed by the answer, and then suddenly, his body went limp. Without thinking, Sonny grasped his wrist and wrapped her fingers around it. She was immediately jolted into a white vortex and out the other side. When the vortex stabilized, she was shocked to see Logan standing beside her on the edge of a small chasm. She studied the space in front of them, spotting Foster standing on the other side.

He seemed jarred by the empty space around him, until he spotted the pair. He judged the distance between them and, realizing he couldn't brook the expanse, withdrew a chain from his shirtfront. With a small jerk, he tore it from his neck and tossed the chain to Sonny. It floated up and across the space in slow motion, as if time had dared to defy gravity and set its own speed.

As the chain floated in her mind's eye, Sonny's breathing also slowed, followed by a disturbing quake that shattered her serenity. Her skin began to prickle pleasurably, and she realized her sensory receptors were in tumult. A second vision was coming on top of the first one, and this new web of images wasn't so new. She had seen and felt them before. They were waves of sexual ecstasy, a flood tide of two bodies exploding in a downpour of fiery sensations.

Disoriented by the explicit images, Sonny struggled to keep the two visions from colliding. The effort took every ounce of her willpower, but she managed to deflect the sensual images and throw them back through the vortex.

The first vision shored up with a vengeance, and Sonny caught a glimpse of the floating chain once more. She opened her hand, palm up, to catch the metal. Moments later, the chain—and the key attached to it—landed in the center of her palm. She closed her fingers around the metal tightly, hoping the touch would kick-start her exit out of the maelstrom. It worked. Like a tornado gone haywire, she was shot back through turbulence and the vapid, endless clatter of bawling winds.

She slammed back into reality, like lightning cracking the skies. When she got her bearings, the New Mexico sky glared hot and blue above her head once more. She immediately heard a series of hacking coughs, followed by painful gasps. Following the sound, she saw Logan's fingers wrapped around her exposed wrist. Idiot! He had thrown himself into the vision with her, and he had scrambled the images. Why had he done such a foolish thing? It was bad enough she had dared to initiate a vision so close to a dying spirit, but for him to jeopardize his health was insane.

Blood drops spattered the tiles around her knees, and Sonny knew she had to don her gloves as quickly as possible. Her nose was leaking like a sieve, and unless she found a way to block the seepage, it would turn into a gushing river. Her body would suffer the consequences quickly after that. It would hurl her through fantasies and trances, two at the same time, and leave her delusional.

Sonny heard movement, and when she glanced up, she saw Logan fumbling through Foster's shirtfront. In seconds, he was hauling a key embedded with an emerald from around the man's neck. A stuttered wheeze permeated the air.

"Don't waste your breath talking, Foster," Logan cautioned, patting his chest. "We'll get you medical help."

A dab of red oozed from between Foster's slim lips, and Sonny panicked.

"Foster ... " She shook his lifeless legs. "Where's the DVD?" His chest rose as if he would answer, and then she heard a long exhalation of breath ... and then only silence. Mesmerized, Sonny stared at the lifeless face inches from hers. He was gone without answering her question.

Tears surged, and she rested her head against the side of the chair. How could she be so unfeeling as to put a DVD above a man's life? Her blurred vision caught the jagged edge of the key peeping from Logan's palm, and she burst into tears. It was despicable to care more about a key than a human life.

A siren wailed in the distance, bringing her attention back to the blood-spattered tiles around her knees. A neighbor had obviously called the security gate, frightened by the sound of the gunshot.

A hankie swam in front of her face, and Sonny took it. She wiped her drenched cheeks, smearing blood from her seeping nose. Alarmed, she held the cloth tight against the bottom of her nose, willing the blood to stop. Her sobs quickly turned to hiccups, and from hiccups to small sniffs.

"Not a word, do you hear?" Logan said, sliding the key into his shirt pocket and buttoning it. "Let me do all the talking when the police get here."

Sonny nodded, the fingers reaching for hers. In seconds, she was on her feet and dumped in a nearby lounge chair. She continued holding the hankie to squelch the blood flow.

"Let me hold the key," she muttered. "You'll be frisked by security; I won't."

"The key stays with me. It goes where I go." He saw her sudden scowl. "And don't even bother trying to sweet-talk me into giving it to you because there is no way in hell you are going to touch this key. Even I felt the twisted energy of that last vision. It about took me down. From here on out, you are going to keep your gloves on, twenty-four seven."

Blind anger singed Sonny's voice. "Don't you dare give me orders, and don't deny that you flung yourself into my vision on purpose."

"We needed answers."

"You could've killed us both with such a reckless act. And for your information, if I want to touch the key, I will. If you don't like it, you can go straight to hell."

A cheeky grin came her way, but he held his tongue.

"What? No sarcastic comeback?" she railed.

"And have you damn me to hell again? I think not."

A siren wailed close by, cutting off Sonny's choked reply. Obnoxious toad! He was making her think he wasn't manipulating her, when in fact he had just done so by not arguing with her.

Hearing the echo of door slams, she whirled towards the doorway. A second later, two strapping security guards charged out of the shadowed hallway and onto the back patio. Their guns were drawn, and Sonny had never seen anything so frightening in her life. *They won't shoot you, Sonny. They can't. They don't have the whole story. Just do as Logan says. Let him do all the talking.*

She closed her eyes, taking small, measured breaths. *That's it. Stay focused. Stay calm. And most of all, stay away from the thought that you aren't Sonny Blake.*

CHAPTER SEVENTEEN

"Ned's acting hinky, I tell you," Brad said. "He palmed off all his appointments on me today. He's never done that before. You know he finds my techniques deplorable. What is the bastard up to? If you ask me, he's had a psychotic break. His behavior's off."

"Off? What does that even mean?" Charlotte asked, dropping the book she had been reading onto the end table beside her. "Ned is Ned. He's always in full control."

Brad turned from the window. "You assured me the hidden cameras would work."

"They *are* working, but so far, they haven't recorded him doing anything suspicious."

Brad turned back to the view outside the window. "Then he's onto us. He knows we've noticed the all-night sessions, and he's tinkering with the video feed. He's a wily bastard, always has been, always will be. You know how he was as a kid." Brad turned from the window. "He's going to center his perversions on Sonny if we don't stop him."

Charlotte sprang from the sofa. "Don't you think I know that?" She moved to the window, studying the canyon floor below them. "It may be time to reveal our suspicions to Dick."

"Logan Reed would be better," Brad stated, settling beside her. "He has Meta Corps clout, and we both know those bastards don't take shit from anyone. We can drop hints in Reed's ear."

"And say what? Ned can't keep his hands to himself?"

"He's doing more than just fondling a patient, Char!"

"Where's your proof?"

"I don't have any yet, but a psychopath never changes his spots. He may go underground for a while, but his urges won't let him stay underground for long. When he resurfaces, he finds a new hunting ground."

"You're right. With old friends, he can blackmail and manipulate," Charlotte said in disgust.

"He needs to be stopped."

Charlotte turned from the window. "You realize that if we confess what we suspect, Pandora will be compromised, and all the good we accomplished with it will be debunked?"

"But we'll be stopping a serial killer for good. We'll be saving countless lives when Ned is behind bars."

"He'll see any threat coming," Charlotte pointed out. "In many ways, he is as intuitive as Sonny."

Brad looked out the window, his glance skimming the mountain range. "Where do you suppose Logan and Sonny went?"

"Who knows?"

"Well, at least Ned can't get to Sonny while she's with Reed." His glance fell from the hill back to Charlotte. "The man appears to be falling for her. If we let him in on Ned's past, it would save us time and trouble, plus keep Meta Corps from debunking Pandora."

Charlotte left the window, plopping back down on the sofa. Her smile was grim. "Pandora can't be saved at this point. Ned has seen to that."

"He certainly took it light years away from its original intent," Brad said, following her from the window and sinking into a wingback by the sofa. "The only sure thing we know is that Ned has reworked Pandora for his own agenda."

"Which takes us back to square one," Charlotte said. "We must do everything in our power to record one of his late-night sessions. Once we have that, we can confront him with it. He'll have no choice but to stop what he's doing and go underground, like before."

Brad fished in his pocket and withdrew a cigarette pack. "I still say we drop hints to Reed. We let the shit fall and see where it sticks."

"How do you propose we alert him without alerting him?" Charlotte asked.

"You'll call Sonny and convince her there's major trouble in the Sans Spring office. She'll have no choice but to go and oversee the crisis. While you're doing that, I'll arrange a meeting with Agent Reed and Lieutenant Cutter."

He blew smoke rings in the air. "This is the last time I intend to help you with anything concerning Pandora," he added. "You agreed when we married that the project was simply too dangerous to continue its practice. Didn't we hurt enough children in the name of science and our egos? I care too much for Sonny to continue to lie to her."

"Do you think I enjoy lying to her? Knowing that if we don't stop Ned, we'll be sending her to a life filled with unimaginable pain?"

"Once I confess everything to Reed, he'll move heaven and earth to keep her safe. You've seen how he looks at her."

"We have to focus on stopping Ned's behavior *now*."

"How do you propose to do it?"

"We'll use Ned's own therapy against him. We'll put Margie Hunt under, take her through Pandora, and record what path she leads us down. If she responds to our questions and commands, we'll have our proof."

"Let's use Sonny instead," Brad suggested. "Let's have her touch Margie and blow Ned's charade out of the water. It's the logical thing to do. He'll be arrested."

"And so will we," Charlotte said, shaking her head. "No, everything I'm doing is to make sure Sonny's safe. Now, go and call Sonny while I contact Margie."

Brad sprang from the chair, stubbing his cigarette out as he passed an ashtray atop an ornate end table. Reaching the door, he paused, but didn't turn around.

"After this debacle is finished, I'm leaving The Sanctuary. If I stay, I won't be able to look Sonny in the eye ever again." He pulled open the door and went through. His thoughts immediately soured. He didn't give a damn what happened to him. As long as the killings stopped, and Sonny was safe, he'd accept whatever punishment Meta Corps dished out. He'd even divorce Charlotte if it meant saving Sonny; their marriage had been unraveling for years, anyway.

Heading for his car, he realized he should've stood up to Charlotte long ago and refused to do her bidding. What she wanted didn't matter in the scheme of things. In her own way, she was as determined as Ned to rework Pandora for her own gain. *No.* He shook his head. Action was needed right now, action against both of them.

Reaching his car, he jerked the driver's door open and slid inside. Instead of calling Sonny, he was going to drive to Cutter's office and spill everything to him. Once he revealed Ned was really Charles Fremont, a convicted felon, Cutter'd leave no stone unturned in making sure Ned got what he deserved. Brad smiled smugly as he backed out of his parking space. If things played out as he thought, Ned would soon be rotting in a lonely prison cell, unable to act out his perverted fantasies. He stepped on the gas pedal and shot down the driveway and onto the blacktop that led to The Sanctuary security offices.

• • •

The tires on the Kia kept up a steady hum on the blacktop, allowing Logan to take a moment to wind down. Today had already turned really shitty, and the interrogation they had just come through had been even shittier. And now, with the ominous cracks of thunder drawing closer, along with a sheer black dip in the skyline, it was clear searching for the Pandora disc would need to be postponed until the weather cleared.

He could smell the change in the air already. Would he be able to drive through howling winds and rain without upending the car and killing himself and Sonny? He didn't relish even trying. If everything he heard about monsoon rains was true, they should've been driving to the nearest motel and checking in. Would the mouse be agreeable to stopping? He stole a peek at her profile. No, she was brooding, lost in thoughts he couldn't begin to understand.

"You need to let it out and breathe," he told her.

"How do I breathe ever again, when I don't exist?"

"You exist," Logan said.

"As what, a sideshow freak? For pity's sake, Logan, I *know* things. How did I not see *this*?"

"We don't even know that *this* is true," Logan said. "Sykes was a bitter old man eaten up by his conscience. He did Para-Corps' bidding, and God knows that pack of radicals spent hours stroking their own egos rather than helping their patients. Why do you suppose the group was disbanded?"

"Went underground, you mean. They obviously haven't stopped."

"Again, we don't know that."

She fell silent, going back to her brooding, and Logan decided not to push the conversation.

"I suppose we should've put a call through to Dick before we left Foster's," she said, startling him. "After all, it's clear Foster's death is connected to Daddy's. Didn't you say you promised him we wouldn't keep information from him?"

Logan slid his gaze back to the skyline. "We'll be doing him a greater service by finding the DVD before our sniper friend has a chance to destroy it."

Sonny sprang up in her seat. "My God, you're right. It's totally possible our conversation was overheard. We've even less time than I thought." She twisted around, and Logan saw her check the roadway behind them. "There's nothing behind or ahead of us, so floor it! We can reach The Harbor in less than fifteen minutes."

Logan gave a twisted smile but held their speed. "And what is The Harbor?"

"My second residence," she stated. She hit the down button for the window. "It's hot in here. Aren't you hot?" She turned her face towards the wind whipping in and enjoyed the breeze.

"Perhaps I should have pilfered a Valium from Foster's medicine cabinet for you," Logan said. "You're sounding more and more like Alice's White Rabbit every minute."

"You'd like that, wouldn't you?" Sonny snapped at him. "Give me a drug to get me out of the way."

Logan sighed, suppressing an urge to box the mouse's ears. "Believe me, if I wanted you out of the way, you would be." He saw the mulish set of her lips and prepared himself for one of her sarcastic retorts. A clap of thunder shook the frame of the car instead, and the pair jumped. The darkest part of the skyline was closing in on them rapidly. "Let's hope we manage to beat the rain. I've never driven in a treacherous monsoon before."

"It's not treacherous until the water has had time to pool," Sonny advised. "Do you need me to drive? I'm in much better shape than you are at the moment. You look terrible."

Logan shot her a lopsided grin. "Sticks and stones—"

A hiss interrupted him. "Turn left at the next light, and then move to the far right lane. There's a shortcut we can use. It'll save us at least five minutes."

Following her instructions, he increased their speed.

"Do you believe Foster's story about me?" Sonny asked, as the vehicle coasted under an overpass.

"I believe he believed it," Logan answered. "But then—" A crack of thunder rocked the skyline, making them exchange tremulous glances. "I thought you said we had time."

"We do. The thunder is just a wake-up call."

Another booming clap permeated the air, followed by a sudden torrential downpour of wind and rain. Logan flicked the windshield wipers to high and then focused his attention on keeping the center white line in sight. Five minutes later, he emitted a vitriolic curse.

"It's a mess out here," he said. "I didn't intend to spend the night trapped in a motel room with you, but the first one we come to, we're stopping." It was clear by the dip of her brows that she was remembering their shared visions. Her eyes narrowed, and he called her on it. "I don't know what's going on in that pretty head of yours, but if you think I'm going to drive another five minutes in this monsoon, you're crazy. And you're not going to either. We're stopping."

She made a face at him. "In that case, take a right at the next flashing light. The Harbor's just up the incline."

Logan studied her shuttered lids.

"We've got to step on it," she urged. "The main part of the storm is closer than I thought."

Logan shook his head. Now she was admitting the truth. They were in trouble. A mile later, they reached the flashing intersection, and he turned right.

"The Harbor's just ahead," she told him. "It will be cozy and dry."

Overhead, another clap of thunder shattered the air.

"We're cutting this awfully close," Logan said. He tried to ignore the word "cozy." The last thing he needed was to be confined in a small space with the mouse.

Sonny leaned over and checked the speedometer. "I don't see why you're so worried. We're barely doing ten miles an hour."

"The idea is to get where we're going alive," Logan countered.

She pointed out the front of the windshield. "Can you see that row of lights up ahead?"

Logan peered through the shimmering rain, grunting when he saw the designated lights. He followed the roadway, his foot tapping the brakes all the way.

"The road's going to fork at the end of the lights," Sonny told him. "Turn right and follow the next set of light poles. We'll come up under a carport."

A clap of thunder shook the car, and the pair jumped again. A river of raindrops slid down the front windshield, trickling down the driver's-side window and onto the frame of the car. Logan heeded Sonny's suggestion and drove the car up the incline rapidly. Sonny's ashen face was enough to convince him they were making shelter just in time.

Concentrating on the string of lights, Logan was soon braking under a sloping carport. He shut off the engine and glanced out the side window. A beautifully carved entranceway stood outlined. Cozy and dry, she had said; she had forgotten to mention the cabin was made of rustic, cedar logs. He heard the passenger door open and swung around.

"It's not wise to be anywhere outside when the full force of the wind hits," Sonny remarked, slipping from the seat. He was out and around the car even as her feet hit the pavement. She flew to the front door, put in a key code, and then quickly waved him inside. "The rain will last for hours," she said, as he strode through the door behind her. "It will give us time to put our heads together. I think I know how to locate the DVD."

"I'm listening," Logan said, distracted by the look and feel of the great room they were now standing in. It was New Age chic, housing a comfortable seating area like its sister hacienda, Serenity. However, the difference ended there. In Serenity, he had seen technology at its finest. Here, the shelves lining the wall contained New Age books, angel statues, and big and small amethyst crystals. Scented candles and metaphysical wall hangings were spaced at sporadic intervals around the room, and they gave the cabin the feel of a mini spiritual retreat. Two floor-to-ceiling bookshelves dwarfed the northeast wall of the room, and their top portions contained wrapped items in a bevy of small cubbyholes. He watched Sonny cross to the shelf, where she scanned the holes with her fingers.

"Up on the mesa, and then later at Serenity, you wondered why Daddy left the Lovers Tarot card for me. I think I can answer that now."

Her fingers paused in their search, and she hauled a rectangular box from its cubbyhole. She spun and headed for the seating area, signaling Logan to join her. When they were both seated before an ornately carved coffee table, she opened the box and withdrew a deck of Tarot cards. She picked up their conversation, riffling through the cards.

"Back at Foster's, when you entered the vision, what did you see?" She let a card fall onto the table in front of them and then continued her search.

"Sykes tore a key chain from his neck and tossed it to us," Logan answered.

Her fingers halted, her gaze lifting to his face. "Right. And when we exited the vision, you immediately looked for the key around Foster's neck, because in your world, clues are tangible things, something you can see, touch, smell, or hear with your own physical senses. But in my world, everything tangible is symbolic."

She stopped speaking, and Logan realized she was making sure he was following her reasoning.

"I'm still listening," he told her.

"Right." She began searching the deck again, finding and dropping cards onto the table. "Now, in your logical world, a key opens a structured door. It could be a door to a house, a car, or even a safety-deposit box. But in my world, a key symbolizes knowledge, and since the key landed in my hand during the vision instead of yours, I believe Foster was saying that we must think spiritually first and then translate that knowledge into the real world. That means, I must think Pandora out spiritually, and you must make use of that knowledge in a practical way."

"And how do you think spiritually?" Logan asked, curious.

She reached into her pocket and hauled out the Tarot cards sequestered there. She flashed them at him. "These are the cards Meta Corps sent. They're from a traditional Tarot deck, because that's the deck most people are familiar with." She laid the five cards out in a line, in a repeat of their earlier arrangement. "Here are the original images," she said. She picked up five of the eight cards she had chosen from the new deck and flashed them at Logan. "These are from the mythic Tarot deck, which contains actual renditions of mythological creatures."

"Like Pandora," Logan stated.

"Right." She laid the new cards over the original five and then placed the sixth card with Pandora's image above the row. She tapped the card. "If we believe Foster's story—and I don't want to, by the way—Pandora was designed to open the mind and empty it." She tapped the Fool card. "The Fool card would then symbolize a fresh new start by taking a leap of faith into the unknown. See how the card depicts Dionysios, leaving the safety of the maternal womb. Like a baby bird leaving the safety of its nest for the first time, it takes a leap of faith."

"The start of a radical new mind treatment," Logan interjected. "Going boldly where no man has gone before."

"Exactly," Sonny agreed. She tapped the next card. "Here, the Judgement card shows the god Hermes in the role of psychopomp, the guide of dead souls. It was his job to summon the dead and lead them to their final reckoning. The figures rising from the coffin reflect our past lives being called up for review."

Logan tapped the other Judgement card peeping from beneath the other. "The wake-up call. But who's blowing the trumpet?"

"In both our worlds, it would be a professional therapist, one with the know-how to lead the client out of their dark world and into the light of a new one."

"Sykes fit that bill to a T," Logan said. "And if we believe him, once you empty the mind, you are free to replace it with any 'light,' good or bad."

She tapped the third card. "This High Priestess goes beyond the one we labeled as 'secrets.' Remember how Foster said a green door was always used to trigger the memory shift? As you can see, this is the only card with an actual door. It shows Persephone entering the underworld through a door and then down a set of steps."

"That's pretty straightforward," Logan stated. "However, she looks like she's going down those steps willingly."

"She is," Sonny agreed. "In myth, she was abducted by Hades, who, after seeing her beauty, desired her as his consort. He brought her to the underworld, where she ate the forbidden pomegranate fruit, and after that, well, she came to his bed willingly."

"Lucky Hades," Logan teased.

Sonny grinned at him. "More Svengali than lucky," she chided. "Now, look at this Death card compared to the first. Here we see Hades collecting coins at the River Styx. In the underworld, no one could enter hell without paying the ferryman, Charon, a toll first. Once the toll was paid, the dead were free to leave their old lives behind and be reborn into a new life."

"Another straightforward strategy," Logan said. "A reprogramming of the mind through a new and unique set of memories."

"Here's where it gets interesting," Sonny said, slapping the new Tower card down. "This image shows the labyrinth, a tower built by King Minos to imprison a horrible creature known as the Minotaur. I won't thrill you with how the creature came to have a man's body and a bull's head; instead, I'll concentrate on the tower built to hide the hideous creature away from the world. Needless to say, as time marched on, the structure and its location couldn't remain in a stagnant state forever, not when it housed such a shameful secret at its core. The kingdom of Minos eventually fractured, and thus the myth of Theseus was born."

"I know that myth," Logan said. "Princess Ariadne gave Theseus a magical golden thread which he used as a talisman to locate the labyrinth and slay the beast."

"And when he did, Poseidon rose up from the sea and used his trusty trident to crack the tower open."

"Thereby causing a collapse of old forms to give way to the new," Logan said. "It's clear the builders of the Pandora paradox thought that if they could take the ugly part of our selves, those false values we hide in our psyche, and rework them in some new, soul-defining way, we'd be … what? More godlike?"

"It's more likely you were right before. They reworked the memories for some selfish reason, something that benefited them, not the patient. But what kind of memories would accomplish that deed?" Sonny asked. "If we believe Foster that I was the first successful transference, why did they choose my memories to move along a spiritual path?"

"Perhaps, when they tried to reprogram your memories, your guardian angels added something to the mix—to protect you. Some sort of talisman. As you said earlier, the mind is an unfathomable world. God knows we haven't even begun to explore a quarter of what's lurking there." He switched thoughts. "Is it possible for the mind to bring along some talisman for protection, in case things go horribly wrong after the transference?"

"You're thinking of my nosebleeds now," Sonny said.

"Don't jump the gun," Logan told her. He tapped the card. "Is the sea god Poseidon symbolic of Sykes' part in the paradox?"

"No. The god's eruption from the sea suggests a powerful, instinctual force emerging from the unconscious, stronger than the will's desire to repress it."

"So the nosebleeds could be a warning to you, a message that Pandora has a time limit."

Sonny's head reared back, and she quickly picked up the last two cards on the table and flashed them at him.

"You've hit the nail on the head," she said, amazed. "These are the two cards we found in the computer. We agreed that the Hermit card represented Foster, but if we substitute this card for it, we see the god Cronos, whose name means 'time.' In myth, Uranus and Gaea mated and produced the first race of Titans. Cronos was the youngest of them. Now, Uranus regarded his progeny with horror, for they were ugly and imperfect, and made of flesh, so he shut the Titans up in the depths of the underworld, so that they might not offend his eyes. As you can imagine, Gaea got pretty pissed, so she fashioned a scythe from her bosom and gave it to Cronos, who, with her aid, castrated his father and cast his bleeding genitals into the sea."

"That's a lovely picture." Logan smirked. "But how does that apply to the nosebleeds?"

"Everything has its season and time—which is true if we think universally. Everything is born: star clusters, new plants, new babies, and then everything dies and gets reborn again in some fashion. I think Foster was referring to that when he said, 'There'll be nosebleeds first.'"

"First? Are we to assume other physical ailments will show up?"

"I hope not," Sonny replied, shivering.

"I won't let things get that far," Logan said. He pointed to the one card remaining in her hand. "And the last card?"

"The Ten of Swords. The mythic image here focuses on the wrath of the Furies. These lovely ladies believed women were far superior to men, so when they learned Orestes had committed matricide, they sought revenge in the best way they knew how."

"They constantly tortured his mind," Logan surmised.

"And then some. As you can see by the image, Orestes is nearly dead from the curse they put on him."

"So who is this lovely creature with the sword?"

"The goddess Athena. She felt so sorry for Orestes that she became his champion and protector. See how she's holding back the Furies' rage against him with her sword of justice, like a bodyguard? Remind you of anyone?" She paused, giving him a measured glance. Logan caught her meaning at once.

"If you're about to say I represent a goddess, don't. I promise you I don't have a noble bone in my body."

"But you do have a gun and a badge," Sonny countered. "And you were assigned to work with me."

"A situation that I'm starting to regret," Logan muttered. Her expression fell at his words, and he held up his hand. "Now, don't go thinking I regret meeting *you*. What I meant is I like my cases where one plus one equals two. I like solving murders that are messy with emotions. Hatred, revenge, jealousy, passion—I can understand those reasons."

"So can I, and it's clear that this *is* one of those cases." She ticked off on her fingers, "First, someone hates me enough to kill me. Second, they took revenge on me by killing my father. And third … " She paused. "Well, I don't know where the jealousy is yet."

Logan eyed her warily. "It's not your aunt, and it certainly isn't your uncle. Your aunt is overprotective, yes, but she's not jealous of you. And as for your uncle, he's more interested in dating you."

"What a rotten thing to say!" Sonny exclaimed. "And how would you even know he's interested in dating me?"

"Because I'm interested in dating you."

Sonny sniffed at him. "Envy is a man's game. Pandora was probably started by a woman, but you can bet an envious man soon stole it from her so he could use it for his own twisted reasons … " The sound of music had Sonny breaking off mid-sentence and glancing towards her purse on the foyer table by the front door. "It's Aunt Charlotte's ring tone," she said.

"Answer it," Logan said. "She's checking to see that you're not buried under a deluge of hail."

Sonny sprang from the settee, grabbed her purse, and returned to the couch with it. "Hello, Aunt Charlotte. Are you safe and dry? No, we're at The Harbor, waiting out the storm ... " She paused, listening, and Logan saw her expression sour dramatically. "No, I haven't heard from him, why should I? Uncle Brad knows how I abhor his checking up on me every five minutes." Her gaze found Logan's. "Do me a favor, Aunt Charlotte. Stay at Rosita until the storm is over. You and Ned can come here when the roads can be traveled again safely."

Logan heard a high-pitched, angry tirade through the receiver. Sonny hung up the phone a moment later, her expression pained, as though she had been wounded.

"What now?" Logan queried, his brows knitted in a frown.

"Ned and Aunt Charlotte are coming, but not until the rain stops," Sonny replied. She turned and left Logan, her walk slow and swaying. Logan followed her quickly.

"What's really going on?" he asked.

"It's me. I'm so tired of being inundated with feelings. It's like I'm mourning my own death."

Logan draped his hands on her shoulders and spun her about. He cupped her face with his hands.

"Look at me," he said. She met his flinty gaze head-on. "You are the most amazing person I have ever met. You live life with an unshakeable faith in the goodness of Spirit, and you carry a burden that would take Hercules down." A flash of lightning lit the room, highlighting Sonny's cool green eyes. He studied her face silently, and she studied him back. He lifted her chin and caressed her bottom lip. "Now, the rain is hammering on the roof, the roads are flooding, and we've some time on our hands. So, pull back your energy, and let me kiss you. No visions. No images. No flying monkeys."

"There might be a white rabbit," she said breathlessly.

"I can handle that," he replied. He lowered his head and planted taunting kisses along her cheek, and then he settled his mouth on hers. It was a light kiss, but a tender, lingering one, and it produced a mutual shudder between them.

Spellbound, the pair stood close, their bodies pressing against one another. And then Sonny slid her arms around his neck, parted her lips, and let him possess her mouth. His heart reacted immediately, and with a lazy, sensuous movement, his tongue entered her mouth. Another shudder shook their frames, and he felt her pull back, as if tugging on an invisible thread, and even though he wanted to unleash his hunger and satisfy it, he didn't. Instead, he lifted his lips, and liking the textures, juices, and spices of her, he gave her a heartfelt hug, which ended with a firm pat on her fanny. She jumped at the tap, a lazy laughter sweeping her eyes.

"Ouch," she declared, a blush of pleasure staining her cheeks.

Logan winced. "Ouch? Don't you mean: 'Wouldn't you like to come to my bedroom and see my sound system?'"

Sonny patted his shirt absently. "Will you wear your Flash Gordon outfit?"

"Is the Pope Catholic?"

She laughed again, shrugging out of his arms. He brought her back quickly, dipped is head, and planted a soft kiss on her lips. When they were eye to eye again, she gave him a dazzling smile.

"Are we attempting one of our rare excursions into humor?" she asked.

Logan grinned. "It's nice to hear you laugh again."

She spun out of his arms, raised her hands over her head, and stretched lazily. "Um, when I feel this delicious, I laugh at practically anything; sometimes nothing at all."

A crack of thunder shook the rafters. Both their grins faded.

"As much as I'd like to glory in the feel of your silken skin," Logan said, glancing out the window, "These bawling winds sound like engines rising, passing through a cry and into a scream. Are they always this hyped up?"

A splatter of hail on the roof was his answer. Seeing him wince, Sonny laughed again.

"There is a strange, dreamlike lunacy to it," Sonny answered, leaving his arms. "As if you've entered the twilight world of the half-alive."

Logan arched his back to relieve a kink. "I see now why you're so fond of siestas," he said. "No one could sleep through this racket."

"But you can recharge your batteries with a quick lie-down," Sonny teased.

Logan twisted his back to relieve another kink. "Well, I'm not the Energizer Bunny, but I'll give it a try." He reached out and snatched Sonny back into his arms. In seconds, he had fallen back onto the couch and brought her with him. "If I can't make love to you all night, at least we can fool around until the clock strikes midnight and you disappear into the night, leaving only a glass slipper behind." His hand swept to the back of her neck, and her chest melded to his. Their lips met in a drugging kiss, and before he could stop himself, his hands were fumbling for the buttons on her blouse. She moved against him, and he thought she meant to halt his fingers, but when she slanted her lips across his instead, he slid his fingers inside her bra and searched for a nipple. The kiss deepened, and his palm followed the curve of her breast, finding a taut nipple puckered with desire. He stroked it, and then, as if hit by a cold bucket of water, Sonny tore her lips from his and sprang from the sofa with a troubled gasp. With a watchful hesitation, she presented her back to him and buttoned her blouse again. Neither of them spoke for a moment. And then she did.

"So dark out there. So dark and so forever."

Sighing, Logan sat up. He'd not ask what that enigmatic statement meant. She was experiencing some distant memory, while his body craved sex. Nothing but a cold shower would power down his current arousal. As for her, he didn't know what would help her senses power down.

"I didn't mean to lead you on, Logan," Sonny stated. "My emotions are a mess, and I've never felt such an exhilarating response to any man. I'm teetering between untethered desire and angry warmth. The effect is like a graveyard."

Seeing her trembling limbs, Logan bolted from the sofa. He stopped behind her. "You don't owe me an explanation—or an apology," he said. "You're still the most amazing person I've ever met, and no pleasurable make-out session will ever alter that fact. I should apologize to *you*, but I'm not going to, because I intend to kiss you as often as you'll let me. And I assure you, you are going to let me." She whirled around then, floored by his words. Seeing her mouth open, he placed a finger over her lips and grinned. "No, it's our fantasies that make life bearable." He winked at her, and her laugh was like a whinny. "Now let me get some shut-eye," he said. "Kissing you has worn me out. And don't stray from this room," he added, seeing her move. "It's clear someone would love to get you alone."

She took up residence in the nearby window embrasure, ignoring him and studying the pelting rain outside.

Grinning, Logan swung his legs up onto the couch. In seconds, he had settled back and let his senses reach into the raging storm. Two minutes later, the real world drifted into oblivion.

CHAPTER EIGHTEEN

The storm raged over the cabin, rattling glass windows and continuing to pelt the ground with hail the size of golf balls. From her vantage point in the window embrasure, Sonny studied the jagged streaks of light permeating the eastern skyline. Would the storm never budge from their location? Its fury had become relentless.

Her gaze scoured the oppressive cloud cover, and she lifted her fingers and brushed her lips. She could still feel Logan's kiss and the excitement that mounted within him. The dormant sexuality of her body had been awakened at that moment, leaving her to realize she liked the curve of his mouth, the rush of warmth between them, and the graceful strength of his hands as he explored her breasts.

A booming thunderclap doused the arcing light, and she winced. She hadn't enjoyed the interruption of the moment, though. One minute, her heart had slammed into her ribs, and the next, a feeling of great torment had saturated her body. A terrible sense of humiliation had followed, and the strong gnawing had severed the wild surge of pleasure between Logan and her.

The sky dumped another round of hail onto the rafters of the roof. Mother Nature had gone wet and wild, and though beautiful to watch, Sonny knew the hidden treachery behind the storm.

She glanced over her shoulder at the man sleeping on the leather sofa. She wished she had his power to ignore problems and sleep like a baby. She hopped from the window suddenly. The room was turning cold under the damp, charged air outside. She passed a wingback chair, grabbed a crocheted lap robe off the back, and laid it gently across Logan's sleeping form. As the coverlet fell, she scanned the dark shadows on his cheek and his long, sooty eyelashes. She wondered how she could be offering the man warmth of a blanket, when by all rights she should be smothering him with it. He had declared his intention to kiss her as often as possible, arrogant enough to believe she would let him.

She listened to his even breathing, observing the rise and fall of his chest. He was dead to the world, and not even rain, wind, and thunder could put a dent in his blissful euphoria.

Whirling around, Sonny's glance found the ornate clock on the mantle. Two a.m. Morning was only hours away. What would be the best way to field Ned's and her aunt's questions without drawing suspicion? She knew if she went at them head-on, she would be goaded into revealing she knew about The Pandora Project.

Had Foster told the truth? Was she Amanda King? *That's the $64,000 question, kiddo,* her inner voice advised.

Yes, and if we're ever to get through the rest of our life without going insane, we need to learn the answer.

Hearing the sound of wind whistling up the lower staircase, Sonny shivered. It felt like the lower outside door had blown open from the howling winds. Though Logan had warned her to stay nearby, she had to check it, or the mud room would be flooded. Besides, she needed time away from the toad. His good looks were a distraction, and she needed to get her mind around Foster's revelation and then create a plan of action to obtain the Pandora disc.

She moved across the room and down the stairs, startled to find the outside basement door standing wide open, raindrops splattering the floor. Lifting her gaze, she saw Ned shaking his trench coat free of raindrops. Alongside him, her aunt was scraping mud off her boots and scowling.

Ned spotted her first, greeting her immediately. "Did you think we would leave you to fend for yourself in this dismal storm?"

"I'm not alone, Ned," Sonny said, annoyed. "Logan's here." He ignored her words, and Sonny hid a frown. This wasn't good. The pair had come to ambush her now, instead of waiting until morning. Ned's grim expression clearly telegraphed some sort of displeasure with her. Had they heard about Foster's death already?

Ned was the first to reach the staircase. "You look tired, Sonny."

Sonny contemplated telling him she *was* tired—tired of all the lies, the mothering, and the smothering … She halted the thought and addressed his concern instead.

"I can't sleep. Storms jar my brainwaves. Why are you two up so late?" She moved off the staircase and joined her aunt, who was making herself comfortable in one of the empty lounge chairs. Sonny hopped into the window embrasure on her left. Her aunt leaned back, addressing Sonny.

"Ned feared you had been caught in the storm; he offered to check on you. I couldn't let him come alone. The roads are under water all around the property. You know how much water a storm like this can drop in a matter of minutes; his van could've fishtailed and slipped into a swale. I offered to follow him, in case his van hit one of those pockets."

"Which it didn't," Ned replied irritably. His eyes became flat and as unreadable as stone. "What have you been doing all day?" he asked, switching subjects and shedding his trench coat. He hung it over the back of a second wingback, rounded the chair, and took a seat. "We didn't see you at lunch."

"I've been showing Logan the sights, touristy things."

"Where did you say the fellow was?" Ned asked, glancing around.

"He's sleeping in the great room."

Keeping her attention on the rain sheets pinging off the window, Sonny crossed her fingers and prayed the pair wouldn't ask her where they had gone. She tucked her feet beneath her, curling deeper into the embrasure, and prepared to do battle with Ned first. He was always the first to use frigid silence as foreplay. It was an irritating habit, but for once she was glad she knew how to recognize it. It allowed her to prepare for the upcoming attack.

"How soon before this case with Logan Reed is solved, Sonny?"

Sonny's gaze flew to Ned's face. There it was. He was asking a question that she could sense had a double meaning.

"You don't have the right to ask me that, Ned," she replied.

The chains of his necklace clanked loudly. "Though it is rare for me to ever interfere in your life, I must be protective of the company now that David is gone. I don't need to tell you things are tense since the staff has heard the news."

Sonny's eyes narrowed. What was he after with this low-key attack? He tended towards straight-on accusations. She cocked her head at him, ignoring her aunt's brief stir in her chair.

"Are you planning to call Meta Corps and have Logan taken off the case?" she asked. "If you are, let me warn you I won't allow it. His reputation would be damaged beyond repair."

"Since when do you worry about a Meta Corps agent's career?" her aunt asked. "You're not falling under his spell, are you?"

Sonny's mouth twitched with amusement. "Absolutely not. I read him the moment we met. He's bright, witty, and extremely good at what he does. He has no ulterior motive in being here that I can see—except to solve a case of serial murders."

"He's arrogant," her aunt chided.

"You forgot extremely handsome," Sonny quipped.

Her aunt grimaced. "Don't take that sarcastic tone with me. This is not the time for you to add romantic stress to your life. Send the man back to New York with your apologies and a promise to help in another case. With David's death, and the press looming, Meta Corps will understand."

"I don't renege on my contracts, Aunt Charlotte, and for your information, there is no romantic stress in my life."

"There will be if you allow Logan Reed to monopolize your time," Ned threw in. "After all, dozens of people outside this company would enjoy harming you, or marrying you, for no other reason than that you're rich."

Sonny stifled a giggle. Ned actually thought Logan Reed was after her money. The thought was so ludicrous Sonny did laugh aloud.

"I'm sorry, Ned. I don't mean to laugh. You're looking out for me, and I love you for it. But you are way off base in this case. Logan is not after my money or anything that belongs to Blake Industries."

"How can you be so sure? He strikes me as a very cunning young man. And whether you'd like to admit it or not, he showed up at The Sanctuary the very moment your father was killed. Perhaps Meta Corps arranged the murder and then sent their best agent to cover their tracks. After meeting you, he may have become fixated on you. After all, you are a stunning woman."

Sonny knew she should be pleased by the compliment; however, she felt her skin crawl at the words instead. Why did the thought of Ned thinking of her as a stunning woman throw her off her game? She felt a light touch on her shoulder, surprised to find her aunt had risen.

"We have been protecting you since you were born, Sonny, and we have done a damn fine job of it."

Sonny glanced at the fingers skimming her collarbone. But what had occurred during those twenty-eight years, she wondered. Altering memories, using patients as guinea pigs? She shook her head to rid herself of the unwanted thought.

"If you're insinuating I am not grateful for the love you give me, Aunt Charlotte, you're way off base. I've always shown my gratitude to you and Uncle Brad. Your kindness after my mother died got me through some dark days; however, I'm grown now, and old enough to have a man sweep me off my feet."

Her aunt scoffed loudly. "It's clear we shielded you too much from the real world while you were growing up. Along comes a handsome agent who plies you with compliments, and you begin acting out—like a teenager."

"Nothing is going on between Logan and me, Aunt Charlotte. We're working a case together."

"A case that no decent empath would've taken," her aunt remarked. She shivered in emphasis. "Peeking into the deaths of young girls can only be considered voyeuristic."

"You think I'm enjoying the brutality of it all?"

"Don't twist my words."

"Then don't stand there and accuse me of being indecent, when the truth is, the victims' families need closure. If I can give them that, I intend to."

Ned's chains jangled loudly again. "Can the argument, you two," he interrupted. "What your aunt is trying to say is that we know how hard you've been working the past year. We don't want you to overextend your abilities by delving into some sordid world of debauchery and murder—especially with the week we're facing."

Sonny hissed her displeasure. "I decide when my abilities are overextended, Ned, not you or the family. I agreed to help Meta Corps because I can. They sent Logan because he's extremely good at working with empaths. It's a perfect match. I only wish everyone would stop treating him like a leper. It's pathetic how badly we treat our guests and endanger their lives."

Ned's head whirled about abruptly. "What do you mean endanger? Has someone tried to harm Agent Reed?"

Sonny suppressed the urge to scream. She had to start paying attention to what she was saying. Any slip of the tongue could send her into revealing Pandora. Ned was now out of his chair and bearing down on her, and she held up her hand, sliding to the edge of the windowsill.

"Don't go twisting my words, Ned. I said what I mean. The entire family has been extremely rude to Logan since he arrived, and it's embarrassing."

Sonny hopped from the window and headed for the staircase. She needed to wake Logan at once. She needed backup, and she needed it now. She heard footsteps and whirled around, surprised to find her aunt following her to the steps. Her tone was emphatic when she reached Sonny.

"There's some trouble at the Sans Springs office that needs handling. This is the perfect opportunity for us to meet with the press and take care of company business at the same time. I'll go with you, of course. Ned can't go. He's knee-deep in appointments, and so is your uncle. Together, we should be able to wrap the problem up in three days, tops. I'm sure Logan will understand if you need a few days to take care of Sanctuary business. He can enjoy all the retreat's amenities while we're gone. After all, The Sanctuary is a perfect vacation spot for overworked agents." She hauled out her cell phone. "I'll make arrangements for the company jet."

Sonny snatched the phone from her fingers. "Are you ordering me to Sans Spring, Aunt Charlotte?"

"Far from it," she said, snatching the phone back. "I'm thinking of the company. David's death has shot holes in so many of our upcoming projects that it'll take us at least six months to recover. Besides, you don't want to end up like your father, do you?"

Sonny pursed her lips. She had already endured two sniper attacks. It was the third she was worried about. If only Logan would hear their voices and come to investigate. Seeing Ned's baffled gaze, she hedged.

"I'm ready to fight back if there is an attempt on my life. You have my word on that."

"You make it sound like we should know that for a reason," Ned said. His tone finally suggested outright hostility, and Sonny knew exactly what his next question would be. He didn't disappoint her. "Do you think one of us killed David and is now intending to kill you?"

Sonny dropped her gaze to the carpet, concentrating on the tips of Ned's patent-leather shoes. "All I meant, Ned, was until Dick finds Daddy's killer, none of us are safe."

"Precisely why you need to go to Sans Spring with your aunt," Ned emphasized. "You'll be safe there. We can't protect you if you continue gallivanting all over the countryside with Logan Reed. You become a target for his enemies, as well as any that might wish to get back at Blake Industries."

Sonny wondered what Ned would say if she told him he should be looking out for his own welfare.

"I want your word you will leave for Sans Spring as soon as this storm stops," Ned stated.

"I'm not going anywhere, Ned, and that's the end of the discussion."

He drew closer, his expression as black as his suit. "Don't go against me on this, Sonny. I can *make* you go."

Sonny had no doubt that he could, but she wasn't going to give him a chance to try. She studied his dark expression carefully, sensing that his demeanor seemed off tonight. *More off than usual?* her inner voice asked. Sonny suppressed an urge to rip off her gloves and touch Ned's hand. His attacks were usually passive-aggressive, but not tonight.

He has an ulterior motive, her inner voice suggested. *He killed your father and Foster, and before he kills you, he wants to be sure his secret is safe.*

What secret? Sonny asked her ego. *It's certainly not Pandora.*

"Your word, Sonny," he pushed.

Sonny shivered, her hand fluttering to her neck. There it was again—Ned was making her skin crawl with his demand. She seized the small spurt of anger rising in her chest.

"I'm sorry, Ned, you will just have to be pissed at me. I'm not going anywhere until after Daddy's funeral."

She gave him one final look and then returned to the window ledge. When she got there, she studied the firebush adjacent to the window. Ned was beyond pissed. She had seen the cold fury in his eyes as she passed him. Was he pissed enough to drag her from the window and out the back door? If he did, he'd have a screaming bitch on his hands.

She heard one last clink of chains and then nothing. She steeled herself for another verbal attack, but kept her gaze focused on the firebush. A moment later, she sensed she was alone in the room and turned. Ned's trench coat was missing from the chair, and her aunt was nowhere in sight.

And they left without dragging you out by your hair, her inner voice said. *What's up with that?*

She heard the sound of two engines starting and sighed in relief. The pair had obviously chosen to brave a staggering hailstorm over her. And thank God they had. A knock-down, drag-out fight would've decimated her already shaky demeanor. She slid her legs up, grasping her knees with her arms. Now all that was left to do was to create a plan that would ensure she and Logan found the Pandora DVD as quickly as possible.

A green flash assailed her mind's eye, and she focused on the image. The green key belonged to what? A green door? She studied the rain-drenched cat-claw bush situated a few feet beyond the firebush. Another flash of green whipped across her mind, this time a green building. Alarmed by the image, the hair on the back of her neck began to prickle. She knew that building. *"So dark out there. So dark and so forever."* The words had her clutching her throat. She quickly reached into her pocket and withdrew the High Priestess card she had placed there. She didn't know why she had slipped the card into her pocket after her discussion with Logan. *It just felt right*, her inner voice explained. *We never ignore that feeling, right?*

Clasping the card tightly, she prayed for protection. *So dark, so dark.* The mantra had her scanning the room behind her with a shiver. And then, searching for a plausible explanation, she glanced down at the Tarot card in her hands again. *The Priestess. The Seeress. The Guardian of the Doorway.* What secret did Spirit want her to see in the card?

She studied the image of Persephone descending the stairs into Hades' domain and shivered. *Down through the rabbit hole, one, two three; out the other side, fiddle-dee-dee,* her inner voice chanted. Sonny slapped her knee with the card. But where would the other side be located? And what would she find if she went there?

She studied the card more closely, trying to think of how the card related to Foster's confession. What had he said about the mind transfer? *It needs a trigger,* her inner voice reminded her. *A green door to send the mind through.*

That's it, she thought, sitting up straighter on the windowsill. Hades dragged Persephone into the underworld to make her his consort. Could it be that simple? Was her real-life Hades bent on making her his consort? She shivered at the thought.

A thunderous clap exploded over Sonny's head, and she bolted from the window. The lights in the room went out, and Sonny fumbled for the wall, hit it, and then used it to move. She heard a rustling nearby and then saw a flicker of a shadow. *Run,* her inner voice warned. *Run if you value your life.*

A hand suddenly snaked around her face, and a white cloth pressed against her nose and mouth. The action cut off her air supply, sending her into panic mode. She dropped the High Priestess card and began clawing at the fabric. Her gloves hit the hand holding the fabric, and she knew instantly who was stalking her in the dark. Ned had come back for her, but if he thought she was going down without a fight, he was mistaken. She tore at the cloth and then clawed at Ned's wrists.

Her actions made Ned bring more pressure to bear on her back, causing the cloth to gouge her lips. Unable to struggle or scream, she recognized the smell of chloroform teasing her nostrils and knew she wouldn't have the strength to hold out. If only she could remove her gloves and send Ned into a frightful vision of demons and monsters.

A cluster of stars brought a lightheadedness with them, and Sonny realized what she did in the next few seconds would determine whether she stayed alive. She focused her senses on memorizing every single minutiae of the darkness surrounding her—Ned's hands, his posture—all the curves and angles. She absorbed the images, cataloguing, collating, and deciphering.

Pinpricks finally skewered her eyelids, sending her body into a meltdown. *You're a goner,* her inner voice warned. She thought so, too, as her knees buckled; however, unlike her body, her inner voice had no intention of going down quietly. *There's hope on the horizon,* it nudged. *Push the card where Logan can find it. He'll understand its meaning.*

Using her right toe, Sonny managed to shove the Tarot card to the middle of the floor without Ned noticing. Seconds later, her body went limp. Being lifted was the last thing she remembered, along with the knowledge that she was descending rapidly into a dark pool of nothingness.

CHAPTER NINETEEN

Logan came out of his deep sleep with a sudden jerk. *Sonny!* The word brought him up swiftly, and he studied the dark and empty room around him. When had the electricity gone out? *Dammit!* How long had he been sleeping? He bolted from the sofa to the front door, relieved when he saw the sedan still parked under the lighted overhang. At least he wasn't in total darkness. For a moment, he thought Sonny had stranded him at the cabin. It would be just like her to think she could solve their dilemma on her own. His gaze searched the room again. Was she off trying to reboot the breaker box?

The nape of his neck prickled suddenly, a sure sign that if he didn't find her, he'd find something unpleasant instead. He craned his neck, listening. The rain had stopped, and the house was too quiet. He began a rapid foot search of the main floor, promising himself he'd not do the obvious when he located Sonny. *Kissing her sounds delightful,* his inner voice approved.

I meant strangle her, he shot back.

He reached the staircase and moved up quickly, scouring each of the three bedrooms. He found each room deserted, and by the time he was on the main level again, his heart was hammering wildly. Where the hell was the mouse?

Spotting a lower staircase, he grimaced. He needed a flashlight fast. Searching a basement area in the dark was foolish. He whirled around, scanning the shadows behind him. Where would the wench keep a flashlight? He didn't have to wonder long, as he spotted a gray panel breaker box next to the front door. He moved quickly, throwing back the panel door and hitting the breaker switch.

The lights popped on, almost blinding Logan; however, he ignored the glare and returned to the staircase. If he found signs of a second car, he would comb the outside area for tire tracks. With so many pools of water still standing, he'd be able to judge whether there was a back road out of the area.

He took the stairs two at a time, halting on the bottom step when he found himself facing a second living-room space. Blasted wench! How many rooms did she need to work in? He stepped into the recreation room and headed for the outside door; however, when a crinkle sounded beneath his boot, he lifted his toe. A Tarot card peeped up at him from the floor. How the hell had the card gotten from the table upstairs to the room down here?

His Meta Corps instincts shored up immediately, and so did the first stirring of real fear. Something had happened to Sonny—something she couldn't control. Had she left the card as a clue? He studied The High Priestess on the face of the card. Everything connected to everything, isn't that what Sonny had said? *Nothing is random.* Hadn't she also said to say what you see?

He studied the card, noting the door stood out. *And every door comes with a key*, his intuition said. His hand shot to his shirt pocket. A green key to open a green door? He let his mind travel back to yesterday. Had he seen a green door at any time yesterday? None that he remembered. *Think, Reed*, his mind pressed. *Think green.*

He retraced his movements in his mind. There was the vision on the mesa, the vision in the cottage, and the fire at Serenity. *No, think smaller*, he told himself. He and Sonny had left the cottage and gone to Serenity. He had driven, and upon arrival, he had smoked a cigarette. *Go smaller.* His mind threw up the memory. He had smoked a cigarette, studying the property as Sonny pointed out its colors. The colors flew into his mind rapidly— purple, blue and *green.*

He glanced down at the card again. Everything connected. A beautiful goddess had been abducted by Hades and given a forbidden fruit to eat, and then Hades had made her his consort. Did a man desire Sonny more than life itself?

You should know, his inner voice remarked. *You desire her more than life itself.*

He grimaced. *Never mind that now. Think who Hades could be.*

He considered his suspect list. Charlotte Blake could be ruled out, unless of course she was manipulating her husband to do her dirty work. But what possible reason could she have for harming Sonny? Sonny posed no threat; besides, she seemed more like a woman on a mission—a woman who might know a terrible secret and was determined to protect Sonny from becoming a victim of that secret. Was Brad Fletcher on the same mission? Perhaps— but with a twist. He seemed genuinely fond of Sonny. But did that fondness harbor a twisted soul? A third name entered Logan's head. It was more likely Ned's soul was twisted. Lieutenant Cutter thought so. So did Blake. Why else focus on Ned's late-night sessions and demand to see his travel receipts? Had Ned been using The Sanctuary as a safe haven, while enjoying a smorgasbord of possible victims, and Blake had found out? It would answer why he'd had to be killed. It would also answer why Foster had been killed. He was holding the mysterious Pandora DVD, which Logan suspected would clearly show the original patient therapy sessions had been reworked by a modern-day Jack the Ripper.

To his credit, Ned spent most of his time paying little attention to Sonny, but that could've been a ruse. If he showed too much attention, Sonny would've suspected him. And once she did, she'd use her abilities to learn his intentions. No, playing a quiet game of hide-and-seek was the smart thing to do. It's what Logan would've done in Ned's place—except for pretending not to find Sonny attractive. After all, what man wouldn't find Sonny Blake so attractive he'd have to make a pass at her at least once in his life?

And what red-blooded man wouldn't want to have incredible sex with her? his ego added. *We do.*

Logan frowned. *Stop thinking with your balls. Sonny's life is at stake. Think of how to find her.* But why would Ned steal Sonny right from under Logan's nose?

You'll be blamed for her disappearance, and ultimately Meta Corps will be blamed. The thought felt so right in his mind that Logan knew he had hit on the truth. Ned Chalmers, or whatever his name was, had gotten access to Pandora and its power and now had every intention of using it on Sonny for his own personal agenda. But what was his agenda? Hatred? Obsession? Jealousy? Revenge? All four?

Logan's adrenalin spiked, and he crumpled the card he held in his hand. He whirled around and dashed back up the stairs. He had to find Lieutenant Cutter and press him into launching a full-scale search for Sonny. If, as he suspected, Ned had built a secret laboratory for Pandora, Logan was sure Ned had taken Sonny there.

Reaching the foyer, Logan grabbed the car keys and bolted for the door. Throwing it open, he was startled to see Lieutenant Cutter's jeep pulling into the carport and braking behind the Kia. Two men exited the vehicle, and Logan's lips puckered in annoyance. Damn! He didn't need Brad Fletcher's accusations right now. For a fleeting second, Logan had déjà vu. He had been down this road before, chasing a female empath in trouble, only to have the incident backfire on him. Would this one end the same way?

He tossed the thought away, greeting the men as they reached the door. "I was coming to see you, Lieutenant," he said quickly.

"Good, because I've come to see you and Sonny." Cutter pushed Logan back from the door and entered the cabin. Brad Fletcher followed quickly on his heels. When the trio was standing in the great room, the lieutenant offered an observation. "You look more rested than the last time I saw you." He looked beyond Logan's shoulder. "Where's Sonny? I thought you two were joined at the hip." He waited for an answer, shocked when Logan suddenly grabbed Brad Fletcher and slammed him against the wall.

"Where the hell has Ned taken Sonny?" he snarled. Brad's hands came up, attempting to derail Logan's chokehold, but Logan threw all his weight against him. "When I let you breathe again, you better tell me where Ned is."

A strong body pushed itself between the pair, attempting to dislodge the chokehold and take command.

"Let him go, Reed, or I'll take a gun butt to your head!"

Logan attempted to shoulder the lieutenant aside but found the body as hard as a stone wall. He eased his chokehold, taking a step back, but his right hand remained plastered against Brad's chest. His gaze took in the lieutenant's dark expression.

"There's no time for pleasantries, Lieutenant. Sonny's been abducted."

"What?" Cutter and Brad exclaimed simultaneously.

"Good God, what have you two been up to since last night?" Cutter asked.

Brad took the moment to shove Logan's hand from his chest. "Damn charlatan!" He pulled his shirt back into place. "Is this how you work with empathic clients? You let them get abducted?" His gaze skimmed the lieutenant. "If anything happens to Sonny, I'll fry your ass."

Logan's snarl came first. "What the hell are you doing here, Fletcher?"

"Enlisting Cutter's help to arrest Ned."

"What the hell for?"

"Among other things, David's murder."

"You have proof, I hope?"

Brad sought an empty chair, his tone disapproving. "As soon as Cutter lets me see the knife in evidence, he'll have his proof. I'll know who it belongs to."

"Forget that now," Logan stated. "We're way past David's death." He tossed the Kia's keys on an end table and signaled to the lieutenant. "Fire up the jeep, Cutter. We've got to search for Sonny."

"Search five hundred acres in the hopes of stumbling upon her? You're daft."

"I've got to find her."

"We will, but first we need a specific area to search. Now, calm down, and sit down. Catch me up on what you know, and I'll help you reason out where we should look."

Reluctantly, Logan sank onto the couch. Cutter was right; they needed a focus.

"David was never the intended target; he simply got in the way." Logan withdrew Foster's key from his pocket and flashed it at the men. When Logan didn't say anything more, the lieutenant bent and snatched the key from his fingers. He studied its odd shape and the emerald jewel embedded in its top half.

"I suppose the key belongs to the mysterious Pandora?"

Brad's gasp split the air. "You know about Pandora?"

The lieutenant's gaze shifted rapidly. "Yes, we know. I could ask you how you know about it, but that would be pointless."

Logan cut in swiftly. "I know you're knee-deep in the project, Fletcher, perhaps even the mastermind behind it, so tell us what you know, or I'll have Meta Corps here in less than an hour. They'll bury you so deep you'll never see daylight again. Now, tell me what you know, stat."

"The only thing I know is that you're a fucking screw-up." His glare drilled Logan's. "Where did you get that key? I know who owns it, and it bloody well isn't you."

Logan grimaced. "You go first, Fletcher, and don't bother trying to con me, because I already know Pandora takes a young subject and reprograms their memories. It literally wipes their minds clean and gives them a new life."

"What?" the lieutenant exclaimed. "Are we moving into science fiction territory now? Next, you'll be spouting that aliens have landed and are living among us."

"I saw the film, Lieutenant, and I'm not talking Tom Cruise here." He motioned to the key in Cutter's hand. "Foster Sykes offered Sonny this key as proof of The Pandora Project. In fact, he admitted his involvement—just before he was shot to death."

Floored, the lieutenant dropped into his chair. Brad, on the other hand, bolted from his.

"Good God! Foster's dead?"

"This morning," Logan said. "Before he died, though, Sykes claimed Sonny was the first successful patient of the project."

"The man was deranged," Brad said, annoyed. "There hasn't been a successful patient yet."

Logan motioned to the key. "According to Sykes, he made recordings of the patient transfers; however, before we could search for the DVD, the monsoon started. We've been stuck here for hours. Sonny went missing while I caught some shut-eye—"

"Fucking screw-up!" Brad cut in. "Your license should be yanked."

Logan cast him a murderous glare. "Sonny left a clue before she was taken."

"You're sure she was abducted and not just tired of your sparkling personality?" Brad mocked him.

"Can the humor, Fletcher," Logan said. "You're wasting my time." He handed Brad the crushed Tarot card. "Sonny left me this clue."

Brad unfolded the card and studied its image. "No one but Sonny can read the truth associated with this card," he said.

"She's one smart cookie, I'll give you that. She knew I'd look at the card and interpret it logically. Now, according to mythology, that card represents Hades abducting Persephone into the underworld. Substitute Ned for Hades."

"See, Cutter?" Brad declared. "I told you Ned was a bastard. Even Reed figured it out. Now, what are we going to do about it?"

"We?" Logan repeated.

Brad fired up. "You won't find Sonny without my help! I know The Sanctuary inside and out. If there's a secret laboratory on the property, I'll find it." He waved at the lieutenant. "I've already told Cutter everything—my involvement—Charlotte's involvement—our fears." His eyes surveyed Logan. "If you are as good as Sonny claims you are, you'll let me help you fry Ned's ass."

"What did he call himself before coming to The Sanctuary?" Logan asked.

Brad squirmed in his chair. "If you think I'm going to reveal the skeletons in my closet—."

"You already have," the lieutenant interrupted. He turned to Logan. "Ned's real name is Fremont—a convicted felon. Spent ten years in prison for sexual battery."

"None of that matters now," Logan said, rising. He glanced at Brad, who had the good sense to remain silent under the scrutiny. "Being around Sonny, I've learned that two plus two doesn't always equal four." He snatched the key back from the lieutenant. "We're looking for a green door, in a green building, with a room housing a chair and green headset."

"Then you want Serenity—Green Arbor, to be precise," Brad said. "It's filled with therapy rooms."

"With Sonny inside one," Logan added.

"You've lost me," the lieutenant remarked.

Logan's jaw clenched. "The day Sonny and I met, she inadvertently whipped us into some damn vision of a therapy session in progress. We didn't see much, but I remember seeing a green headpiece on a young woman's head. We were hurled back out of the vision as fast as we went in, and when I asked, Sonny had no idea what the vision meant."

An irritated growl sliced the air. "Are we going to stand here talking about her visions, or are we going to save her?" Brad chided. "Ned has a huge head start. It might already be too late."

Logan bolted to his feet. "For once, Fletcher, you and I agree on something. We've got to *act.*"

Two minutes later, the trio was inside the waiting jeep.

"I hope you have some plan of attack for when we get there," the lieutenant said, firing up the engine.

"By the time we get there, I'll have thought of one," Logan assured him.

"It's easy to see why you have no friends," the lieutenant said, backing down the incline. "It takes sharing to have one of those."

"Have you been prying into my background, Lieutenant?" Logan queried.

"Absolutely," Cutter replied. He spun the wheel and dropped the jeep into drive. "While I was talking to your boss, I asked him to e-mail me a copy of your personnel file."

Logan's gaze impaled the lieutenant's, while a chuckle sounded from the back seat.

"You're a fucking good cop, Dick," Brad said.

"And you're both fucking pricks," Logan quipped. The lieutenant grinned and jammed on the gas.

The jeep picked up speed, with sirens howling and lights flashing. Reaching a blinking yellow light, it sailed into oncoming traffic, dodging an SUV as it screeched to a stop. It then headed for a second intersection, where it veered right, up onto an entrance ramp. In seconds, it was passing a road sign that read: SERENITY, 5 MILES AHEAD.

Seeing cactus stalks whizzing by at breakneck speed, Logan did the only wise thing he could. He buckled his seat belt with a muttered curse.

•••

A thrumming saturated Sonny's consciousness and she awoke with a jerk. Her gaze collided with a stark white wall, and she wondered who had the audacity to repaint her room while she slept. She felt an itch along the bridge of her nose and attempted to scratch it. However, she found her wrists shackled to the arms of a large chair.

Glancing down, she tested the metal clamps and then gave a frustrated groan when she felt how tight they were. Her glance dropped lower, to her tightly bound ankles. Her brain threw up the memory of being smothered by an obnoxious smell and then being dumped into the family limo. The remembrance of the abduction rankled, and a dangerous glint surfaced behind Sonny's eyes. Ned had killed her father and was now bent on harming her.

Sonny swung her head left and right, surveying the room around her. Was escape possible? Sure, if one could find a door. She let her gaze follow the seam of the walls, searching for a break in the smooth plaster. When she saw none, she knew the room was airtight. Room! To call this chamber a room was being generous, she decided. Outside of the chair she sat in, there were no furnishings, no wall hangings, and very little light. And the chair she was shackled to? Well, it was uncomfortable, to say the least.

Sonny let her gaze wander upward, feeling something heavy bump against her temples and neck. What had been settled on her head? A million answers swam through her brain, each one more terrifying than the last, but her brain finally settled on the truth. Ned was going to use the Pandora process on her to turn her into … what? A vegetable?

The thought was so frightening Sonny began straining at the clamps. If she couldn't find a way to loosen the cumbersome links, she'd be a goner. *Calm down and think rationally,* her inner voice demanded. *People who give in to panic end up hurt or dead.*

Right.

She took a deep breath, and thankfully, her nerves steadied. *That's it, keep breathing,* she told herself, *and keep focused. Think what you can do to save your life. Think what Logan would do to save your life. Logan!* Was he looking for her? A pool of tears welled at the thought. Perhaps he didn't care enough to mount a rescue. Her pulse tripped. No, he took his job seriously, and he'd leave no stone unturned in finding her. It was a matter of pride.

Another unwelcome thought swam through her head, and she attempted to push it away. No matter how bad things got, she'd never admit out loud that she had fallen in love with Logan over the last two days. Besides, hadn't Logan made it abundantly clear he didn't trust women with empathic talents? She wouldn't add more fuel to his dislike by declaring her love for him. *But he kissed us, wants to go on kissing us,* her inner voice reminded. *You heard him; he's going to kiss us as often as we let him.*

Forget that now, Sonny told her ego. *Concentrate on discovering where we are and how we can get out of here.*

Sonny's gaze snapped back to the white walls. Was she underground, in a basement or bomb shelter? Or was she tucked away in plain sight in one of her own dream lab wings? It was terrifying not to know. And terror, she knew, bred stupidity. If she didn't somehow manage to figure out where she was in the next few minutes, she'd never be able to logically mount an attack against Ned.

The thrumming noise intensified, emanating from a place above her head. Sonny glanced up, noting a curlicue of a light socket hanging from the ceiling. What was its purpose? A light vibration along her temples gave her an answer.

It's part of the Pandora process, her inner voice advised. *A laser beam that alters brainwaves.* Horrified by the thought, Sonny struggled against the clamps again. She needed to squeeze out of them before her mind was devoid of any rational thought.

A faint draft of cool air suddenly caressed her face, and she swiveled her head towards the gust. She watched the wall transforming from plaster to plate glass. Looking through the glass, she caught sight of three religious paintings of Jesus Christ, and to their left, she saw a staircase trailing upward. To her right, there were two computer stations, two metal desks, and four wingback chairs. *My God!* She recognized the furniture pattern. She was in Green Arbor—in one of the designated therapy rooms, or was she? There was a cold composition to the air, as if she was below ground, not above.

The walls around her settled into place, opening up the room and making her squint under the sudden splurge of light. *You're nothing more than a lab rat in a chair*, her inner voice taunted her. She heard the sound of a door opening behind her and knew Ned had finally condescended to show himself.

A second later, he appeared in front of her.

"I'm sorry it's come to this, Sonny, but you gave me no choice. I'm tired of waiting for you to figure out what I've done and take action against me. It's too bad, really. With your incredible talent, we could have owned half the world. In time, you may have even enjoyed sleeping with me."

"The thought sickens me," Sonny snarled.

His tone lightened, though his expression remained antagonistic. "I'll have to be extra careful in programming you," he mocked her. "But I promise you, when I'm done, you'll enjoy having sex with me." Stunned by the pronouncement, Sonny could only stare at Ned. A finger snapped in front of her face. "I want you to know that I had no idea your father knew about my late-night sessions with women. I have always been extremely careful in conducting the trysts. But he had the audacity to follow me to one of the sessions and then blackmail me with what he saw."

"Daddy always was a good judge of character," Sonny said. "You're lucky, though. He didn't kill you."

"No, instead he realized stealing your skill was my end game. Thanks to his interference, I've had to push up my timetable."

Sonny cleared her throat. It was time to put forth a bluff. "I hope you've done your homework on Pandora thoroughly, because I know I have. You see, Pandora can be reversed, with the right trigger. Thankfully I know it, and what I know, Logan Reed knows, which means he will be here on your doorstep before you have time to finish the mind transfer."

Ned's expression veered from annoyance to outright anger. "You won't recognize him when he comes, though. I'll see to that."

The statement ignited a fire in Sonny's belly. "Stop boring me, Ned. You don't have anything to threaten me with. If by some miracle the procedure works, and I'm no longer Sonny Blake, I won't recognize you, so any threats you make now are falling on deaf ears."

Ned's gaze softened. "You've got it backwards, Sonny. I don't *want* to use the Pandora procedure on you; I *have* to. You need to see the darkness as I see it, and once you do, you'll beg to move through it with me. With your ability to manipulate time and space, we'll consummate the magic in both body and soul. I promise you, your new life will be incredibly rich, and every night when you lie down to sleep, you'll thank me for sharing that richness."

"What the hell are you talking about?" Sonny asked.

"See for yourself," Ned answered, stripping off Sonny's gloves and pocketing them. He strode from the chamber, and Sonny congratulated herself on buying herself a few more minutes. Her fingers brushed the cold steel of the chair arms, and she was tossed into a familiar vortex. When the vision settled into focus, she was standing behind a glass window, watching a hypnotherapy session in progress.

The woman in the therapy chair was young, beautiful, and scantily clad. Her slim tank top barely contained her bulging breasts, and her short shorts could only be labeled as erotically indecent. A small, green headset protruded from her scalp, and her face glowed with an inner radiance. Beside her, Ned studied her face and figure. Overhead, his prerecorded voice took the woman through a series of mind scenarios.

"And where are you now?" his voice asked.

The young woman's answer was a flat monotone. "I'm on a boat. Phil and I are sailing to Bermuda. The sky is blue, and the seas are calm. Phil is at the wheel, and it's almost lunchtime—"

"And where are you now?" the voice suddenly asked.

"I'm having sex with Phil." The young woman's breathing changed.

Reacting, Ned stepped forward and slipped his hand beneath the young woman's tank top. He fondled an unseen nipple, his eyes glued to the woman's animated face.

"Phil's a wonderful lover ... " Ned's hand shifted under the material. "He knows just where I like to be touched ... Ohh ... We're climaxing now ... Ohhhhh ... "

"And where are you now?

Ned's fingers increased their fondling, but the woman in the chair remained oblivious to the stroking.

"I'm in the park with Phil. It's Sunday. We always go to the park on Sunday. The kids are playing nearby, with our dog, Scruffy. We've brought a picnic lunch. We'll stay until four ... "

"And where are you now?"

Ned's fingers withdrew from the tank top, and with a quick jerk, he pulled the material down, exposing the woman's breasts. The eager look flashing in his eyes hurled Sonny's mind out of the vision and back to the real world.

She came back to reality with a jerk, hit by an electric shock that jolted her forehead. She was pitched backwards in the chair, and her eyes flew open. She knew exactly why Ned had stripped her of her gloves. He had wanted her to see firsthand what he intended for her. It was miles from Pandora's original concept. He had reworked it for his own manic desires. *No wonder he never came within ten feet of us*, her inner voice advised. *He was afraid we'd catch a glimpse of his aberrant behavior.*

A second jolt of electricity sliced across Sonny's forehead. To her relief, God was kind. She lost consciousness immediately.

•••

Logan whipped through the front door, barreling towards the green door ahead of them. It had been a long drive to Serenity—the longest of his life. And now, he was facing the longest minute of his life, praying that he'd find Sonny alive on the other side of the door. He raced across the tiles, thrown off guard when he saw the door had no keyhole. Behind him, he heard a familiar growl.

"Have we guessed wrong?" the lieutenant asked.

Brad snatched the key out of Logan's hand and placed it in a slot beneath a matching green jewel carved into the archway. He spun the key, waiting for the tumblers to roll. When they didn't, he glanced at Logan.

"Give it time," Logan countered. "If I've learned anything from Sonny, it's that Spirit shows a way when there appears to be no way." He stepped forward, twisting the key back to its original position. It popped back upright.

"If you're wrong, Reed," the lieutenant said, "I'll see that you never work in law enforcement ever again."

"Ditto," Brad added.

Lifting his hands, Logan silenced the men. As if by magic, Sonny's voice filtered through his mind. *One plus one equals two.*

Nothing is random. He spun the key to the right again, and then listened carefully for the tumblers to roll. A second later, they did. The door sliced open in front them, revealing a staircase. Sonny was right. Spirit was always on duty. It was sending them deep into the bowels of the earth. He stepped forward, feeling a tug on his sleeve.

"Let me go first," the lieutenant said. "You're in no shape to be making any rational decisions. If we find Ned down there, you'll probably shoot first and ask questions later."

"I have no intention of shooting him," Logan responded. "I might strangle him, but either way, I'm going down these steps first."

"You're a fucking prick, Reed," Cutter said.

"Right back at ya," Logan said, withdrawing his pistol from his waistband. He took the first steps down; however, when he and Cutter reached the bottom steps, they found a long tunnel stretching before them.

The lieutenant quickly drew his pistol. "This adventure is getting too damn creepy," he stated.

"Yes, and neither of us brought a coin to pay the ferry master," Logan quipped.

"I'd ask you to explain that," Cutter whispered, as they stepped off the staircase and entered the tunnel, "but my instincts tell me it's some spiritual proverb you learned from Sonny."

Reaching out, Logan felt the wall beside him. He began tracing its length. Behind him, the lieutenant did the same. The trio headed off, following the wall to keep their bearings, and as they moved, Logan prayed the end of the tunnel wouldn't be the end of his relationship with Sonny.

• • •

Sonny felt a faint tingling along her scalp and stirred. Who was interrupting her dreams? Her eyes shot open, and she blinked rapidly to bring her surroundings into focus. As her vision cleared, she was hit with a reflection of herself strapped to a chair. Her brain came awake at once. *You're still Sonny Blake.*

Beyond the reflection, she saw Ned seated at a console station and wondered why she still knew who she was. Had something gone wrong with the mind transfer? That had to be it. The mind zaps had been excruciating, leaving her body engulfed in a raging fire. Another two or three doses of that kind of punishment and she would beg to be somebody else—anything to stop the pain.

She heard a crackle in her ears, and Ned's voice came online.

"You can stop this, Sonny. Just say the word. You can remain Sonny Blake and share the darkness with me. I can tweak only some of your memories rather than all of them. I can reprogram you as my wife. We'll go underground, to a place in Mexico. The choice is up to you."

"Go to hell, Ned," Sonny spat. She saw movement beyond the window and felt a light tingling along her scalp. Ned had started the process again. A myriad of sensations whipped through her mind, followed by a set of multiple thought patterns ebbing in and out of clarity. Behind her eyes, she felt a vague stirring and wondered whether it *was* possible to sabotage the transfer.

The image of a poster flashed across her mind, and she grasped on to the image. Right. *Twilight Zone.* She recalled the episode she had once seen during a Syfy marathon on TV. The frightened subject of a mind experiment had implanted a code word in his subconscious that, once triggered, totally reversed the mind alteration. Could she do the same? She found herself suddenly smiling. It would be a kick if she could.

She felt a delicious euphoria steal over her body as she felt the chair fall back. What word could she use as a code word? Her brain threw up a name. Logan? Not a common enough name. She could wait eons to hear that name.

Mouse? Perfect.

She sent the word into her ebbing thoughts. *When you hear the word 'mouse,' you'll remember everything. You'll have Sonny Blake's life back again, and everything will be as it was.*

Sonny closed her eyes and began drifting down a wide, pain-filled rabbit hole.

"Good-bye, Sonny."

"Good-bye, Ned," she whispered softly.

•••

With a tightly clenched jaw, Logan halted before another door without a keyhole. He studied the seams of the door, noting a pinprick of light peeking through. It would take thirty seconds to open the door, and for once in his life, Logan asked God to grant him a favor that didn't center on his own ego. He just wanted to be in time.

He turned the knob, and finding it unlocked, he pushed the door open. To his surprise, he found another set of steps leading down. Now they really were descending into the bowels of hell. He heard the lieutenant's footsteps hitting the steps behind him, while up ahead, he could hear a distant thrumming.

When he reached the bottom of the steps, a blazing stream of light blinded him. Logan shaded his eyes. They were in a small laboratory filled with computers. Logan's intuition kicked in, and he raised his revolver, searching for a sign of Sonny. Alongside him, the lieutenant's gun came up.

The pair made their way further into the room and then halted at the sight of a handgun pointed in their direction. Reflexes flaring, both Logan and the lieutenant aimed their weapons at the same time.

"Don't be a fool, Ned," the lieutenant warned. "You won't get both of us."

A wry smile cracked Ned's lips, and he pulled the hammer back on the revolver. His gaze never left theirs as he moved his free hand and dangled it over a red flashing light on the console beside him. Very slowly, he let his fingers slide onto the gun's trigger.

In that moment, Logan knew Ned would pull the trigger and press the button at the same time. A quick look to his right and Logan saw what he was guarding so fiercely. The Pandora process was underway, and Ned had every intention of seeing it finished before he died. And now that he was cornered, he did intend to die.

Seeing Logan's bright stare, Ned's smile widened. "If I can't have her powers, no one else will. So the burning question is which one of us will pull the trigger first?"

Logan didn't have to think twice about the answer.

CHAPTER TWENTY

The blowback of the gunshot rang in Logan's ears and caused his eyes to water. Ned stumbled back, clutching the console desk to keep from going down under the impact of the bullet ripping through his left side.

Seeing the stumble, the lieutenant dove forward, wrestling the gun from his fingers. Logan heard a muttered growl as he watched the ensuing scuffle and Ned's collapse to the floor. The lieutenant hovered over his body.

"Jesus, Reed! That was one hell of a shot. I thought you meant to kill him."

Logan studied the red stain seeping from Ned's shirtfront. "You mean I didn't?" he asked sarcastically.

"No, but you've wounded him to the max," Cutter said, bending over and lifting Ned's shirt.

"Killing him would surely kill Sonny," Logan stated.

"Sonny!"

Beside him, Brad Fletcher bolted around the glass partition. In seconds, Logan had rounded the window with him. Reaching the table, he stuffed his revolver into his waistband and ripped the headset from Sonny's scalp. Grabbing her neck, he shook her roughly.

"Sonny! Can you hear me?" She remained motionless under his clamped fingers, and he gave her body another vicious shake. Her mind was as far away from reality as the moon was to the earth, and he didn't have a clue of how to bring her back to him. "Fight, Sonny. Fight your way back to the present. You do it all the time." He waited for a response, a tic, a twitch, but nothing came. Her eyelids remained closed, her body a limp rag doll in his arms.

At that moment, Logan experienced true panic, a cramping in his stomach that nearly doubled him over. Not even when he had found himself face down in the gutter, his blood staining the cracks of the pavement, had he given into a sense of panic this great. Now, his heart was pounding, and his blood was turning to ice. If Sonny woke and didn't recognize him, or any part of her old life, he'd never forgive himself. No, she had a pulse—thready, but there. And if she didn't wake?

Stampeded by the thought, he gave her shoulders another shake. "Sonny!"

"Bloody hell, Reed! Are you trying to shake her teeth loose?" Brad snarled. "Step back or you'll kill her for sure!"

The demand burned Logan's ears, and slim fingers hauled him back from the reclining chair. Logan balked at the manhandling, yet gave way as Brad stepped around him and took command. A second later, Logan found himself caught up in the blatant efficiency of the man.

Brad lifted Sonny's right eyelid and checked her pupils. At the same time, his fingers grasped her right wrist and began monitoring her pulse. His stilted call to her was a trifle softer than Logan's.

"It's Uncle Brad, Sonny; focus on my voice." He brushed her cheekbone, and Logan felt his throat constrict at the caress. Time was running out. "Come back, Sonny," Brad demanded. He paused, waiting for a response, and Logan was surprised to see an amazed look cross his face as he dropped her wrist and turned from the recliner. Had he convinced himself Sonny would respond to his voice and no other?

Blocking out Brad's stricken expression, Logan brought his mind from the emotional back to the rational. Sonny wasn't going to waken, at least not without major medical help. The important thing now was to get her that help. He motioned to Brad.

"You conduct sessions like this every day, Fletcher. Can't you reverse the programming, or at least slow it down?"

"Not without a trigger word, I can't. If Ned used one, there's no telling what it was." He motioned to the window. "Does he look like a man who'd give up that information? He'll die first."

Logan agreed, but not aloud. Instead, he signaled through the window to the lieutenant, who immediately took out his phone.

"Code blue, Daniel Six," he ordered through the mouthpiece. "I repeat, I need Trauma Hawk at Green Arbor stat. Code blue, code blue."

The call was relayed quickly, and Logan's gaze lit on the sea of bodies suddenly cluttering the stairwell. Where the hell had all the backup come from? Crime-scene crowds interfered with investigations and made his job of ferreting out secrets almost impossible.

His gaze finally settled on the lieutenant's imposing form, and his expression soured even more. If he thought his mood was black, it was nothing to the fractured scowl staining the lieutenant's face. He still held his hand over Ned's bleeding wound, but he was barking orders at breakneck speed. Bodies left and came back, only to be sent off again.

Realizing he stood no chance of conversing privately with the lieutenant, Logan's gaze shifted to the man on the floor. A female officer suddenly blocked his view as she fell to her knees beside Ned and offered the lieutenant assistance in staunching the flow of blood. Ned remained unconscious at her probing, and even though a sheet of glass separated them, Logan could see a scowl etched on Ned's face. Was the bastard worried he hadn't finished the job? Logan's mind elaborated the thought. Had something gone wrong with the transfer ... or had something gone right? It didn't take long for the hairs on the back of his neck to prickle, a sure sign he had hit on something.

"He's not going to make it, Reed," the lieutenant said, wiping his bloodied hands on a towel as he settled beside Logan and watched the female's efficient ministrations. Logan didn't offer a comment. "You're scowling. What are you thinking?"

"His mind zap didn't work."

"Not that we know of," Cutter said, tossing the towel into the corner of the chamber. "However, if the bastard lives through this, we'll fry his ass for murdering David and attempting to kill Sonny."

"Look at his face," Logan said. "Even unconscious, he's worried. It's as if he suspects the mind transfer didn't have time to work."

"He swamped her mind, Reed," the lieutenant said. "Just look at *her* face. It's devoid of life. If she wakes, what will she be? A vegetable?"

Logan snarled at the insinuation. "It will take more than two or three mind zaps to take Sonny down. The question is did he have time to execute the entire program before we arrived?"

The sound of thundering rotors and loud sirens filtered down to the basement.

"Trauma Hawk," Cutter said, moving away.

Logan grasped his arm. "Ned doesn't ride in the chopper with Sonny," he stated.

"The man needs surgery, Reed."

"He doesn't ride with Sonny," Logan emphasized. "Send him by ambulance."

"He'll die along the way," the lieutenant advised. He eyed Logan's frigid expression. "Jesus! You're hoping he dies along the way."

Logan headed towards Ned's prostrate form. Seeing his approach, the officer who had been tending his wound rose and stepped away.

"He's coming around," she told Logan as she passed him.

Logan glanced down and saw pain-filled eyes staring up at him. The voice was barely audible as it spoke.

"I was sure you wanted me dead," he whispered.

Logan dropped to his haunches. "Killing you would've served *your* purpose, not mine, Chalmers. It would've been foolish to kill you this soon. And trust me, I'm not a fool."

"Thank you for not killing me this soon," Ned said sarcastically. He broke off, his face mired in pain.

"Yet," Logan emphasized, hearing a raspy pant. "I haven't killed you *yet*."

Ned's mouth twisted into a lopsided grin, and a spurt of blood spread across his lips. "Once the program is set, it can't be undone," he wheezed. "There'll be no miracle. You won't save Sonny. She's one with the darkness now."

"I believe you," Logan said. "But I also believe that you would never damage her brain entirely."

He heard another busted wheeze. "You can't imagine the thrill—the power one gets from killing empaths I had to have Sonny's."

"By turning her into a brand new person?"

Ned's eyes were dilating now. "I would've been good to her." He tried to raise his hand, but it fell back quickly. "With her talent and my cunning, we would've been unstoppable."

A scuffle sounded behind them, and when Logan turned, Brad was pushing past two security officers and bearing down on them. When he reached Ned, he dropped to his knees.

"How could you do it, you bastard?" he demanded, his accusation scathing. "How could you send Sonny's mind to God knows where?"

Ned's wheeze was filled with matching contempt. "At least I'm no sniveling coward." He coughed up blood. "I was willing to gamble that Pandora was still viable, and I was right. Pandora works."

"So you fried Sonny's brain all in the name of your precious ego?"

Ned coughed up another stream of blood. "Go away, Brad," he gasped. "Let me die in peace."

Incensed, Brad reached for Ned's neck, but Logan's hands stopped them mid-flight.

"No one wants the bastard dead more than I do, Fletcher, but if you strangle him, he'll find peace. And I don't want him to ever have peace, in this life or the next."

"Let me kill him then," Brad said, knocking Logan's fingers from his. He lowered his voice. "He deserves to feel the same pain Sonny did."

"He will. He's going to bleed to death right here on the floor. I intend to see to it. He'll never make it into surgery."

A rasp whistled through Ned's lips. "Dark … ness."

The stutter was barely audible, but it still rocked Logan's ears. He glanced at the face, suddenly devoid of life, and breathed a sigh of relief.

"The bastard got his wish. He's trapped in darkness for eternity."

CHAPTER TWENTY ONE

Something warm tickled her face, and she opened her eyes. At least she tried to. A horrendous pounding erupted deep in her head, and a tiny voice urged her to sleep. She sank into a wonderful euphoria, until that same tiny voice came again, demanding she open her eyes. Once again, she felt the same warmth on her face and attempted to lift her lids. When they shot up, she saw a white ceiling.

Flinching under the light, she immediately closed her eyes and fell back to sleep. But the tiny voice came again, urging her to stay awake. She opened her eyes, and this time, they stayed open. The white ceiling shimmered in a blur and then shifted to the top of a glass-paned door. Somewhere close by, she heard a light scratching sound. She followed the sound and saw a tree branch bobbing against an open patio door. A sprinkling of light peeped across a stone wall, capturing her attention. Sunlight. It was morning, and the sun was rising. But what sun? And where?

She let her gaze drift left and studied the tree branch. Where was she? She tried to think and found herself hit with that same pounding in her head, although it wasn't quite as painful this time. She closed her eyes, seeking release from the tiring ache, and the tiny voice let her.

Soon, too soon for her liking, the voice came back, prodding her to wake up. The thought made her suddenly cry. It felt as if her mind was trying to test her in some way, trick her.

She attempted to raise her hand and brush the annoying wetness away, but found she didn't have the strength. What was wrong with her hands? She glanced down and spotted bandages covering both of them. She flinched under the jolt erupting in her head. For a moment, she thought the tiny voice would advise her to go to sleep, but when her gaze remained focused on the bandages, the pain drifted away. Why were her hands wrapped? Had she tried to commit suicide? Yes, she must've. That's why her brain was testing her. She had lost touch with reality and tried to kill herself. She had been locked up because she was crazy. Her glance found the open doorway again. No, that couldn't be the answer. There weren't any open doors in insane asylums—just cells, little cells, with shackles and chairs. And pain, intense pain.

The throbbing pain in her head ignited again, sending her into a dark place with shackles and chairs. Think. No, don't think, it's too painful. Go to sleep. No, don't go to sleep. Think. Too hard to think. Better to sleep. Yes, sleep. No, think. Find the answer. Too hard. Must sleep. No, better to know the answer. Time to remember the answer. Yes, time to stop sleeping …

A musky aroma wafted into her nose, and she opened her eyes. Aftershave. Who was wearing it? She attempted to turn her head and found her neck muscles stiff and sore. What the hell had happened to her neck? She glanced down, surprised to find IV lines protruding from under her bandages.

Slowly, her mind began to backtrack. She had been driving on a sharp curve. Blinding lights had hit her head-on, and then, intense pain and … nothing. The rest was lost, at least for the moment. She tuned in to the rhythmic tick of a heart monitor above her head and lowered her chin. A set of wires jutted from the top of her hospital gown onto the pillow under her head. By some miracle, she had survived a car accident. She had been brought to a hospital. But when? And how long ago?

She felt the sheet around her toes rustle and followed the sound. Her eyebrows shot up when she spied a white-coated figure standing at the foot of the bed, totally engrossed in the clipboard he was holding. His expression telegraphed concern as he lifted each of the pages and read them. Was she in that bad of shape? Perhaps the accident had left her paralyzed. No, she realized. She could move her arms and had wriggled her toes slightly. You couldn't do that if you were numb from the waist down. It had to be her head. It had taken a walloping hit during the accident, but how long ago? Days? Weeks? Was that why the doctor's brow was so furrowed?

She let her gaze travel the strong lines of his face. Confident, trustworthy—everything a doctor should be. She'd speak to him. Let him know he needn't worry anymore; she was fine. She felt her eyelids flicker down. A second later, she heard movement, and a strong grip encircled her wrist.

A deep voice called, "Try to stay awake if you can."

She followed the instructions, opening her lids to find a pair of gray-green eyes leaning into her.

"You must focus on my voice ... No, don't try to speak. You must save your energy. You've been a very sick young woman, but you'll get better now that you're awake." He cast a harried glance over his shoulder and then reached up above her head. He must've adjusted her IV, because she felt a euphoric dizziness consume her.

"Don't ... make ... me ... sleep ... " she mumbled.

"My God, she's awake! Awake!"

Scuffling sounds ensued, and then two tall figures leaned over her bed and assessed her face. More doctors? She must've really banged herself up during the crash to garner so much attention. There was even a doctor on standby, just inside the door. Why hadn't he rushed to the bed in concern like the others? A blinding pain erupted in her head at the question, and she reeled back into the pillow. She felt her pulse taken quickly and turned her attention to the doctor on her right. She heard his soft mutter.

"Take it easy. Do you know where you are?"

She attempted an answer, surprised to find her voice hoarse and strained.

"Hos ... pi ... tal."

She heard him mutter, "Thank God," beneath his breath. In the next instant, she found her fingers raised and pinched by the female doctor on her left.

"How do you feel? Can you remember your name?"

She didn't answer right away, stunned by the doctor's show of affection. The woman was holding her fingers as if she personally cared what happened to her. Did she know the woman? Her gaze scanned the beautiful face. She seemed familiar; however, she couldn't put a name to the face. The confident doctor spoke again.

"Stay focused, if you can. I realize the medicine makes your mind drift, but don't space out on us now." Her gaze swam back to his, and he gave a sigh of relief. "Do you know who you are?"

"A ... manda ... Amanda King."

Disbelief, shock, and disappointment flooded his face all in the space of a few seconds, and Amanda had the feeling she had said something horribly wrong. The doctor on her left dropped her fingers as if burned and took a step back. She saw the same dismay register on the woman's face, and then she was turning, looking off to the doorway at the figure just out of the range of her vision.

"Can you remember what happened to you, Miss King?" the doctor asked.

"Car ... accident ... Headlights ... Confused ... "

Again, she saw disappointment flood the doctors' faces. What had she said to make them so worried? Unexpected tears pooled around her eyelashes, and the female doctor stroked her wrist.

"Don't cry, Miss King. You're safe. Your body's been through a rough shock, that's all. Can you tell us how old you are?"

Amanda stirred. The doctor was testing her memory. "Twenty-four."

A gentle pat touched her hands.

"Good. That's enough talking for now. You just close your eyes and sleep. We'll talk again when you've rested."

Once again, Amanda saw the confident doctor reach above her head and adjust her IV bag. A blissful euphoria invaded her limbs, and she floated away. As her eyelids flickered down, she heard movement around the bed. The doctors were leaving.

"I'm sorry. I wish the news could've been better. However, I did warn you."

"Don't be sorry," a new and deeply pleasant voice advised. "She's alive, her brain intact, and nothing else matters."

Umm, a doctor who really cares, Amanda thought, attempting to open her eyes. Was it the doctor at the door? She'd steal a peek; he sounded nice. Though her brain asked her to open her eyes, her eyelids remained shut. Once again, she floated on a cloud. Umm, they were giving her glorious drugs. She'd thank the nice doctor at the door tomorrow for such exquisite, mind-altering drugs.

• • •

The first call for boarding passengers pealed from the overhead speakers, and Logan sprang to his feet. The hour wait had been interminable. Reaching down, he hoisted his duffel bag to his shoulder. Half turning, he extended his hand to the man standing beside him. The lieutenant greeted the gesture with a frown.

"I wish you'd stay a bit longer, Reed. Sonny's making incredible strides in her recovery."

"I've already overstayed my welcome. I'm needed back in New York."

"Bullshit! The agency can stand another week or two without you. What's your hurry all of a sudden?"

Logan clutched his shoulder strap, lifting it to a more comfortable spot on his collarbone. "I've been assigned a new case—an empath missing from the Bronx."

The lieutenant shook his head. "Let the agency assign the case to someone else! You need to stay a few more days."

The overhead speaker echoed a second boarding call, and Logan checked the crowded doorway. He wished he could tell the lieutenant the truth, that he didn't have the courage to stay a few more days. A hole as big as Texas had been punched in his heart the moment Sonny had roused with no memory of her life as Sonny Blake. The knowledge he had lost her for good was slowly eating away at him, and if he didn't leave today, he might never leave.

The cost of staying would be the loss of his soul, and perhaps Sonny's. Besides, he simply didn't have the heart to stay now that they were sure she would never recall anyone from her former life. It was ironic really; he had found his life again, thanks to her, but the cost had been the loss of hers. His gaze swam back to the lieutenant.

"You've got my number, right? In case she needs anything."

"Hell, Reed, what else could she need? You've seen to it that her monies have been transferred from her old life to her new one. How did you arrange that, by the way? Not even Brad could circumvent the roadblocks being thrown at us."

Logan managed a wry smile. It hadn't been easy. But, in the end, his money and Meta Corps' clout had talked in a gigantic way. His bank account had dwindled substantially, but it was a loss he was willing to take.

"The less you know about how it was accomplished, the better," he finally stated.

The final boarding call blared, and Logan extended his hand again. This time, the lieutenant took it. A flash of humor crossed Logan's face.

"You have a home in New York City if you ever need one. You'd make a damn fine Meta Corps agent."

Cutter's mouth twisted wryly. "Don't have the stomach for it. I like protecting John Q. Public."

"Well, if you change your mind, Meta Corps could certainly use a rent-a-cop with scruples. By the way, I did a background check on *you* last week. You spent years off the radar. Down in some hellhole in Somalia, wasn't it?"

"What are you implying?"

"Not a damn thing. Blake was lucky to have you protecting him; so was Sonny."

The lieutenant grimaced. "A lot of good it did. I let Ned get away with assaulting our female guests for years. There'll be hell to pay for that—in this life or the next."

"Not if I have anything to say about it."

Cutter's mouth quirked with humor suddenly. "When you get back, tell Dresden I said you're not such a screw-up after all."

Logan grinned, shifting the duffel again, and heading towards the steward collecting tickets at the entrance ramp. Left with only a boarding pass, he turned and sketched a wave, surprised to find the lieutenant close on his heels. He allowed a lopsided grin to surface.

"I'm a big boy, Cutter. I can ride a plane all by myself now." Logan dipped his head. "Another time, another place, Lieutenant."

This time, Cutter didn't move, merely nodded. Logan continued down the walkway, finally giving a last look towards the terminal doorway. The lieutenant had literally disappeared into the crowd. And now it was his turn to do the same. It was time to pick up the pieces of his life and move on.

Buckling his seat belt two minutes later, Logan glanced out the window. He wasn't sorry to see the last of New Mexico, but he wasn't all that anxious to see New York City again, either. He frowned, his thoughts drifting to Sonny. Just as her mind had been wiped clean and been reborn, so had his. Thanks to her, he had finally learned what it was to put someone's welfare above his own and not care. The love he had for her would sustain him in the long, lonely days ahead. *One day at a time, old man*, his inner voice piped up. *You'll forget all about her if you just take it one damn day at a time.*

CHAPTER TWENTY TWO

Amanda studied the scrub brush outside the window and wondered how much longer Dr. Ramsay was going to make her wait. She was tired of sitting, and certainly tired of having to engage in long, drawn-out therapy sessions. Had there been a snag in signing her discharge papers? The thought caused her heart to flutter, and she rubbed the area absently. Why did the thought of leaving the hospital fill her with such dread?

Ever since Dr. Ramsay had announced she was well enough to leave and resume her life, she had been deluged with sheer terror. What was there to be afraid of out there? Nothing. The flutter in her heart stilled. Driving wouldn't be an issue, either. It was something else. Something she couldn't put a name to.

She sprang from the chair, drawn to the wall mirror as if magnetized. She studied her reflection, surveying the spiky red locks. She had obviously wanted a dramatic change in looks before coming to New Mexico, and she had achieved it. The new color was vivid, and the cut flattering to her face; however, she couldn't recall which salon she had visited to have the work done. The new look was such a stark change that she couldn't help checking her image in every mirror she passed. She raised her hand and traced the outline of her face. Same eyes, same nose, same mouth. Yet, she had sensed, since her illness, it was not the same face. Why that was, she didn't know.

Dropping her hand, she turned from the mirror and sought the cushioned wingback she had just vacated. Dr. Ramsay had assured her any feelings of unease she had would fade away in time. And he had been adamant that her head injury was healing as it should. She had been relieved at the information, but sometimes she felt as if they were keeping something from her. Not telling her the whole truth about the accident. Did she remember the accident? Not fully. But Dr. Ramsey had assured her she would.

A light tingle brushed along her scalp, and she raised her fingers to her temple and rubbed it vigorously. These damn sudden splurges of head pain weren't helping, either. She hated to think they were a permanent fixture in her life. No, Dr. Ramsey had been adamant that they would stop in time, too.

"Another headache, Miss King?"

Amanda dropped her hand, turning to the doorway. "Only a slight one," she replied. "All in all, the headaches do seem to be dwindling."

"Good." He proceeded to his desk and took a seat. "Don't forget to rely on your Tylenol tablets, though. They'll help immensely." He flipped open the folder he had carried into the room. "I've been going over your therapy reports, and you've made excellent progress this last week. There's no sense dragging out your stay here. It's time for you to re-enter the world." She saw him scribble his signature on the bottom of a sheet and felt that same prickle of fear. "I'm okaying your release for this afternoon, unless you have objections?" He paused, and hearing no reply, he looked up.

Amanda wondered what he would say if she told him she did have objections. That something frightening was waiting for her out there. It had no name, face, or form, but she knew it was stalking her.

"Are you having second thoughts about leaving, Miss King?"

She brought her wandering mind back to the present. "No, of course not. I'm feeling fine, only ... "

"Only?"

"There are still so many unanswered questions."

He settled back in his chair, dropping his pen and focusing on her face. "Let's hear a couple."

"I have this odd feeling of not belonging anywhere. And I've developed an obsession with studying my reflection in mirrors, windows, anything that gives off an image. My hair ... " She touched her head, her sentence trailing off.

"Head injuries often trigger memory lapses. We've talked about that. The important thing to remember is to let your mind and body heal at its own pace. When it's time for you to know the answers to the fears you are experiencing, your subconscious will let you know. What else is bothering you?"

"Why I was in New Mexico. Was I on vacation?"

A bewildered frown coated his features and then was gone, almost immediately. Once again, Amanda felt that odd stop in time. As if he was wracking his brain for an answer that would satisfy her, as well as keep her from asking any more questions about the accident. What was it about the accident that nobody wanted her to learn? His gaze caught hers.

"You're the only one who can answer that question, Miss King. Where you're from you've told us; however, who your friends and family are ... " She saw him shrug. "We haven't a clue." He saw the quick bite of her lower lip. "You mustn't worry over it, though. The answer is bound to come once you pick up the pieces of your life at home. It sounds harsh, I know, but four weeks ago, neither of us knew of the other's existence. I wish I could give you all the answers you need, but it's literally impossible. What I can do"—he reached over and pulled a business card from its holder—"is give you my card and tell you to give it to your regular doctor when you arrive back in Vermont. I'd like him to call me so I can be sure you're being properly treated. Hearing from your family would be nice, too."

Amanda took the card and pocketed it, knowing she'd never use it. Once she left the hospital, it would be as if she had never been here. She'd return to the miserable existence of fending for herself at whatever job she could find. Why had she told Dr. Ramsay she had family waiting for her in Vermont? She knew why. Shame. He had been good to her. Plus, she didn't want him to know that she had had several flashes of young girls in an orphanage over the last several days. The image hammered at her brain and wouldn't let go.

"Miss King?"

She glanced up, noting the curious gleam in his eye. "What you really mean, Doctor, is that you need to relay instructions to my doctor on how to take proper care of a woman who's losing her sanity."

"Now why would I let you out of here if you're insane?" He laughed.

"You wouldn't ... or shouldn't."

"Precisely." He leaned forward, crossing his arms on the desk. "Being afraid to go back into the world after a horrendous accident is perfectly normal. I'd be worried if you weren't experiencing feelings of doubt, but you'll work through them. You're a strong, gutsy woman." He closed the folder in front of him, and Amanda wondered how he had come to the conclusion she was gutsy when he barely knew her. "I've arranged for a limo to take you to the airport ... No, don't object. It's waiting outside, near the west entrance. Any fears about being in a car again?"

"No, of course not," Amanda stated. "The accident wasn't my fault."

"See there. You are better. That was a definitive statement." He gave her a smile, and Amanda returned it. She had accepted his charity of a plane ticket home, but how on earth would she repay him for a limo ride? She couldn't. She'd have to dismiss the driver upon her release. She turned her attention back to him and saw he was now riffling through the top left drawer of his desk. Finding what he sought, he withdrew a large manila envelope and handed it off to her.

"The police managed to retrieve your purse from the wreckage. Lieutenant Cutter dropped it by an hour ago and asked that I give it to you upon your release."

Amanda breathed a sigh of relief. Her purse! Thank goodness! Her wallet was in her purse, and it contained money. Her brain elaborated on that thought. Her purse also contained her driver's license. There'd be a picture that would assure her once and for all that she was Amanda King.

Taking the envelope, Amanda ripped the edges, pulling out the purse and rummaging through it. Cosmetic bag, keys, wallet. She grabbed the wallet and opened it and then searched for her I.D. card. Finding it, she pulled it out and stared at the photo. For a fraction of a second, she got that insane niggling that she was looking at a stranger. And then the inkling passed, and she read the address on the license. *165 Park Street, Burlington, Vermont.* She studied the rest of the contents. More keys, cell phone. She riffled further, spotting a bulky envelope near the bottom.

Pulling it out, she peered inside. A small gasp escaped her lips when she spotted a huge wad of hundred-dollar bills staring up at her. She glanced up to find Dr. Ramsay watching her with a troubled frown.

"There must be some mistake, Doctor. I'd never carry this much cash in my purse. In fact, I'm sure my bank account contains less than this. This isn't my money."

"Not your money?" He straightened suddenly, all business. "Perhaps, at last, we have hit on one of the most important things your mind has forgotten. Could you have been on an extended vacation, or perhaps moving into the area? The cash might be a down payment on a house."

"No, absolutely not! I don't take high-priced vacations. No ... " She dropped the envelope back in the purse. "This is not my money. The police have made a horrible mistake. They've mixed up purses somehow. There's no other possible explanation. This envelope is not mine."

Seeing her agitation, Dr. Ramsay sprang from his chair and came around the desk, patting her shoulder when he reached her.

"Don't upset yourself, Miss King. I'll make a quick phone call and see if Lieutenant Cutter is still in the building. His brother is a doctor on staff here, and he often drops in for a visit when he's in town. If there's been a mistake, he'll rectify it."

Amanda felt a surge of anger at the lieutenant's carelessness as she snapped the purse shut. "I'll make sure he rectifies the mistake," she stated strongly.

'There's no sense in losing your temper over this," the doctor said. "And by the way, it's nice to know you have a temper. It means you're finding your old self again."

"My old self! What on earth do you mean by that?"

He looked startled at the question, but forestalled any comment by lifting the phone receiver on his desk. "Jenny, see if Dick Cutter is still in the building ... He is? Good. Call down and tell him I need to see him at once." He cradled the receiver and wagged a finger at her. "Now I won't have you getting upset when the lieutenant gets here. It sets back all the wonderful progress you've made this last week. In fact, just to be sure, I'll catch the lieutenant at the elevator and warn him not to upset you in any way."

He exited the room so fast that Amanda had no time to tell him she wasn't worried about being upset. She was mad that her life had spun out of her control and into others' hands. She slid back on the seat cushions and held the purse firmly in her lap. She'd demand answers from the lieutenant as soon as she saw him. She was clearly not ready to be discharged in her doubtful state of mind. She would discuss that fact with the doctor when they were alone again.

A moment later, Dr. Ramsay re-entered the room with a tall, massive figure with hair the color of a field of oats. He came her way and perched himself on the edge of the mahogany desk, studying her face while the doctor took his seat behind him. Once he had, the lieutenant acknowledged her, his voice striking a familiar chord inside her as he spoke.

"Saul tells me there's been some mix-up with your personal belongings, Miss King."

Amanda nodded, taking the purse from her lap and handing it off to him. He took it and began inspecting the contents, and she used the moment to muster her flagging courage. This was not the time to be intimidated by massive muscles and brawn. A mistake had been made, and she must set it right. No matter how much poorer it made her.

Snapping the purse shut, the lieutenant's gaze returned to hers. "I'm afraid I don't see anything amiss, Miss King."

"Then you are a bigger lunatic than your men," she replied tartly. Her tone was smooth but insistent. "Now that I'm on the mend, I think I deserve full disclosure about my accident."

The lieutenant shifted on the desk, a deep furrow creasing the bridge of his nose, and then, to her surprise, he twisted around and spoke to the doctor.

"Do I have your permission to speak frankly to Miss King, Saul?"

Amanda saw a hesitant nod and shivered under that same sinking sensation that had haunted her ever since she had opened her eyes and found herself a patient in a strange hospital bed in a strange town.

"How much of the accident do you remember?"

It was her turn to be floored by a question. "Hardly any of it, but Dr. Ramsay assures me my memories will come back, given enough time."

"Would you like a remembrance to hold on to until that occurs?"

"Certainly."

He leaned forward, fiddling with the straps of the purse. "The accident occurred on Saguro Drive. A careless tourist on horseback lost control of her horse and lumbered into the path of oncoming traffic. You swerved left, the car coming east swerved right. You went over an embankment, while the other car managed to plow into a sand dune." He held the purse out to her. "The money is yours, Miss King. The gentleman in the other car left it for you."

"Left it?"

"I know it sounds preposterous, but there are still some Good Samaritans left in the world. The driver walked away from the crash, and you didn't. Once he learned how injured you were, he left the money for you."

He waved the purse at Amanda, who took it back slowly. She clenched her jaw to kill the sob rising in her throat. An absolute stranger had taken pity on her. It was humiliating.

"But why did he do it?"

"I guess he thought you needed the money more than he did. We'll never know. He left Taos not long after the accident."

Amanda sat for a moment, trying to absorb the lieutenant's words. She had been given five thousand dollars by a total stranger. She could go where she liked and do what she liked with it. She was free. Her eyes suddenly ringed with tears. She couldn't keep the money. She had to return it. It was a matter of pride.

"Do you remember the man's name, where he came from?" she asked quietly.

"I believe he came from New York City, a detective of some kind." The lieutenant fished in his pocket. "The name was Reed, I think. I might still have my notes containing his name and address, if you care to write and thank him."

"Yes, thank you, I would."

Amanda mentally crossed her fingers. She had no intention of writing to the gentleman, not after the lieutenant's refusal to give the money back to him. She was going to go herself and *make* him take back the money. She couldn't become any more indebted to him than she already was.

She heard the sound of rustling pages and succumbed to the worst wretchedness of mind she had ever felt. She wanted the money desperately, but she mustn't keep it. If she ever was to grow whole again, it had to be through her own efforts, not through the kindness of strangers. The money had to be returned with her most heartfelt "thanks, but no thanks."

Girded by her resolve, she was pleased when the lieutenant muttered, "Ah, here it is."

He flipped the pad to a blank sheet and began scribbling. Thank goodness she had convinced him she intended to write her mysterious savior.

The lieutenant tore the sheet from the pad and held it out to her. Taking it, Amanda forced a bright smile to her lips. The lieutenant wasn't as intimidating as she'd first thought. He had a kind heart. It was too bad she had to deceive him in such an underhanded way. She tucked the sheet safely in the purse and stood, offering her hand to the lieutenant, who shook it briefly.

"Thank you, Lieutenant. And thank you, Doctor, for the plane ticket home."

"You can thank that young gentleman you're writing to for that. He bought you the plane ticket."

Amanda suppressed an angry retort. Her mystery man had taken a lot upon himself. Money, a plane ticket. Had he bought the clothes on her back, too? He must've. She didn't have the sophistication to buy clothes as chic as these.

"Did the gentleman happen to pay for the clothes I'm wearing, Lieutenant?"

"Why, yes. And he paid your hospital bill. Didn't he, Saul?"

Amanda saw a flicker of unease cross the doctor's face. "I can't divulge that kind of information. You know that, Dick."

Amanda felt her courage deflate quickly. "He must be very rich and very sure of himself."

"And very stupid," the lieutenant added.

"Why do you say that?"

"He forgot to take you with him when he left."

Amanda saw a mischievous gleam enter the lieutenant's eyes, and she blushed profusely. He was teasing her, and she hadn't the foggiest idea why. Nor did she know how to respond. To her surprise, her ego surfaced, making her feel an emotion she hadn't felt since waking up. She laughed at the lieutenant's remark. However, when a second laugh threatened to bubble up in her throat, she choked it back. She had almost forgotten how good it felt to laugh. Perhaps sharing her body with an alien ego wasn't so bad after all.

She gave a last nod to the pair and exited the room, letting the door fall softly shut behind her.

• • •

Watching the door close, the lieutenant inhaled deeply.

"Was that wise?" The question echoed from the chair behind him, and Dick turned, meeting the doctor's worried gaze.

"Absolutely not, but then I've always been a sucker for happy endings."

"Having her write Agent Reed could set back her recovery. I took an oath to help patients, not aid in confusing them with bogus fairy tales. What if she decides to visit him in person and return the money?"

The lieutenant began twirling a metallic paperweight by his knee. "I'm counting on that. They belong together, Saul. And sometimes love needs a little push."

"Even if she gets there and never remembers the truth?"

"Even then."

CHAPTER TWENTY THREE

Ignoring the persistent ringing of his phone, Logan shrugged into his denim jacket. Whoever was calling would have to leave a voice mail. He was already running thirty minutes late, thanks to a late-night cat-and-mouse game through Chinatown. Why were young girls always drawn to that part of the city? He hoisted his pant leg up and slipped his revolver into its holster. He knew the girl's reason, of course. *Romeo and Juliet*. Family clashes. Two pissed-off teens on the run from their parents.

Swinging around, Logan snatched up his keys and wallet from his desk and tucked the wallet in his back pocket. Whirling around, he was startled to find his secretary, Monica, standing in the open doorway.

"Not now, Monica," he threw at her. "I don't care who it is."

"It's Dresden. He's asking to see you."

Logan made a face, sliding his keys into his front jeans pocket. "What in the hell have I done wrong now?" A smile broke out on her face, and she shushed him with a wagging finger. "Alright, you win," he growled. "I'll be a good little boy."

She made a face at him and then backed out the door quickly. The lines of concentration deepened along Logan's brow. He had kept a tight rein on his temper since his return and a low-key attitude when in the office. He hadn't pissed anybody off, especially Dresden. A muscle quivered in his jaw. Then again, he and Dresden had barely exchanged four words since his return. It was possible Dresden believed he still held a grudge for being sent to New Mexico. That had to be it. He wanted to clear the air between them.

Perching on his desk, Logan began whistling softly. He had to get Dresden out of his office ASAP. He wasn't ready to talk about Sonny and New Mexico yet. Not with anyone. Quicker than he liked, he heard Dresden's booming laugh and took a deep breath. Moments later, Dresden's imposing form dwarfed the doorway, and Logan hopped from the desk.

"I'm on my way out," he said by way of greeting. "I've got my teens cornered in Chinatown. If I delay, I'll never smoke them out."

"I won't hold you up long," Dresden said, stepping back. He pushed his companion into the room. "Miss King, here, assures me she will take only a moment of your time."

"Miss King?"

Logan's throat closed up. Jesus! Sonny? Here? What the hell had happened?

Bowing out the door, Dresden cleared his throat. "I'll leave you two to your discussion."

For the first time in his life, Logan was speechless. What the hell could the mouse possibly have to say to him in her present form? It was clear by the tilt of her brow and the uncertainty of her expression that she didn't recognize him. It was also clear she was having trouble finding the right words to start the conversation between them. Should he push the issue first?

As if pulled by a magnet, she suddenly moved to the other side of the room and began studying the large, framed picture hanging there. Logan's gaze fell on the image. The Lovers card. He was a glutton for punishment, he mused. Upon his return, he had bought a deck of mythic Tarot cards, made a portrait-sized copy of the image, and hung it up, as a token of his time with Sonny.

"It's a blow-up of the Lovers Tarot card," he stated, breaking the silence.

She whirled around at the pronouncement, and he saw a blush stain her cheeks. "It's quite a unique photo," she remarked. Her gaze swung back to it again. "I wonder if it's proper to hang such an erotic picture in your office, though."

Logan hid a smile. That sounded a lot like the old Sonny. He perched himself on the edge of the desk again, deciding to let her continue the conversation. After all, they were nothing more than strangers now—ships that had passed in the night. He crossed his right ankle over his left, noting she had turned to face him again. He noticed the skin pulled taut over the elegant ridge of her cheekbones. She had lost weight since he had last seen her, and he guessed the mind transfer had taken its toll on her demeanor.

He wished he could bring the confident gleam back to her eye. The mouse standing before him had lost all her polished veneer. Ned Chalmers had wanted to make her a passive, nebbish mouse, dependent on him for everything, and he had certainly achieved it.

Watching her recross the carpet, he saw her glance at the mirror hanging on the wall directly in front of her. She seemed to lose herself in the reflection, and he sensed she was distracted; perhaps she had even gone away from the room itself, lost in some kind of mind fugue he couldn't begin to fathom. When she continued staring at herself, Logan knew, if the conversation was ever to keep going, he would have to continue it. She was simply not up to the task. That she had been discharged from the hospital before she was fully recovered was evident. What the hell had Ramsay been thinking? He'd place a call to Taos the moment she left the office and demand an answer.

"You're probably wondering why I'm here, Mr. Reed."

Startled, Logan glanced up. She had come out of her trance and was now seated in a chair in front of him. "Naturally," he replied. "A detective thrives on a good mystery."

She almost smiled at his statement, and for a brief moment, Logan was reminded of the day they had met. She had almost smiled at him that day, too. She opened her purse and retrieved a manila envelope from the interior, and then, straightening, she held the envelope out to him.

"I appreciate your generosity, Agent Reed. However, I can't accept money from a complete stranger. It's a matter of pride."

Logan studied the envelope but made no move to take it. "There seems to be a lot of that going around these days." He hopped from the desk then, away from her and towards the door. "The money is yours to do with as you wish, Miss King. You can keep it or throw it away; it's your choice. If you can't use it, there are a number of charities in the area who would appreciate the donation."

He reached the door, taking a moment to glance back over his shoulder. She was standing now, holding out the package, but her sad expression had shifted to a scalding fury.

"Do you mean to say that you are refusing to take the money back from me?"

He jiggled the doorknob. "Looks like it."

She stepped forward, waving the envelope at him. "No one refuses to accept five thousand dollars."

"You just did."

She snapped her mouth shut, obviously floored to find her own words thrown back in her face. She let the package fall to her side, and Logan sensed he had won the battle between them. It was a hollow victory, though—and unfair. She didn't remember their feisty arguments. He did.

When she continued to stand transfixed, he jiggled the door handle to gain her attention. She was back in one of those damn fugues again. How often did they occur? She'd had two since he had been with her, and they had been together less than five minutes. Didn't Ramsay give her medication to combat the damn trances?

"You won't take the money back?" she asked again.

Jesus! She was out of the trance and back with him. He could hear tears laced in her voice, and when he scanned her face, he saw her brush away a wet spot. That small movement was his undoing. A sudden flash of an erotic kiss assaulted his mind, and his stomach clenched tightly. The image also sent him moving back to her side where, when he reached her, he cupped the side of her face. His voice was husky and warm as he spoke.

"Trust me, mouse, the money won't break me. I want you to have it."

She froze at his words, but her hand didn't. It came up and settled over his caressing fingers. A second later, the pair was pitched into a vortex and out the other side. When the vision settled, they were side by side, watching themselves have sex in the middle of a big, round bed lined with white satin sheets. To say the sex was mind-blowing was an understatement. Their thighs were soaked, and their breaths were caught in long, surrendering moans. The turbulence of their passion seemed to burn away the room around them.

As quickly as they entered the vision, they were flung back out. The woman touching his fingers collapsed, and thinking fast, Logan snatched her up. A full-blown seizure seized her body, and he lowered her to the floor. He slipped his arms beneath her back, attempting to soothe her contorted body. Where was her tongue? He needed to keep her from choking on it.

He reached up, startled when the seizure left as quickly as it had come. When she didn't move or rally, an icy tremor of fear swept through Logan. They had been down this road before, and it had ended badly. He grabbed hold of her chin and shook it.

"Don't you die on me, mouse, you hear? Do anything, but don't die on me!"

Her eyes flew open, scaring the hell out of him. A sob tore from her lips, and she flung her arms around his neck, clinging to him as if all the demons of hell were chasing her. He pressed his hands against her spine, listening to the deep sobs wracking her frame. Christ! That had been close. He felt a cool wetness on his neck.

"What hap-happened to me?" came a stuttered hiccup.

"You blacked out momentarily, but you're coming round again."

She wound her arms tighter around his neck, her lashes fluttering against his cheek. "Thank you ... for not abandoning me."

"All in a day's work, Miss King."

Her body stiffened, and she pulled back to glance at his face. "Who the hell is Miss King?"

A myriad of emotions swept her face, and then, as if a light switch had suddenly popped on, she scrambled from his arms, kicked at his legs, and scooted along the carpet away from him. She was on her feet in a flash.

"You arrogant clod! If this is how you protect your female clients, it's no wonder they shoot you. I've a good mind to buy a gun and shoot you myself."

Surprise siphoned the blood from Logan's face. He'd recognize that shrewish tone anywhere. "Sonny?"

She made a face at him. "I don't know. Maybe, maybe not. Let me think on it."

"With what?"

A stunned silence greeted his ears, and then she exploded in icy fury again. "What a filthy, rotten thing to say! I'd like to see you stay sane after having a trillion gigabytes of electricity jolted through your brain." She glanced down at her hands suddenly. "Good God, where are my gloves? I need my gloves."

Logan sprang to his feet. "Simmer down, mouse! You're breaking my eardrums!"

"I *need* my gloves."

Hearing her panicked tone, Logan rounded his desk and flung open his top drawer. He hauled out a sealed package of gloves and tossed them to Sonny, who took one look at the gloves inside and glanced his way.

"Don't ask," he warned, slamming the drawer shut. "You already own every inch of my heart. If you think I'm giving you any more power over me, think again." He winked at her broadly, and stunned, she snapped her mouth shut, tore open the package, and donned the gloves. Finding them a perfect fit, she glanced at him again. He shrugged at her. "Just a safety precaution," he said, "in case your memory returned and you came looking for a broken-down detective who loves you more than words can ever say."

A fresh set of tears glistened on her eyelashes. "You can't imagine how horrendous it was," she told him. "The pain was so great, I prayed for the mind transfer to work."

He shot to her side and took her in his arms. "But your mind found a way to come back to me. You beat Ned at his own game."

She stilled his mouth with her fingers, her glance narrowing. "What happened to him? Where is he?"

"Spending an eternity in Hades, I hope." Her fingers dropped away, and she shifted in his arms. She was running away from him again. He brought her back into the circle of his arms. "Nothing matters now but that you're with me again." His tone hardened, like steel. "I'm not letting you go again. The last time damn near killed me."

He heard a sob tear from her throat. "We barely know each other, Logan."

"That's not true," he said. "Thanks to your empathic skills, I've seen *all* of you, and I'm pretty sure that you've seen *all* of me."

Her lips tilted for a half second but then turned down again. "It'll never work. You're needed here; I'm needed in New Mexico. I have to go back and put things right."

"You needn't worry. The Pandora Project will never see the light of day again."

She pulled from his arms. "It's not that."

"What then?"

"Ned used The Sanctuary to sexually abuse our guests. By now, the media will have crucified the retreat and our staff."

Logan's hands spanned her waist, drawing her back to him. "The media has been dealt with by Meta Corps. There'll be no slander, and your aunt has taken the reins of The Sanctuary. She and Brad have things well in hand, so stop all this stubborn mouse nonsense and say you'll marry me."

"It's too soon. We just met."

"And the sky is falling, blah, blah, blah. What's your point?"

"I'm sure I have one, if you'd just let me—"

"Kiss me," he said, cutting her off mid-sentence. "What?" She looked so adorably flustered, he repeated himself.

"Kiss me."

He waited for her lips to lift, and when they didn't, he took the initiative. The way to have the last word with a stubborn wench was to put her mouth to better use. He smothered her warm lips, letting his hands trace the soft lines of her hips to the hollow of her back. A small moan came from her throat, and she molded herself against him. Her touch was his undoing. In minutes, his fingers were fumbling with the buttons of her blouse, and all thoughts of chasing two lovesick teens through Chinatown frittered away.

"If you're going to make love to me, you should lock the door," Sonny whispered breathlessly, a moment later.

His finger halted, and he studied the upward tilt of her mouth. "Later."

"Now."

"Later."

His mouth nuzzled hers, and then a whisper fanned his lips. "The door, Logan ... "

"Later," he said, slipping his fingers into her bra.

"I said *now* ... "

His fingers halted, and he sighed dramatically. "You are the most aggravating mouse." He left her side, locked the door, and then headed back her way. "However, there is no way in hell you're going to talk me out of making love to you," he said, sweeping her into his arms. "Don't even try."

He dropped her onto the office sofa and then followed her down. In just under a minute, his naked body claimed hers, and, just like their shared visions, he brought her to the brink of climax and then pushed her over the edge.

THE END

PRESENT DAY—WASHINGTON D.C.

Hacking coughs split the air, followed by a series of raspy moans. A second later, a loud sneeze bounced off the green walls of the room. Fumbling in her jacket pocket, Brianna pulled a tissue out, and swiped her runny nose. This cold was getting the best of her, and she wished with every fiber of her being that her spirit guides would whisk her away to some tropical island where they never heard of burning lungs and clogged nasal passages.

She dropped her forehead to the desk, and gave into a second set of coughs. If she ever learned who had given her this nasty virus, she would place a curse on their head that couldn't be reversed. Her office door creaked and Brianna realized her assistant, Janet, was responding to her lacerated coughs. She took a deep breath, willing herself to shore up her energy. A strange rattling in her lungs made her clutch her chest again, and all thoughts of making conversation fled into a graveyard of dead sentences. She hated being sick. It was a tremendous drain on her system. And to make matters worse, she was becoming light-headed. If she didn't know better, she'd think something bad was in the wind.

"That cough could use a little Wiccan magic, blue eyes."

The voice was raspy and deep, and Brianna's head snapped up at the statement. She studied the chubby figure crossing the door frame, and voiced her surprise.

"Good heavens, Tommy, who told you I was sick?"

"I have my sources." He approached her desk, studying her cracked lips and ruby-red nose. "I warned you not to travel at this time of year. Perhaps now, you'll listen to me." Her laugh turned into spastic coughs, as Tommy dropped into a chair across the desk from her. He plopped his briefcase on the edge of her desk, and slid back in his chair. "Well, let's get to the point while you still have breath to speak with. Do we have a deal or not?"

Brianna dabbed at her dripping nose.

"Not—and he wouldn't say why, damn him!"

"Probably doesn't like doing business with witches." Tommy teased.

Brianna frowned at his words.

"Don't make me sorry I told you about my background when we became partners, Tommy. And for your information, the coven I grew up in frowns on using magic to manipulate people for one's personal gain."

"Too bad. You could use a magical make-over right now. Your hair is a mess, your mascara is flaking, and your tall frame is hunched over like Quasimodo."

Brianna raised a hand to her hair, brushing a stray tendril behind her ear.

"Don't be shy, Tommy. Tell me what you really think."

"Don't make jokes. When you're unwell, I take it very seriously."

"That's because I'm rarely ill." She stifled a pressing sniffle, and tossed her tissue into the trash can under her desk. A light chuckle sounded as Tommy crossed his legs, and fidgeted with the seam of his trousers.

"I warned you to take your time with this buyout. There is no hurry to liquidate all of your assets at once just because you've decided to make major changes in your lifestyle. Hurried choices can be disastrous, you know."

Hearing his words, Brianna shivered. A moment later, the air around her head stirred, and she glanced up. There it was again— the feeling that something was brewing in the wind. Was spirit attempting to warn her she should be on her guard? Or was she being warned it was much too late to worry? She heard the loud mewl of a cat's cry in her ears, and drew in her breath. There. That disturbance was definitely a ripple of something sinister. Where had the cry come from? Janet's office?

Strong hands gripped her fingers, startling her.

"Here now, what's wrong? You've gone completely white."

"Did you hear it?" Brianna queried.

"Hear what?"

"A cat crying. It sounds hungry—or in pain."

"I didn't hear anything. Are you sure you heard a cat?"

"I heard a cat, dammit!"

A hand waved in front of her face.

"Hey, don't bite my head off. I'm no warlock with super-sonic hearing, you know."

Brianna grimaced, clutching his hand.

"Don't humor me, Tommy. I have a feeling something's wrong."

His expression turned serious.

"I'll have Janet call maintenance to check the nearby offices."

He sprang from his chair and exited the room, leaving Brianna to bite her lip in frustration. Why had she snapped at Tommy? He was her best friend, and his friendship meant everything to her. Besides, cat cries just didn't dance on the wind, no matter how real they sounded. She was ill, and the cries were just figments of her sick body.

Tossing back her shoulders, she made a face at the painting on her wall. She may have heard a cat crying, but without knowing the source, there wasn't a thing she could do about it. She felt a light touch on the side of her cheek, and jumped.

"You're spicy hot," Tommy stated. "That's not a good sign. Fevers often cause hallucinations."

"I am not hallucinating, Tommy, I heard a cat . . . no, don't say anymore. I know it sounds crazy."

"Damned crazy," he muttered.

"Well, it wouldn't be the first time I've been called crazy, so sit down, and stop worrying about me."

"I can't help it. You're the most rational person I know—next to me—and if you're hearing cats that aren't there, there is great cause for worry."

"It's more than being sick, Tommy."

"What the hell does that mean?"

"It means that I have this feeling of dread that I can't shake—as if someone has just died."

Tommy angled around the desk, and retook his former seat.

"You're on overload—too much work, and too little sleep, and for what? Why are you pushing things at such a breakneck speed?"

Brianna didn't answer right away. She could tell Tommy the truth—that she had been feeling a disturbance somewhere in the fabric of time for months, and was worried by it. He would understand her fears. After all, they had no secrets from one another. He might be a man of art and science, but he had added the power of magic to his vocabulary since meeting her.

Still, she didn't want to involve him in her childish fears unless she had to. If only she didn't sense that the disturbance concerned him in some way. She could feel it pulling both of them towards the past, instead of the future. And worse, she felt herself being dragged back—towards old relationships that she had vowed to keep buried forever. Besides, she shouldn't be able to gauge energy levels anymore. Yet, she could feel the energy in the room around her as if she had conjured up a cone of power, complete with the Guardians of the Watch Tower. No, she stopped her thoughts. She had no intention of revisiting that kind of pain ever again. Not for anyone. She gave a tired sigh.

"Have you ever made a decision you wish you could take back, Tommy?"

"Only every time I sit across the bargaining table with you."

"I'm serious."

"So am I." He heard her sigh again, and threw out his hand. "Okay. Are we talking a complete do-over here? Or just a small, magical tweaking?"

"I'm talking a total re-do, a chance to relive a moment over again, and make a different decision."

"My God, woman, you own two foundations and a wildlife habitat. What else do you want?"

"Mind-blowing sex would be nice."

She heard a busted chuckle.

"Surely you can conjure up a willing partner with some simple romance spell you know." He saw her frown and held up a finger. "None of that matters now. What matters is your damn decision to alter your life."

"Don't get me wrong." Brianna stated. "I am genuinely proud of what I've accomplished with the foundations. But somewhere along the way, the dream became so twisted that it no longer resembles the dream I started out with. Now, I just want to find my roots again and start over—preferably with a quiet, respectful man who loves children."

Tommy scooted his chair forward, and then settled back.

"You need a strong-willed husband, blue eyes. Any other kind, and you'd run rough-shod over him." He switched thoughts rapidly. "Now that you're revamping your life with mind-blowing sex instead of business, I guess a merger of Sage Industries is out of the question, huh?"

"I haven't sunk that low yet." Brianna snatched a tissue from its holder and blew her nose. "Well, you've heard my bad news; how did it go in Texas?"

"Damn charlatans. They let me fly all the way out there, and then just as we hit the bargaining table, they sent word they were passing on the buyout."

"Did they give a reason?"

"They said they're looking to liquidate their holdings, not acquire more."

"It was a good deal, Tommy."

"For you, it was. But let's face facts. Big corporations bypass great deals all the time. It's not personal. It's just business. We'll find another buyer. D.J. Corp isn't the only game in town."

"No, but he's the best. His projects are always environmentally sound. He doesn't drill the hell out of the land or the sea, and his wildlife habitat in Wyoming has an ecosystem to die for."

Another sigh emanated.

"I did my best in Texas, Brianna. I hope you believe that."

Brianna gave a matching sigh.

"I know you did your best." She squared her shoulders. "Let's start making phone queries again. Perhaps D.J. could recommend another corporation that might serve as well. What do you think?"

"I'll call Jake Rogers and find out." He reached in his coat pocket and withdrew his Blackberry. He began making notes on the pad, and Brianna took a moment to study her calendar.

A second later, the phone jangled on the desk, startling them both. Annoyed, Brianna snatched up the receiver, and held it to her ear.

"What is it, Janet?"

"Brianna?"

The voice was low and unfamiliar, and Brianna tucked the receiver closer to her ear.

"Who's this? Can you speak up? The connection's bad."

The voice came online again, steady and loud this time.

"Brianna?

Her pulse skittered.

"Papa?" She clutched the front of her blouse. "Am I dreaming your voice? How in the world did you find me?"

"I've always known where you were, Brianna—right from the day you left my side. I've followed your career closely over the years, too. I'm extremely proud of who you've become."

Brianna's chest tightened. *Déjà vu, Brianna,* her inner voice nudged, *déjà vu.*

"What's wrong, Papa? Why are you calling?"

"There's been an accident."

Brianna squeezed the front of her blouse, his words freezing her brain. Sudden tears welled up, followed by another heaviness centered in her heart.

"Its mother, isn't it? I felt something in the wind—a hint of something bad. How s-serious is it?" she asked.

"Very serious. The entire congregation has fallen ill."

"Good heavens! What from? Have you determined the cause?"

"Our best guess is a busted ritual."

A shadow of alarm touched Brianna's face, and a warning voice whispered in her head again. *Déja vu, Brianna, déja vu.* To her dismay, her voice broke slightly.

"And m-mother?"

"She's gravely ill. I don't think she's going to make it. That's why I'm calling."

Brianna bit her lip to control a sob.

"Can she be moved to a critical care unit in Tucson for treatment?"

"No. She collapsed while performing a ritual, and until we determine what occurred prior to her collapse, we can't let outsiders get involved. We attempted to intercede on her behalf, and well, I don't need to tell you what can happen when an intercession fails."

Brianna's eyes bordered with tears again.

"You must call 9-1-1 immediately. Mother needs to be airlifted as soon as possible. I can meet you in Tucson some time tomorrow afternoon." She glanced at her calendar. "I can catch the red-eye flight out tonight."

A weary sigh emanated in her ear.

"That won't do, Brianna. I'm suffering from the energy sickness, along with the members. I am unable to travel at the moment."

Brianna heard a raspy cough and winced.

"You must let me come home, Papa. I can help."

"I wish you could, but when you left, all ties to the coven were broken."

An unexpected surge of anger had Brianna lashing out.

"That was fifteen years ago. It has no bearing on this incident. I have read the Book of Shadows, and I know what's written in terms of who succeeds whom in a crisis. There's no doubt in my mind, I have to come home and assess the situation."

Her father's cough came through the line again.

"It took a long time to put the Dark Time behind us, Brianna. Please don't make a mockery of our laws by going against them again. I only called you . . . in case this is goodbye."

Silence descended on the other end of the line, and Brianna suppressed a sob.

"Papa . . ."

The line went dead, and Brianna's hand shot to her mouth. He had hung up on her. Her hand suddenly fell away. It was clear the Dark Time had descended again without warning, and this time, her mother's essence had taken the hit. She replaced the receiver slowly, wishing she could replay her father's words in slow motion. Her mother had been performing a ritual when it tanked. No, her mother didn't make mistakes like that. Then what? *A clever attempt at murder?* Her inner voice threw up. She shunned the thought, but then thought better of it. Why would the Elders attempt to alter a ritual if they didn't suspect foul play?

She banished that thought, too. She wasn't going to start suspecting that a sinner had entered the clearing and attacked her mother. Her mother's collapse had been an accident caused by spirit, and her father had let the Council try to reverse the outcome—with disastrous results. What had made him do such a foolish thing? She wouldn't know until she asked him in person. Or saw her mother.

Snatching up the phone again, she punched in Janet's extension.

"Ready for the next dose of Nyquil?" Janet teased.

"No, I need you to call the airport and book the earliest flight to Tucson for me. And book a rental car."

"Will do." The line went dead and Brianna replaced the receiver.

"Do you want me to fly home with you?"

Brianna glanced up, suddenly remembering she wasn't alone in the room. She covered her mouth with shaking fingers.

"Thank you, Tommy, but no. You've got to stay here and find a buyer for my company. It's more important than ever now. I'll sign the power of attorney over to you before I leave."

He leaned forward in his chair.

"Are you sure this is what you want to do?"

Her voice drifted to a whisper.

"I'll conjure a protection spell for the pilot and passengers before we take off," she replied.

"That's not what I meant, and you know it. We're talking about you walking back into the lion's den when you've vowed to never go into the den again. Bad blood doesn't dissipate over the years, you know; sometimes it just hibernates."

Brianna began chewing on her lower lip, her eyes darkening with pain.

"I have to go home, Tommy, and that's that."

He didn't offer any other comment aloud, but she saw him frown. She looked away, clamping her lips to imprison a sob. The past was the past, and though she needed it to stay dead, she couldn't sit and wait for word of her mother's death. She felt ice spreading through her stomach at the thought, and she suddenly burst into tears.

Alarmed, Tommy sprang to his feet and circled the desk. He threw his arm over her shoulders, comforting her with his warm embrace and sly wit.

"Here now, blue eyes, forget what I said. If you have to go home, I'll support you. I'll even find one of those magical books of yours and conjure up a spell for you to use." He squeezed her shoulders, and Brianna slipped her arms about his waist and hugged him.

"You're the best, Tommy. I knew you'd understand." She brushed her cheeks against his belt buckle. "If I don't go, and Mother dies, I'll never forgive myself."

"And if they slam the gates in your face?"

"I'll lose my soul."

"What's one little soul among many?" Tommy teased, shaking her shoulder.

Brianna squeezed his waist.

"You are treading on sacred ground with that statement, Tommy. Every soul counts in the scheme of things."

"Even your damaged one?"

"God, I hope so," she said, slipping her hands from Tommy's waist. She leaned back in her chair, swiping her drenched cheeks with a tissue. "All better now," she said, tossing it under her desk. A long sigh emanated as Tommy re-circled the desk and fell into his chair again. His sly wit re-surfaced at once.

"I know we've bantered about witches and warlocks over the years, but just how good of a witch are you, anyway?"

Brianna's head shot up, a mischievous glint entering her eyes.

"Change the subject, Tommy, or you'll find out first-hand just how good I am."

He held up his hands, making a cross with his fingers.

"Stay back, you evil, blue-eyed vixen."

Brianna laughed at his sarcasm.

"Crisis averted," she croaked.

"And without using black magic against me." He gave her a toothy grin, dropped his hands, and hopped from his chair. He hauled up his briefcase, rapping it on the edge of her desk before turning.

"Just say the word, and I'll fly home with you, Brianna."

She studied his serious expression.

"This is something I have to do alone, Tommy. And," she pointed a finger at him. "You need to find a buyer for the company ASAP."

He nodded, then turned from the desk, and exited the door. Watching him go, Brianna gave a relieved sigh. Thank goodness, Tommy knew when to push, and when to back off. If he had pushed things, she would've come unglued, for sure.

Torn by an influx of conflicting emotions, Brianna began drumming her fingers along the desktop. What had really happened to her mother in the circle? She didn't know; she only hoped that when she arrived in Green Sapphire, she'd find that the Elders had misread the signs, and things weren't as bad as her father implied. Her mind replayed Tommy's words: "And if they slam the gates in your face?" She frowned immediately. If, when she arrived, she was barred from the property, she would work her way south along the back roadway, and enter the compound through the outer property bounds. She was going to determine for herself what happened to her mother, and nothing and no one was going to stop her. No one was going to hurt her mother and get away with it.

For more books by Rachel James, check out:

The Kindred

In the mood for more Crimson Romance?
Check out *Flame Unleashed by Jillian David*
at *CrimsonRomance.com*.